SAMANTHAZADE

SAMANTHAZADE

Leo G. Taylor

Boyen D. Brook Publishing

The name Boyen D. Brook and the "Kilroy Was Here" face
in association with the stylized reflecting pool beneath it
are registered trademarks of Boyen D. Brook Publishing.

Printed in the United States of America

First printing 2019

ISBN 978-1-948576-02-4

Cover Art: Photo by Rachel Crowe on Unsplash

CONTENTS

CHAPTERS

CHAPTER ONE:

A WALK ON BALD MOUNTAIN

"I SUPPOSE AS A PSYCHIATRIST you think it's abnormal for me to relate to this child as my son, don't you?" Charles Ogden asked the woman sitting across from him.

"The parameters of normality are sometimes rendered arbitrary by circumstances," Dr. Samantha Dale answered. "In your case, as one of the wealthiest men in the world, and one of the most intelligent I might add, such boundaries become meaningless."

"I'd accuse you of flattery," Ogden replied, "except that I sense that you are saying that as a way of softening the blow. You aren't going to accept my proposal, are you?"

"Not in the usual sense," Samantha answered, "but I am prepared to give you what you want. I don't like the idea of terminating the life within me, regardless of where it came from. And Hugh Turley couldn't handle it in the long run. He isn't made that way."

Ogden's craggy features softened with relief. "You're right," he said. "That's all I wanted in the first place. What I want is the boy, and a marriage that lasts just long enough to take undisputed legal possession of him. A marriage that remains unconsummated, and therefore without that additional bond. The alternative would just bring on complications in this instance. I know you're in love with Turley."

Samantha relaxed noticeably. She was happy to have Ogden confirm what she had suspected all along. He wanted the baby she was carrying and nothing more. Just as much as she wanted to be rid of it.

"I acknowledge at the outset," Ogden continued, "that the major impediment to a traditional marriage is the fact that the child you are carrying is the result of rape by my son. A brutal rape, with the intention of murdering you later. After he'd let his pack of equally brutal henchmen have their fun with you, that is. It is understandable that you would continue to associate that trauma with the criminal's father, even though I am in many respects the direct opposite of my plainly psychotic son. You would always see the similarities, and that would constitute a continuing problem. Even if I weren't more than twice your age."

Samantha Dale sensed the effort it took Ogden to make such an admission about his dead son. She resisted the urge to try and make it easier for him with a word of comfort, however. She'd made her position clear, and now it was time for Ogden to state his entire case.

"Plus," Ogden went on, "there are other impediments to a traditional marriage as well. I'll admit to a weakness: I've crashed my libido with a steady diet of championship belly dancers and roller-skating carhops. On that account alone a normal marriage would be disastrous for both of us. I'd have a hard time passing up the side dishes in favor of the entrée."

Samantha smiled at the analogy in spite of herself, but immediately recovered. "My great concern," she went on, "is that Turley will think less of me if he knows the truth. He can take rejection a lot better than he could take the cold business relationship we're cooking up here. I know him, and I know that's the way he'd think about it. I'm sure he'll be waiting for me. My gamble is that he will forgive me when he learns the truth."

"Okay, I get your point," Ogden answered. "We'll throw in the frills, then, for the sake of appearances. Marriage at Winchester Cathedral, a whirlwind tour of Europe. Back here to deliver the baby. Then we'll terminate the relationship just as decisively. Irreconcilable differences, we'll say. Divorce and settlement. A good settlement".

"Agreed," Samantha said. "Let's talk about that last point."

ON RARE OCCASIONS I'll oversleep, and it happened that morning. I skipped my morning run to check into Word to the Wise Investigations early. My body vetoed the plan, though, and after stashing my car in its absurdly expensive parking slot I went for a jog through Central Park.

On Bow Bridge, of all places, I slipped on something unexpectedly slimy and fell flat on my back. "Are you all right, sir?" asked a young man of about twenty as he helped me to my feet.

I brushed the kid off before I could think about it, and he walked away whispering to his girlfriend about those hostile New Yorkers.

What had gotten to me, besides the embarrassment of taking the fall, was the kid's evident concern for the welfare of an older guy. Was I starting to look that old?

Perhaps. I'd begun to notice a down-in-the-mouth look in the mirror. There were matching peaks over each eyebrow that marked where hair grows back into scars. A short beard covers a scar on one side of my chin and another that broadens my mouth half an inch on one side. My hair is still dark though, and thick enough to keep it cut short. Thirty-five is close to the end of a boxer's career.

Maybe it's like that for a private detective who tends to lead with his chin more often than he uses his wits. And that's the way it played out not two blocks away from the park. The rain had only been falling for about five minutes when I saw the woman step out from the curb and realize her mistake. As she moved back from an oncoming car, she lost her balance and dropped the bundle in her arms. It bounced in an elastic way that, coupled with the horrified look on her face, made me think it was a baby.

The woman was frozen, there was no time to scoop up the baby, and a car was on the way. The chance for a slide recovery looked good to me at that moment, and I went for it.

But I had mistimed the move badly. The car got there too soon and my head collided with the front tire. I think maybe the vehicle had been accelerating.

I'd been moving fast when I hit the pavement, so the impact sent me into a spin. My shoulder made it around just in time to get pinched and rejected by the back of the right rear wheel.

The spin continued. Both right wheels from the following car brushed my off leg as I completed the slide, ending up nestled against the curb with my face in something that stank.

Miraculously, the two cars had passed over the precious bundle without touching it. Looking both ways, as she should have in the first place, the woman picked it up.

The bag had been torn by the fall, and her dozen-or-so skeins of newly-purchased yarn peeked out in places. She seemed more concerned about them than she was for me. With a look that told me she'd taken me for some sort of nut or pill-head, she moved on. Nobody else on the crowded sidewalk even turned to look. That's New York for you.

I tidied up my clothing in the reflection of a store window. I'd reacted in time to avoid getting my arms run over, and the head didn't count. It had already been used to repel every kind of object short of a bullet. The crimp in my suit at the shoulder would take a lot of ironing, but it was hard to tear fabric made of anti-ballistic carbon fiber.

Yes, I was definitely in a funk. I was permitting the loss of my main squeeze to get to me as badly as it would have done to that kid on the Bow Bridge. It was time to get over it and go on about my business the way any tough big city hard-boiled detective ought to. Except I wasn't sure what that would be.

At the office my secretary, Ida Wilde, had already settled in for the day. She'd set up an appointment for me in about an hour, she informed me, and I went into the inner office to spruce up and try to get that wrinkle out of my suit.

The client arrived. A young woman named Haldis Pike. She wore a conservative tweed outfit with the hemline below her knees and owlish horn-rimmed glasses. She'd put her hair up in a tight bun. She wore practical shoes, and was tall enough to nearly look me in the eye. I couldn't guess her age. It could have been anywhere from twenty-five to forty.

"I think my uncle killed my father in the woods," she said without preamble.

From the looks of Ms. Pike, I hadn't expected that direct a statement for openers.

"What were the circumstances?" I asked.

"My Uncle, who calls himself Norman Granville," Pike explained, "went into the woods of upper New York State with my father. Later that day some men carried my father out, poisoned."

"Not that it matters," I asked, "But is this Norman Granville you're referring to the famous Shakespeare critic?"

"Yes," Haldis answered.

It was a personal connection. Once removed, that is. By coincidence Granville was the author of the textbook used for a college Shakespeare course I had taken. The professor had followed the book so closely that Granville himself might have been teaching the course. And I had repeatedly crashed on the rocks trying to catch up with where the professor was going in his commentary. The idea that I'd have to contend with a mind like Granville's if he'd really gone rogue was intimidating.

"What makes you think your father was poisoned?" I asked.

"My father would never have eaten toxic mushrooms," Pike answered, "and that's what killed him."

Just like Claudius and Hamlet's father, or at least that's the connection I should have made. But instead I had a flashback to my first assignment as a rookie cop, paired with a veteran on patrol. His name was Matt Jacobs. I'd heard mutterings around the precinct and was ready for what happened. I'd watched him carefully that first day. He'd probably thought it was a case of hero-worship. Then he'd taken a pill out of a case and started to swallow it.

That's when I'd given him a full bitch-slap across the face, which I had to do to keep him from actually getting the pill into his mouth.

Jacobs had been so startled he'd reached for his gun, so then I'd had to slug him. I'd knocked him out, so I'd had to shake him awake.

"What's up?" he had asked.

"Just this," I had answered. "I'm not riding with a guy on dope, so get used to this happening every time you try to pop one of those."

"You . . . obscenity Blue-Flamer!" he had begun, but then, feeling the effects of that punch, he tempered his response. "Why hell, slugger, I'm not riding with you anyway," he answered. "Do you think . . .?"

"Then you'd have to explain it to the Captain," I interrupted, "so like I said, get used to it."

My partner had broken his habit and stayed off it for good, but not before his locker room complaints to the other guys had stuck me with the nickname "Boy Scout." That name wasn't meant as a compliment, but I carried it for the next four years without letting anybody know it bothered me.

So that's what flashed behind my eyes when Haldis Pike told me about her uncle poisoning her father. A brother doesn't give his brother poison, any more than he'll watch him take it. He'll slap it out of his hand first.

I must have changed my expression as the memory of that first day on patrol came back to me, because Ms. Pike cocked her head like a dog, watching me. "The motive," she continued, "is that my father was about to agree to leave his money to a charitable foundation instead of splitting it between my uncle and myself."

I opened my mouth to ask another question, but a light on my desk distracted me. It signaled that an unannounced visitor had come into the outer office.

"Excuse me for a moment, Miss Pike," I said.

I brought the visitor up on the monitor. He was a distinguished-looking man of about fifty, well-dressed.

"That's him," Haldis said at my elbow. She had come around the end of my desk to look at the monitor. "That's my uncle."

On screen Ida was inviting the newcomer to take a seat.

"Go ahead and let him in," Haldis continued. "I might as well say it to him as to you."

I hit the button that signaled Ida to admit the visitor to my office. I opened the door, Norman Granville came in, and we exchanged introductions.

"I was concerned about you, Haldis," Granville told her. "You seemed distraught and . . ."

"I have a history of questionable life choices, Mr. Turley," Haldis interrupted. "That's what my uncle is going to tell you, after dancing down the primrose path for a while. But the fact still remains that my father died because he was about to devote his half of the inheritance to charity, rather than to assign it to the brother who had already spent half the family's wealth."

"There you have it, Mr. Turley," Granville answered. "Haldis has presented the quandary that awaits you upon acceptance of the case: is it murder or misunderstanding?"

"Well put, Mr. Granville," I replied. "Would you mind telling me what happened on that trip into the woods, and why you were there?"

"Not at all," Granville replied. "It might save you a great deal of trouble. Harley was preparing for a field trip, to make observations, to take specimens, and to write notes for his studies. He was a writer, you see. I accompanied him to help."

"A writer?" I repeated. "You mean he was Harley Pike the botanist?"

"Yes," Granville replied. "Author of numerous books on edible plants; the man who was single-handedly restoring the damage to the popular field guide to edible plants market that was done by the demise of Euell Gibbons via stomach cancer. Now the death of Harley Pike to mushroom poisoning will crash the market again."

"And boost the career of Red Herring," Haldis commented, "who wrote the guidebook for disguising the issue."

Granville ignored her remark and went on. "I cooked for Harley on the trip, as well as just helping to carry things," he said. "Unfortunately, I knew little about the foods he gave me to prepare. Alas, what Haldis says is true. It was I who gave

Harley the dish that killed him: a plate of mushrooms that proved to be deadly poisonous."

"You see, Mr. Turley," Haldis said. "He admits it."

"I learned in hindsight, Mr. Turley," Granville explained, "to my infinite sorrow of course, that Harley had mistaken the poisonous mushroom species Omphalotus illudens, containing toxic muscanine, for Chanterelles. The two are somewhat similar in appearance, it turns out. But I would have no way of knowing the difference. It was far from my area of expertise and it simply did not occur to me to question Harley's evaluation. I personally witnessed Harley collect the mushrooms and identify them. Who was I to contradict him?"

If Granville was guilty, I realized, all this business about identifying the species of mushrooms would be considered speculation in court. The thing that would matter was what was actually in Harley Pike's stomach.

"You're a good cook, right?" I asked him.

"If you can call training as a Cordon-bleu chef being a 'good cook'," Granville answered, "yes."

Clifton Webb, I thought: that's who the guy reminded me of. Granville had a way of making you feel like a worm, even with a reasonable answer spoken in a civil tone of voice.

Behind his back, Granville delicately lifted aside the sheet of paper I had used to cover the digital recorder I had activated a moment before. Just as delicately he held it in front of him and continued: "And if you are attempting to get me to state unambiguously that I prepared the meal for him, I readily attest to that fact. Harley was the expert, not I."

"But you didn't eat any of them, right?" I asked him.

"That is correct," Granville replied, setting the recorder back on the desk. "I happen to be allergic to mushrooms. I invite you to verify this by talking to my doctor if you wish." He gave me the doctor's name and I wrote it down.

"It may be," however," Granville continued, "that I can clear the air with a word or two of explanation. Bald Mountain was not even our destination when we departed. When I heard that we were in that area I simply had to see it. We left the highway and proceeded down Route Nine-W. A crowded parking lot

revealed that ours was a popular destination. This simply
increased my anticipation. In my mind I could hear the New
York Philharmonic playing "Night on Bald Mountain" as we
approached the path; 'Cornell' the sign read, and the path was
marked with blazes. It was an old mine trail, somebody said.
We followed a footpath up the hill. Steep, it was, and consisting
of bare rock alone. The water of the stream below sparkled as it
ran over shelves of rock. We bore left, away from the stream,
for a half mile or so. The rocks presented themselves as a long
hallway with steps every few yards. Birdsong enveloped us,
melody and counterpoint as immersive as the crisp, clear air that
invigorated our footsteps. Ahead of us were the big bare knobs
of the mountain. The going got steep and leveled out. Then it
got steep again as we turned on to the switchbacks of an old
mountain road. It was lined with pine trees that had been
twisted into grotesque shapes by some passing storm,
heightening our sense of adventure. At least you know, Haldis,
your father spent the last day of his life on Bald Mountain,
overlooking the Adirondacks. 'If only Haldis were here to see. .
. .'"

Haldis had tightened her grip on my arm. "He almost had me
going until he reached his dramatic climax," she said through
her teeth. "Will you take the case, Mr. Turley?" she asked,
glaring at Granville.

I nodded yes. Even though I was dry-mouthed at the prospect
of facing Granville's kind of speaker in a courtroom.

CHAPTER TWO:

THE HOOK

IN RESPONSE, GRANVILLE drew himself up to his full height. "Then I shall await further developments, Sir," he told me. "Good day, Haldis." He gave us both a curt little bow and left.

"Where did the incident take place?" I asked Haldis.

"Officially, in the woods beside Bald Mountain Pond," Haldis answered. "That's what they said at the hospital at Saratoga. Two men besides my uncle were with him when the doctors examined him there. But my father was unconscious and he died less than two hours later, before I could get to him."

"Where are your father's remains?" I asked her softly.

"In the Manhattan Precinct Morgue," she answered. "I had him taken there by private ambulance as soon as it was possible."

"So, you suspected Granville from the very beginning?" I asked.

"Yes," Haldis went on, "and here's another thing. Granville set a landmine for you as he left. He conveniently neglected to tell you that my father was losing his eyesight. That provides a good reason for Dad to have asked my uncle to drive him. My uncle would like to let that slide by and then drop it like a bomb in the courtroom."

"Good point," I told her. "Who were the men who helped at the scene? Do you have that information?'

"Yes," Haldis answered. "An orderly at Saratoga Hospital got their names and addresses. Actually, they are both from New York City."

"That's a break," I told her. "I'd better question them and go from there."

Haldis got up to leave and I escorted her to the door. She hadn't reached the elevator before a man passed her, coming toward me. Jordan Deaver, an ex-cop. He'd been a police sketch artist until he'd taken early retirement after serving his twenty.

"How's the art career going?' I asked, as he paused at the threshold. Deaver had left early so he could concentrate on painting, or so he'd said.

"It's, ah, so-so," Deaver answered. "Say, I need to see you."

It was poor timing. I wouldn't have accepted another walk-in case, because it seemed likely I'd have my hands full with Haldis Pike's problem. But Deaver had been a cop, and that meant something.

"Go on into my office," I told him. "I'll be there in a second." I gave Ida the contact information for the two men who'd tried to help Harley Pike, and told her I'd take any meeting she could set up with them, and as soon as possible.

Back in my inner office, Deaver looked even gloomier than he had outside. "I'm no monk," he told me, "but I've had too many bad experiences with women to go into another relationship."

Too bad for you Pal, I thought. You can't win unless you have the guts to stay in the game. But I didn't say it. I'm a private detective, not a cheerleader.

"It's always 'How does this look on me?'" Deaver continued, mimicking the kind of feminine chatter he found to be irritating. "Or it's 'What are you thinking about right now?'" he went on. "And the old reliable 'we never talk anymore,'" he concluded. "That stuff drives me crazy. In addition to which, I've switched to painting, and I wanted to get a feel of the streets. So, I go the prostitute route."

Deaver had surprised me with that one. Drawing a picture of a suspect from a verbal description takes brains as well as talent, and I had figured him for a much smarter man than this. And I also hadn't pegged him as a guy with that strong a libido. Maybe the trouble was he'd retired too early. The guy couldn't be much over fifty.

"So, you're being blackmailed?" I asked. It was a good guess, based on the past several cases I'd had that were connected with prostitution, but it turned out to be wrong.

"No," Deaver replied. "I was going about it in a pretty anonymous way. They were just working girls on the street. No names, and not even in very good light."

"Back alley stuff, then?" I asked.

"Exactly," Deaver replied. "After two marriages where I was going nuts from listening to silly blather all day long, my priority was just getting it done and going on my way. Sketching suspects from descriptions is a discipline that calls for concentration. You get word pictures that are muddled, that are iffy, that you have to guess the meaning of. By the end of a shift you've had enough of that. After the breakup of my second marriage I was looking for a way to take care of my needs with a straight transaction. Forget hotel hallways. People are there, looking at you. I opted for street trade. The regular way. No, uh, oral stimulation. I'd have gotten pretty ticked off if I looked down there and found out I was getting my kicks with a man dressed as a woman."

So far, the conversation seemed to be going nowhere. "Am I going to be editing your memoirs here, Deaver?" I asked him, "Or are you about to connect this to a case?"

Deaver's face reddened. "I see your point," he replied. "Okay, here's the problem. I think I may be targeted for a hit."

"That's better," I told him. "And it's connected to your dealings with a prostitute, right?"

"Yeah," Deaver replied. "To make a long story short, I got used to a regular, named Ginger. She was good at finding dark places in an alley. We'd do it standing up, which was my favorite. Never had anybody catch us at it until . . . well, until the time that hell broke loose, two nights ago."

"So, what happened?" I asked him.

"A car drove into that dark alley with its lights off," Jordan answered. "I would have thought that the alley was too narrow to even get a car into."

"Somebody who knew the neighborhood, then," I said.

"Yeah," Deaver replied. "Well, it turned out that the alley was big enough to drive into and open a door to get out. And that's what happened. While I was, well, immobilized. A man got out of the car and then the driver shot him. Killed him. The gunman didn't see Ginger and me until the muzzle flash from the gun lit us up."

"Did you see the shooter?" I asked. "I mean, well enough to recognize him?'

"No, not at all," Deaver replied. "My back was to him and I could only see out of the corner of my eye. But I don't know just how good a look he got of me in that moment. He could see Ginger's face, but not mine."

"Then what happened?" I asked.

"We got out of there fast," Deaver answered. "Past an old freezer somebody had junked. His car couldn't get past that."

"And you say he might be planning to try and kill you?" I pursued.

"Yes, I think so," Deaver answered. "Because the next day Ginger was shot and killed."

"Too bad," I said. "Was her killer identified?"

"No," Deaver answered. "It was a drive-by. No witnesses."

"And what makes you think you're a target as well?" I asked.

"Just a feeling," Deaver answered. "Like somebody is watching me. And of course, the fact that the killer in the alley may think I can identify him."

"I see," I told him.

Deaver paused for thought. "Ginger was special," he continued. "She went to extra effort to be accommodating. She was . . ."

Deaver's voice trailed off and caught in his throat. I got the idea then. There was truth in the well-known rhetorical question "why do you think they call them hookers?"

"I'll look into the problem, Deaver," I told him. "But I won't enter it into my records as a case yet. It's probably just a matter of getting the word out that you're no threat as a witness. If the perp gets the message, and if he believes it, you'll be off the hook. I think I've gained enough street cred over the years to get it done."

Deaver looked relieved, and left in a better frame of mind. Part of it, I guessed, was the fact that he'd gotten something off his mind that he couldn't talk about to just anybody. And if not me, then who?

CHAPTER THREE

GENUS NERIUM

"THE TWO MEN WHO HELPED carry Harley Pike out of the woods live in Queens," Ida told me, "and on the same street." She handed me the address in case I'd forgotten, which I had. "The one I called, Hal Smoots," she continued, "said he'd arrange with the other man to come over so you could talk to both of them at once. Is one O'clock all right?"

"That's good, Ida," I told her. "I'll take an early lunch, and make that for sure."

I walked over to the hotel where Louis Goldman worked, and got him to sit down with me in the dining room. Louis hadn't always been a hotel detective, and he still had an ear for news.

"Yeah, Turley, I think I can help," Louis told me after I'd explained the problem. "I caught a rumor on the street that a young would-be pimp recently got himself killed by trying to set up shop in a place where he wasn't wanted. That would account for the man who checked out in the alley during this dame Ginger's interrupted trick."

"So, if there's any truth to that rumor. . ." I replied.

"Then the killer is an established pimp," Louis finished for me. "The answer to your client's little problem might be connected with Ginger herself."

Louis left to get back to his duties and I stayed to have a good meal. The dining room wasn't crowded at all. The reason, I decided, was that the guy at the piano either wasn't any good or the piano was out of tune. A hooker tried to get me going, but it was early and she wasn't Samantha Dale. Busted on two counts.

I ransomed my car and drove to Queens to talk to the two men who'd tried to help Harley Pike. The meeting took place in Hal Smoots' garage. He was a shade tree mechanic and spoke against the background of two enormous engine blocks suspended from chains behind him. The other man who had helped, Truman Guinn, was sitting there too.

"How did you happen to meet up with the two brothers?" I asked.

"We were coming back from fishing down at Bald Mountain Pond," Hal answered. "I smelled something cooking."

"That's all?" I asked. "Nobody called you over there?"

"Nope," Guinn confirmed, "just the scent of food. Spices or something special like that were getting cooked up at a campfire down at our left as we came away from the pond. And here we were with a string of fish and sharp appetites."

"I looked down there into the trees," Hal said, "and at first I thought I saw . . . well, a leprechaun. Because this guy in under the trees was dressed in this fancy outfit, and the sun was slanting in on him through the trees, and I couldn't get any scale in there."

Guinn took up the story. "I said 'hey, Hal, let's go over there,'" he continued, "'and see if this guy wants to cook up a couple of these fish and share them with us.' A couple of them were still flapping, that's how fresh they were."

"Yeah," Hal added, "and so we went over there and put the proposition to them . . . there were two guys . . . and that's when we found out there was a problem."

"But the guy who was digging was a neat freak," Guinn went on. "He hadn't finished breaking up camp. He hadn't even put the fire out yet, because he was still burying his garbage."

"I could see that the guy with him wasn't feeling so good," Hal said. "He was sweating and red in the face."

"Yeah, and leaning back against a tree," Guinn said.

"So, we asked him how he was doing and he was out of his head," Hal continued. "'We'd better get this guy to a hospital,' I told the man in the fancy outfit."

"The way he looked I don't think he had any other clothes," Guinn said. "The guy we saw cleaning up the camp, I mean."

"And then the guy who'd been burying the garbage waved his hand," Hal went on. "In kind of a fancy gesture to show us we should put out the fire for hum. Like he didn't even want to waste words telling us to do it."

"We put dirt on the fire and then stomped on it," Guinn said. "And stashed our fishing gear in behind some trees."

"Threw the fish we'd caught into the woods, too," Hal said, "for the possums to eat. We were going to be busy carrying that guy out of there, we knew, even though the trail would be downhill once we got over the hump."

"You mean you weren't going to have to go back over the mountain, then?" I asked Hal.

"No, the trail out of there was just kind of around the edge of the mountain," Hal replied, "so you could go over and then loop around back to the parking area. It wasn't more than maybe two miles."

"Right," Guinn confirmed. "The guy in the fancy clothes wasn't going to be any use at that job. He looked like an office worker, maybe."

"So, then you packed the sick guy out right away?" I asked.

"Soon as we could, yeah," Hal answered. "Picked him up and got out of there."

"Did he say anything while you were carrying him out?" I asked.

"Nothing worth listening to," Hal answered. "He was out of his head."

"The poor guy was talking about a giant," Guinn added. "He thought the trees were giants like in the movie from New Zealand, you know. He could hardly talk. He tried to say some other stuff, but he was just mumbling."

"I guess that'll have to do for right now," I told them. "Would you guys like to go back up there later and get your gear back? I've got some other things to do first, but maybe early tomorrow."

"Yeah, I don't want to lose that gear," Hal answered. "What about you, Truman."

"Yeah, I could do it," Guinn answered.

"I'll keep in touch," I told them.

I drove to the Manhattan District Morgue. On the way there I called Ida and had her consult the computer for a rundown on brands of canned mushrooms. If Granville had pulled a switch, he'd hardly have tried to smuggle poisonous mushrooms to the camp he was planning to set up. For one thing, how would you get any of those in the city anyway? No, a guy like Granville wouldn't risk coming up with actual poison mushrooms and slipping those into his victim's food out in the woods. He'd just use regular ones and add poison. It was an almost perfect plan. All I had to do was find the flaw in it.

While I was waiting for Ida to do her research, I called Granville's doctor. He confirmed the fact that Granville suffered from a long-standing mushroom allergy. It had been brought on perhaps by Granville's exposure to mold and fungi present in the collections of centuries-old books and folios he encountered in his studies.

I parked, and just as I was getting ready to walk into the morgue Ida came back to me on the phone with a list of canned mushroom brands. It was staggering. Something like fifty brands. It was beginning to look as if this was going to be a tougher problem than I'd figured on.

In the morgue I talked to Coroner's assistant Alonzo Shad, who had performed the autopsy. I knew him from an earlier case. I asked him what had killed Pike.

"I'm not completely sure," Shad told me. "We found half-digested remains of mushrooms in the victim's stomach. That supports the theory of accidental poisoning. What puzzles me is how that could have happened when he was an author of books on wild foods. Without question he would have known the difference."

"Don't worry," I told him, "The guy I'm sizing up for this knew that Pike was losing his eyesight. He's the guy who cooked that last meal."

"What's your theory?" Shad asked.

"I think my suspect slipped poison into the food," I answered. "If I could get the coroner's lab to analyze half-digested store-bought canned mushrooms . . ."

"I can save you some time," Shad interrupted. "You're thinking about comparing canned mushrooms microscopically with wild ones, to prove that the victim ate those instead of the wild ones. The flaw in that plan is that there are too many varieties available in the stores."

"You're telling me," I replied.

"You'd never get a court order to get that analysis done here," Shad continued. "It's too speculative, and we're too busy. If you have a bunch of analyses done in an independent lab, you'll have to present all those analyses in court. That introduces an element of doubt in the outcome right away."

"How's that?" I asked.

"If your suspect's lawyers have to introduce the other brands to try and complicate the issue in court," Shad explained, "it'll be him doing it, not you. That will make a world of difference to a jury. I'm not a lawyer, but from what I've seen here, that kind of distinction makes a very big difference to a jury."

"What if I came up with the exact brand he had used to put the poison in, and you analyzed that?" I asked Shad.

"Then you'd have him cold," Shad returned. "We have a good example to compare here, with those stomach content samples. And no two brands are going to be identical, microscopically."

"So, if the killer used store-bought mushrooms and poisoned them . . ." I began.

"And you can find out what brand they were," Shad finished for me, "you've got him."

"And what if he managed to substitute poisonous mushrooms from the woods for the ones Pike found?" I asked.

"Then your case is blown," Shad answered.

I had to agree. It was time to get back to Smoots and Guinn. I called and they agreed to head out early the next morning to go back to Bald Mountain.

"Park your car here and we'll take my van," Hal told me the next day at his house. "The wives want to go along, okay?"

I wasn't in a position to dictate conditions if I wanted them to go. "Sure," I answered, but I hadn't realized we'd get a surly teenager thrown into the deal. Hal's fifteen-year-old son Brad stepped reluctantly aboard at the last moment. He didn't even say hello, because he evidently wanted to stay home and play video games or whatever kids that age do now. As it was he'd managed to bring a phone along to play with on the way.

The wives chatted and were in good spirits. It was nice to go on an outing that didn't involve handling fish, the gist of it was. But the kid maintained silence. Only once did he look up to ask me a question that seemed to have occurred to him in the course of his game. "Did the police ask you to help catch the Crankpot?" he wanted to know.

Brad was referring to the hunt for the city's latest serial killer. "No," I replied. "We're a small security firm, and that's a job that would take more organization than we're capable of."

It was a bad answer, and the kid knew it. He went back to his phone. He probably had decided I was just chicken. And he was right. A sniper who kills at random is nobody you want to focus attention on you. A local TV announcer had made just such a mistake a couple of days before, and paid the price. "That Crankpot is a crack shot," he had remarked to his co-host. Not only had he been besieged with complaints from the public for the glib remark, but the next day the sniper had killed him from a block away while he was crossing the street. Yes, that Crankpot was a crack shot all right.

It was early, and we made good time. When we reached the point on the interstate where we were to get off on Route Nine-W, Hal spoke up. "Here's where we got off to go to the hospital," he said. "Funny, though; Granville tried to get us to turn left and head up to the hospital at Glen Falls. That would have taken at least a half-hour longer."

"Yeah," Guinn put in. "Granville was convinced that the hospital in Saratoga was just for mental patients."

"Or at least that's what he tried to put over on us," Hal added. "I'm glad we didn't go all the way up to Glen Falls. As it was, Truman and I had to flip a coin to see who hitchhiked back to Bald Mountain to pick up the car."

"It gets to be a long night when you start it out carrying a grown man on your back a mile or two," Guinn said.

"Why was it you didn't split up and one of you follow the other to the hospital?" I asked him.

"I don't know," Hal answered. "There was just something about the situation that didn't seem right. But I couldn't put my finger on it."

"I felt the same way, too," Guinn added.

I got the picture, but there was no way testimony as vague as that was going to help in front of a jury.

We soon pulled into the Bald Mountain parking lot. Cars were already there. I jumped out to take a look while the others were deploying. The air was wonderful.

"Here's the thing," Hal said behind me. "Turley's on a tight schedule, I know, so we've got to backtrack along the return loop over to the place we're going. But you girls can go on up and see the surrounding territory from the peak of Bald Mountain. That is, if we can get Brad to go along and protect you."

"Yeah," Guinn said. "Can you handle that, Brad?"

The kid said he could, so we split up the party and got going.

Truman, Hal, and I made a wide sweep to the left along a pathway of bare rock. Tall pines shot up around us at odd angles, as if they had gotten stuck that way when they were trying out for the Disney movie named after the mountain. Our destination was probably less than two miles. I had barely gotten into the rhythm of walking before Hal brought us to a stop.

"Okay, the grove of woods we found them in is just over there," Hal announced, "a hundred yards off the trail."

We went over and the two men showed me where Granville had buried the garbage. Guinn detached a folded Army surplus trench tool from his belt, adjusted it for digging, and handed it to me. The men went to collect their gear while I shoveled.

I got down to some flattened tin cans and other trash. I picked them up and examined them. Their labels were still intact. They were about right for the remains of one good dinner for two men, but nothing about them suggested mushrooms.

I leaned against a tree and thought about it.

I dug down further and after going down six inches found a flattened and burned can. It had no label.

I thought about what Shad had told me at the lab. About how I had no official standing to have a speculative series of tests done at the Coroner's lab. My case had just gone back to having an independent research lab do fifty or more analyses of mushroom brands. And how would that look to the jurors? Coming from a police lab they might accept the conclusions, even though the regular research lab might do a more accurate job. Juries are conditioned by TV to see the police lab conclusion as official.

Smoots and Guinn came out of the woods with their gear, and gave me some that Granville had left as well. It contained cooking gear which had been cleaned until it shone.

We sat and waited, listening to the wind, a distant woodpecker, twittering birds, and a fish slapping the water somewhere behind us. We were waiting for the wives and the kid, because I hadn't found anything there to use as evidence.

Our serenity was shattered by a scream from up the trail to Bald Mountain. "Maisie," Hal shouted.

We raced up the trail, Hal well in advance, to see Hal's wife cringing away from something near her feet. It was a huge snake, over five feet long, with a cobra-like bulge a foot or so behind its head. Hal lunged at it with a heavy branch he'd snatched up in mid-stride, but found himself knocked off his feet by a low tackle from Brad.

Hal untangled himself and leaped to his feet, confronting his son in a fighting stance. "What the hell. . ?" he foamed, astonished at Brad's unexpected rebellion.

"Sorry, Dad," Brad said quickly. "You were about to kill a black racer, and a really nice one. We caught it when it was distracted by taking down a. . ."

Brad looked at the retreating snake, barely visible now in the leaves.

". . . Muskrat, I'd say," Brad continued. "We're not far from the lake."

'That's . . . uh . . . okay," Son, Hal answered, dusting himself off. I had an idea he'd be a little more circumspect in the way he approached his son from now on.

Bradley Smoots had come down the trail from Bald Mountain Peak with a fresh new attitude about the outdoors. What he knew about wildlife he'd probably learned from books or the internet. Getting out and interacting with it was a whole new world, he'd found. Fresh air and a little authority had done wonders for him.

And the best thing about it was that he'd made the discovery in time to get back out in the woods with his dad in the future. If our little party hadn't accomplished any more than that on our outing, the trip was still worth it. The six of us continued down the trail to the parking lot and got out of there.

"What was it you said Harley was talking about on the way to the hospital," I asked Hal again.

"Something about the trees," Hal answered. "Green giants," he called them."

"And you thought maybe he was thinking about that Tolkien book and the movie they made from it?" I asked.

"Yeah," Hal answered. "Movies, that is."

Brad was whistling in the back seat. "What's that tune you're whistling, Brad?' I asked him.

"Just a commercial," Brad answered. "For Green Giant Niblets."

Green Giant, I thought. Green Giant mushrooms! Somewhere along the line, after being hit with a massive dose of poison, Harley Pike had seen Granville disposing of a can of mushrooms. He'd tried to communicate the message in the only way he had left.

Night was falling by the time we got back into the city, but the Coroner's lab doesn't keep banker's hours. I got them to conduct a single analysis on one brand of mushrooms. The results were conclusive: Harley Pike had died from a dose of poison. Mixed with the mushrooms were fragments of some other plant substance.

"What's that?" Shad asked, pointing to the knapsack I'd left on a chair beside the door.

"That's the knapsack Granville left in the woods," I answered.

Shad examined it with a flashlight, discovering one tiny leaf wedged in the lining. "What's this?" he asked, carefully removing it with tweezers. He took it to a nearby microscope.

"Yes," he said, "That's what I thought it was. It's oleander. You've got him."

CHAPTER FOUR:

THE LOW NUMBER

TEMPLE WORTHINGTON moved his hands across the keys of the big Steinway, trying not to look bored. Night life was a welcome part of his usual gig, and now here he was, playing in the middle of the day in the lounge of a hotel museum.

"Somewhere there's music," Worthington began softly, but then stopped. His fingers continued to play the song automatically, but his vocal apparatus ceased to function as he witnessed the arrival of a cloud in the room. It had drifted in slowly and paused as if to see if there was anyone inside it recognized.

The cloud was about five feet tall, and hung suspended about three feet off the floor. Following close behind it a man squirted it with a plant mister, evidently attempting to herd it back into the gallery it had come from.

Worthington regained his composure and played on. "Somewhere there's heaven," he continued, catching up with the song.

In a little while a woman walked by, covered from head to toe in corn syrup, with strips of newspaper stuck to her bare skin.

"What in hell . . .?" Worthington muttered under his breath. A nearby bellhop overheard the comment, and filled the befuddled pianist in on the mystery. "They're staging artistic happenings in the gallery," the bellhop explained. "It's called performance art. They'll be doing it for a while."

The bellhop moved on and Worthington played some more. "That stuff was old-hat fifty years ago," he muttered, after a minute or so. "Art or not, it's amazing that such screwy goings-on can be so distracting and boring at the same time. If this keeps up, I'm going to have to quit this gig and go somewhere else."

A moment later a young man came in and sat on the couch in a corner by the door. The newcomer took a camera from one pocket and a metal cylinder about eight inches long from another. Unfolded, it proved to be a selfie stick.

"Thank you," Worthington said modestly to the one lone octogenarian dowager who had applauded his efforts. "Here's one for you. 'Somewhere over the rainbow,'" he began.

The young man attached the camera to the selfie stick and produced a revolver from the inside pocket of his coat.

Worthington suppressed a sigh. "Not another one," he thought. "This stuff was played out before Perry Como broke his knee."

The young man pointed the gun at his head and lined up the camera for the picture. But instead of pushing the shutter button he pulled the trigger, and blew his brains against the wall to one side of the pianist.

Worthington wiped a drop of red liquid from behind his left ear and continued without missing a note. "Hmmm, it even smells like blood," he thought. "Kind of metallic." He paused for a second and looked at the man on the couch. He turned back and started playing again. "Well, they're getting a little more interesting," he said to himself. He went on with the song. "There's . . . a . . . land that I've heard of . . . once in a . . ."

THE PHONE RANG just as I was heading out the door for my morning run. The call was from Captain John Fowler.

"I'm glad I caught you," Fowler said. "I wondered if I could get you to drop in on a crime scene for me. It won't be for pay, but I guess you know that already."

"I'll do it, John," I told him. "How can I help?" Not only did I owe Fowler a favor, bit I'd been a cop once and it felt good to be able to call a Precinct Captain by his first name and get away with it.

"It's a double shooting," Fowler answered. "It concerns a potential race flare-up. Caucasian kills two black men. Dr. Raymond Renfro, the classic mild-mannered professor, versus two burglars. If you can help put a lid on it, I'll be in your debt."

"I'll see what I can do," I replied.

Fowler gave me the address and a few details. I took the time to change, but breakfast would be a couple of protein bars on the way to Renfro's house.

It was just my luck that two blocks past my house I passed a woman pushing a shopping cart. Guilt gripped me at the reminder of Samantha Dale's do-it-yourself rescue from a houseful of goons. And it meant I'd be seeing Samantha's face on the body of every woman on the way there. Watch out, pedestrians, for the tough, hard-boiled detective. He's love sick.

The cop outside the crime scene stopped me, but Lieutenant Dan Roberts, the officer in charge, saw me and waved me in.

"Nice to see you, Turley," Dan said.

"I got a bug in my ear from the top, Dan," I told him. "I guess maybe he mentioned it to you."

"Yes, he did, Turley. Thanks," Dan replied.

"So, what's it all about?" I asked.

"This one could blow up," Dan told me. "A couple of black men expired on the scene and, given the current climate the deaths could spark racial unrest."

Dan was referring to the murder of several members of a black family the previous day while getting off a bus. It was another outrage from the serial killer called the Crankpot. Eager social justice warriors had already seized upon the opportunity to spread the rumor that the shootings were the work of a police sniper.

"You're right about that," I replied. "The coroner's not even here yet, and I had to shoulder my way through a crowd to get in. What's the story?"

"I'll fill you in on that later," Dan told me, "but you're wrong about the coroner. He's been here and gone, along with the dead guys. We got them photographed and marked their positions on the floor as soon as we could, hoping to prevent trouble here."

"Fast work," I remarked. "Does this house belong to Renfro?"

"Yes," Dan answered. "Dr. Raymond Renfro, Professor of Romance Literature at N.Y.U. Let's go back to where it happened, the den." He led me through the house to a back room.

The room looked more like a personal museum than a den. Stuffed fish and deer heads hung on the walls, sports trophies lined the shelves, and a hall tree displayed a variety of head gear that ranged from a ten-gallon hat to an olive-drab kepi. I looked twice, because something wasn't consistent in the pattern and I couldn't tell what it was. Perhaps it was just the fact that the room didn't seem to match up with the identity of a Professor from an ultra-liberal University.

Chalk marked the two places on the floor, close together, where the men had died. The room was cold.

A man rose from a chair in the corner to meet us. "Dr. Renfro here," Dan told me, "has shot two burglars in his house. If you would, Dr. Renfro, please tell Mr. Turley here how it all happened."

"Not so fast," said a voice behind us at the door we had just come through. We turned to see a man in an expensive silk suit. He was carrying an even more expensive-looking briefcase. Renfro's lawyer.

The attorney introduced himself as William Wyler Wilson, handed us both a card, and took Renfro aside to begin a consultation with him in the corner. They had barely begun to converse when a rock crashed through the window and a voice outside yelled "back-shooter."

"That does it," Dr. Renfro blurted, standing up. "I'm not taking this. I want to explain just how it happened, detective." He looked at Wilson. "Again," he concluded.

Attorney W. W. Wilson rose haughtily to his feet. "Well," he said, "It looks as if I'm not needed here." He left the room slowly, as if expecting Renfro to change his mind and call him back.

"Here's how it happened," Dr. Renfro said, turning toward Roberts and me. "I have a long and narrow house, as you can see."

Renfro stopped, noticing the lawyer lingering in the door behind him. He looked at the lawyer. Wilson finished leaving.

Renfro continued: "In the winter I heat only the front part. I don't often go into the back. This morning I came into this room and surprised two burglars at their work. Or rather, I should say I was the one surprised, because by the time I noticed something was wrong the larger of the two had grabbed me from behind. The other man pointed a gun at me and threatened to shoot."

Dan gave me the truth sign behind Renfro's back. Renfro hadn't repeated any of the speech by rote, but the details were the same as before, Dan was telling me.

"Tell him which gun, Dr. Renfro," Dan suggested.

"Certainly," Renfro replied. "A Colt Peacemaker that has been in my family for generations. The one Lieutenant Roberts is holding."

Dan held the evidence bag with the gun in it up to the light for me to see. "Look at the serial number, Turley," Dan said.

"I already have," I told Dan. "With that low a serial number, and in such good condition, that gun would sell for more than the house we're standing in."

"Sure," Dan agreed. "Dr. Renfro, if you don't mind me asking, why do you choose to live in this neighborhood when you could sell that gun and move to a safer one?"

Renfro seemed surprised at the question. He looked from the stuffed elk head to the hall tree and back at us. "My family were here way back when this was a fashionable district," Renfro answered. "People around here tolerate me because I'm inoffensive. I'm sort of a pet, I suppose, not threatening to anyone. And I teach a non-threatening subject at a very liberal University. That Colt has become such a familiar object that I had almost forgotten its intrinsic value until Charles Ogden offered to buy it a few months ago."

"I see," said Roberts. "Please continue."

"I hesitated," Renfro continued, "and Ogden withdrew the offer. But only because he had found a better example."

Renfro's throat was dry. He drank from a nearby bottle of water and continued: "The man who was holding me asked 'what do we do now?' across my shoulder to the other man. 'Get rid of the witness,' the smaller man answered. 'Antique guns don't have to be registered. We got it made.'"

"The smaller man taunted me," Renfro continued, "by asking 'where do you want the bullet?' He thought it was funny to point my own weapon at me, the one he was in the process of stealing."

Feet were clumping around in the next room. Dan and I thought it was the lawyer again, but it was only another cop walking around.

"It was a bitter thing," Renfro continued, "to know I was going to die by means of an object I had cherished for so long. My great-great-grandfather bought that gun new, the first year it came out, 1873. I'd played with it all my life. My emotion caused me to say something that surprised even me: 'in the neck,' I said, 'so you'll hit the man behind me.'"

Roberts looked at me. He liked that come-back.

"This caused the assailant to break out laughing," Renfro continued, "and the man behind me loosened his grip for some reason. I took my chance and grabbed the gun."

"And then?" Dan asked.

"In a flash I had it in position, cocked," Renfro said. "This caused the man who had been laughing to pull his gun. I shot before he could. In response the man who'd been holding me let loose and grabbed for his own gun."

Renfro took another sip. "Go on," Roberts said.

"I shot just before the second man could," Renfro told us. "He fired several times, but only into the floor."

"Some story," I said.

"Wait a minute," Dan said. "You haven't heard it all."

"Right," Renfro said. "What happened after that is the reason for that commotion outside."

"Yeah," Roberts prompted, "tell Turley about the other man."

"A third man was hiding upstairs in the spare bedroom," Renfro continued." Renfro pointed to a stairway at the far corner of the room. "When the shooting started, he dropped from the window up there and disappeared. I saw him poke his head up in the window the rock came through over there, but when he saw the gun in my hand he took off."

"Can you describe him?" I asked.

"A young man, twenty at most, wearing a red cap," Renfro answered.

Again, we were surprised by a voice behind us. "A white man killing two black men," the cop we had heard before spoke up. Officer Grant Byars. He had come to the back to offer his input. It was going to be needed. Byars was the only black man on the crew.

"Self-defense, but no witnesses," Byars continued.

"That story's not going to fly with that crowd out there. It will fall upon their ears as murder and oppression."

"That's right," I said, "and build from there."

"Any ideas then?" Roberts asked Byars.

"Two of them could shoot each other, though," Byars answered. "It happens every day and nobody says anything about it."

"We'll see," Dan replied. He turned to Renfro. "Dr. Renfro, could you stand being a hero twice in one day?" he asked.

Renfro put his hands in his pockets and looked down at the floor. I tried to put myself in his place: a bookworm, a man who lived a life of adventure at remote second hand in his studies. It would be hard for such a man to push away the one opportunity to be recognized for an act of courageous defiance against deadly odds. But Renfro was up to it. He straightened up and faced us with a level gaze. "All right," he said. "Nobody wants a riot."

"Let's get it over with," Dan said. "Byars, can you get your partner in here?"

"Yes, sir," said Officer Byars.

Edwards, the Officer who had arrived on the scene first, came in. "How can I help you, Lieutenant Roberts?" he asked.

"You've seen what's outside," Dan said. "We can get out of a hole here, but it's up to you two. Especially you," Byars. You're black, so you get the veto if you want it."

"Hell, Lieutenant," Byars said, "I don't want to work inside a hornet's nest any more than you men do."

"Goes double for me," Edwards said.

Then an image clicked in my mind. "Wait a minute," I said, "I've figured out what's wrong here." I crossed to the hall tree. "Dr. Renfro," I asked, "Is this your cap?"

"Yes, certainly," Renfro returned. "It's a hunting cap that my father . . . wait a minute. That cap is red, but it's certainly not the one that was hanging there."

Lieutenant Roberts approached the hall tree and looked at the cap. He put on latex gloves and examined it. "What do you make of this, Byars?" Roberts asked.

Byars bent over to examine the cap. "It's a baseball cap designed to look like a do-rag," he said. "Somebody will make a million on that idea."

"Then he was wearing my dad's hunting cap," Renfro said. "The man in the window."

Byars looked me up and down. "Too big," he said. "Lieutenant Roberts, it will have to be you. Would you mind exchanging clothes with me for a little while?"

Byars was dressed in a police uniform. Roberts and I understood immediately what he was offering to do.

"Byars, I can't be responsible for something that dangerous" Roberts told him.

"So how does a man move up in this dog and pony show, anyway?" Byars asked.

That was enough for Roberts. The two started stripping. Byars went out the back door, wearing Dan's clothes and the do-rag cap.

"Turley, float out front and watch him," Roberts told me. "If you can without seeming to, that is."

"Will do," I told him.

I went out through the front door and watched, as casually as possible. Byars evaluated several prospects who weren't wearing caps before he spotted the young man in a red hunting cap who was hanging back in the shadows. The young man noticed the do-rag cap and said something to Byars.

I looked away, so as not to bring attention to the meeting. When I looked back, they both had disappeared. I waited for a commotion to begin, but it didn't happen.

When I thought enough time had elapsed, I went back inside. Byars was already in the back room with his captive in tow.

Edwards was taking photographs of the young man while Roberts and Byars were changing back into their own clothes. Dan was talking to the young suspect between garments. The scene looked strangely like the dressing room of a community theater.

"If a riot breaks out because of that back-shooting story you've been circulating," Roberts was telling the young man, "then you're on the hook for it."

Roberts adjusted his tie and took the camera Edwards was using. "Look here," he said to the young man. "Look at the two guys you came in here with. They both got shot in the chest. And they shot each other. We know you were upstairs in the bedroom when the shooting started. Want to talk about it?"

The young man looked away and said nothing.

Edwards handed Dan a cell phone with some information on the screen. Roberts inspected it in silence.

Roberts looked back at the young suspect. "You don't have a record, Latavius," he said. "And you don't have to have one. You talk, you walk."

The young man looked up at Byars as if for confirmation. He seemed to like what he saw. "I heard voices," Latavius said, "but I didn't know what the gunfire was actually about. I didn't lie about it on purpose out there. I just assumed the first explanation that came to me was the correct one, I guess."

Roberts handed the phone back to Edwards. "If you like

being an apprentice thief, Latavius," Roberts told him, "we can arrange for you to have a very long apprenticeship. Participating in a felony that results in two deaths would get you twenty years. Or you can go back out there and spread the story the way it happened and stop a full-blown riot. What's it going to be?"

Catch and release. We'd be sorry if this guy's name came up later in connection with some heinous crime, but at that moment it seemed like the right thing to do. Latavius Patton took the deal and slipped out the back way.

The decision having been made, we went through an alternate story, fleshing out the scenario Roberts had sketched for Latavius. Some of it was in pantomime, because a cop we didn't trust was standing two rooms away.

When we had finished Roberts stood for a moment with his arms crossed, mentally reviewing what he had just seen. "Good," he said. "Let's do it before this thing gets away from us."

We went outside and Dan questioned Renfro. We were standing close enough to the police cordon that an eavesdropper could hear him, but far enough away to make it look good.

Renfro stood for a minute or so, supported by Roberts, and took several deep breaths.

"Have you just about recovered from that fainting spell?" the Lieutenant asked Renfro.

"Oh, yes, I'm beginning to feel much better now, Officer. Thank you," Renfro answered. "The fresh air was a wonderful idea."

"Good," replied Roberts. "Now let's wrap this up, so we can get out of here. Tell me what happened."

"Yes, Officer," Renfro answered. "This morning I went into the back room and was surprised to see that two burglars had broken in. I hid and watched then through a curtain I hung back there to keep the cold air out."

"That was courageous of you," Roberts commented.

"Thank you, Officer," Renfro replied. "It was a very frightening experience. They had found an antique firearm I own, worth many thousands of dollars."

"You had better put that gun in a bank box after this," Roberts told him.

"Yes, Officer, I shall," Renfro replied. "They were surprised because they had found something more valuable than they had expected, and they had a falling out about it. To my horror, the smaller man shot the big one with my gun."

Roberts wrote that down in a notebook. "Then what happened?" he asked.

"The smaller man held the gun and looked at it," Renfro continued, "perhaps thinking about its value. He didn't notice that the other man had risen to his feet. The wounded man snatched my gun away from the other and shot him in return. As he fell the smaller man drew his weapon and fired, but only at the floor."

"And after that?" Roberts asked, still writing.

"I was afraid there might be others," Renfro said, "so I grabbed up my gun and looked around. But there weren't, so I called the police."

"I see," said Roberts. "Did you get all that down, too, Officer Byars?"

"Yes, Sir," Byars answered.

Roberts closed his notebook. "All right, Dr. Renfro," he said. "Just in case the robbers did have accomplices, I'm going to detail an Officer to stay here tonight."

Renfro agreed, but I didn't think a cop would actually show up. Renfro would save the city some money by declining the offer. He wasn't exactly the nebbish we had all taken him for. I'd already noticed that he had a few more guns around the place, tucked into various niches. Lucky for him the one he'd had to use was that Colt with the low number.

CHAPTER FIVE:

BLOOD ALLEY

I PHONED THE OFFICE to catch up on developments. "A man named Alonzo Shad called in," Ida reported, "to tell you cross sampling confirmed that the poison that killed Harley Pike was oleander."

"That's early," I replied. "Anything else?"

"Just that Shad thinks they have enough to convict," she answered, "and that they're in the process of getting the warrant right now."

I pulled into an eatery and made up for my missing breakfast. Then I went back to Word to the Wise. There I learned that when the police had gone to pick up Norman Granville, they found he had dropped out of sight. The guy had good intelligence, in more than one way. But at least Haldis Pike would get the money. Or rather, some foundation would.

I hit the street. It was time to do some looking around in that area of town where Jordan Deaver's lost love had gotten herself killed and stick my finger in the wind.

I like to keep tabs on people I've had trouble with in the city. I had learned from a database that Mack Morgan, the older brother of Lamont, was part owner of the hotel I'd taken Samantha's sister Penelope out of a year ago. It was located in an area close to the alley where the murder Jordan Deaver had witnessed had occurred.

I made a second visit to Mack Morgan's sleazy dive. At the desk I asked the clerk where the manager was. With a jerk of his head he gestured toward a door behind him to one side.

I walked in. Mack Morgan was seated at a desk in the corner to my left and two huge men were parked in chairs in the middle of the small room watching TV. My mouth dropped open when I got a good look at the one closest to the TV. I thought I was seeing a ghost.

Mack Morgan nearly did a spit take when he saw who had come in. "You!" he exclaimed, and turned to one of the seated men. "Earn your pay, Bomber," he shouted. "This bastard killed two of my brothers. I want him on the floor quick, ready to work on."

Bomber, the man closest to me, sprang to his feet and took a step to his right. He launched a monstrous roundhouse sucker punch from waist level. He moved quickly for a man his size, but he was so confident of his strength that he didn't bother to cover up with his other hand. I hit him with an overhand right that landed on the corner of his jaw, just under his ear.

Bomber's jaw sank into the side of his beefy head and he toppled toward the wall. He crashed into it, broke a hole in the drywall, ripped more of it out on the way down, and came to a stop with his head hidden inside the wall. He displaced some wiring on the way, causing the glass shade to pop off of a wall sconce lamp a few feet away. It was an antique, refitted from an old gas lamp. The shade fell to the floor and shattered, a beautiful object, cut glass and maybe a hundred years old.

We stood there a moment, the three of us who were still conscious, like a theatrical tableau. Mack Morgan was half-way out of his chair with his hand twisted back by mine, in case the object he had just taken out of his pocket was a weapon. It wasn't. He had tried to ditch his keys and pocket change, afraid I was planning to repeat the treatment I'd given his brother Lamont before.

Morgan was watching the other big man in the room, the lumbering hulk who looked exactly like the third Morgan brother, Davon. A guy I'd tricked into killing himself and Lamont Morgan some six months ago.

The big lug was just standing there with the heavy chair he'd been sitting in dangling from his hand like a toy. Tears glistened in his eyes as he watched the fallen Bomber.

"He cut Bomber's head off," the man said, and a tear spilled over and ran down his cheek.

"It's okay Rooney," Mack said. "Bomber's head is just stuck inside the wall."

"Oh, all right, Mack," Rooney replied. His expression brightened and he sat back down to watch TV.

"My brother," Mack said. "The only one left you haven't killed." Seeing I wasn't interested in the keys, he put them back into his pocket.

"Twins," I said, relieved that my mind hadn't been playing tricks on me.

"That's right," Mack replied. "If it's any of your effing business. Lamont and I kept one each, because we had to peel them off of each other when they got together."

Too much information, I thought. But I didn't say that, because it wouldn't have been polite. "Tell me about a girl named Ginger," I told him. "Used to wear a green cap with a silver stud on it."

"Ginger lives in the Blue Diamond," Mack replied, "across the street about three doors down, as far as I know. Her real name is Viola de Gamba."

Definitely not her real name, I thought, but I wasn't going to waste time teaching Morgan about music, humor, or Italian. "Thanks," I told him, and left.

The desk clerk at the Blue Diamond was a woman. Her sleepy eyes belied the fact that she'd had so many face lifts that her eyebrows threatened to disappear beneath the Orphan Annie wig piled up on her head. It was some kind of problem with her muscles, because she wasn't trying to squint. She was trying not to.

"Ginger?" she responded to my inquiry. "I guess you haven't heard yet. Third floor. Three-oh-nine, but she's dead. Got killed."

I turned toward the stairs.

"Too bad," I heard the woman mumble as I walked by. "Nice girl, Ginger. A good whore. Lose Ginger, lose Moselle too."

When I got to the third floor the door to three-oh-nine was slightly ajar. I approached cautiously but the person inside heard me anyway.

"That's about everything, Carl" a musical voice called from within. The girl with the voice opened the door and looked at me. "Oh, I thought you were someone else," she said.

I looked past her into the room. "You one of Ginger's?" she asked.

My being a client of Ginger's was the handiest interpretation at the time, so I did my best to look crestfallen and see what comfort she might be disposed to offer. "You'd be Moselle, I guess," I told her meekly.

"Oh, Ginger mentioned me then?" Moselle asked, a look of pleasure briefly illuminating her features.

I answered with a small lying grunt.

"Ginger thought she had a new sponsor, a young man she liked," Moselle told me. "But it didn't pan out."

Pretending to suppress a sigh, I looked at my feet.

Moselle and Ginger must have been close. She looked back into the room and heaved a sigh herself, a genuine one.

"I've got two brothers in the car outside, waiting to take me back to Minnesota," Moselle told me. "I thought you were one of them. I don't like this town anymore."

"Did Ginger leave anything?" I asked. Conveniently, Moselle took this as the moping of a disconsolate john and took pity on me.

"What's left is under the bed," Moselle answered. "I'm afraid to touch it."

Footsteps sounded behind me. I checked to be sure. It was Moselle's brother Carl all right. "This guy bothering you, Moselle?" he asked.

"No Carl," Moselle answered. "And have some respect. He got hung up on Ginger."

Carl favored me with a brief glance of pity and took the half-carton of soft drinks Moselle was carrying.

"Bye now," Moselle said, and walked past me to exit with Carl.

Under the bed was a cardboard dress box with various keepsakes in it: a cheerleader's pom-poms, a program from a popular Broadway show, and a small sketch I was pretty sure was from the hand of Jordan Deaver. What interested me most was a photograph of Ginger with a broad-shouldered man with slightly slanted eyes. His bushy hair made him distinctly identifiable, a puffy black mop with a skunk stripe across it from front to back. The white part occupied exactly the space a Mohawk would have if the rest of his hair were removed.

The photo was marked "Neron and me." It had been torn straight across in the middle, carefully put back together with transparent tape, and torn roughly apart a second time. It was still in two pieces now. Ginger hadn't repaired it a second time. There had been two breakups then, the second one final.

Coupled with what I'd heard on the street, the photo gave me a starting point. Twenty minutes ago, I had seen the man in the photo getting out of a long white pimpmobile less than a block from the Blue Diamond.

I folded the sketch up tightly and jammed it into my pocket. Then I hit the street, preparing to ask around some more. I headed north, intending to inspect the alley where Ginger's new pimp had gotten his career so abruptly terminated.

A noise that sounded like backfire came from across the street. I couldn't associate it with any nearby car, and then caught on that it was an echo from an alley just ahead on my side of the street. This one was almost too small to accommodate a golf cart, much less a car. It was down a block or two from the one I was headed for.

I slipped into the alley, close against the wall, and made my way silently down the narrow cleft between high brick walls. Jordan Deaver was there, bending over the still form of a man surrounded by a spreading pool of blood.

Deaver noticed me as he stood up. He retreated from the slowly encroaching flow, making sure the muzzle of the thirty-eight he was holding pointed away from me.

"Turley," he said. "Well, I guess I've screwed the pooch this time." He dropped the thirty-eight onto the broad back of the recently departed Neron the Pimp.

"What the hell goes on?" I demanded. "First you ask me to do a job, beating around the bush for fifteen minutes, and then you go ahead and do it yourself."

"I haven't been able to sleep," Jordan replied. "It affects my judgement."

"How did you find out it was this guy?" I asked.

"That white stripe in his hair," Jordan answered. "I realized it was what I had seen when I turned toward him that night. I had taken it for a stray reflection before. When I saw him out on the street just now it all came together."

"I see," I told him. I looked the alley over in both directions. No one else had recognized the sound as gunfire.

"So, what happens now?" Jordan asked.

"Is that your gun?" I inquired in return.

"No, it's his," Jordan answered. "I got him in here by shoving a piece of pipe into his back and telling him it was a forty-five."

What next indeed? I wondered. Anybody can get tough for a day, but I couldn't imagine Jordan Deaver holding up for long in stir. What the hell? I decided. One more unsolved murder wouldn't make any difference to N.Y.P.D., and the city wouldn't miss the pimp.

"What happens now is that I lose a client," I told him. "Is that the pipe you used?"

Jordan glanced down at a short length of pipe near the body, stuck in the blood. "Yes," he answered.

"Take a hike," I told him.

Jordan couldn't quite believe what I had said. He sidled away, looking back at me a few times like a scared dog. When he reached the street, he composed himself, strolling off in a casual posture with one hand over his face.

It was the kind of alley you wouldn't normally go into voluntarily, so I didn't expect any company. Beyond question, Neron was dead. He had caught a slug through the aorta and had bled out all at once.

No licensed investigator would admit to removing evidence from a crime scene, so let's just say I spent the next ten minutes in that alley reflecting on philosophical issues.

For instance, I thought about just how lucky I was that Arnold Gassner and I had spent only one night at each of the brothels we had visited on our ill-fated world tour. I thought about the huge hook Ginger had left sticking in Jordan Deaver's vitals. And about how there are some waters that are best left untested.

CHAPTER SIX:

THE HAT TRICK

I TURNED MY CHAIR AROUND and looked at the cityscape framed by my office window. Letting Jordan Deaver walk away from that alley had somehow seemed a just act at the time. But then, an act you could do time for is never a good thing. I sat there wondering just how badly I was off my game. It wasn't the proper frame of mind for a private investigator to be in.

Mental fatigue, that's what it was. Or maybe I'd committed the worst crime a private eye can afford: letting a woman get to me and turn me soft. Whatever the problem was, it had made me subject to mistakes. What I'd done for Deaver yesterday was a very dangerous thing to do in a city with as many security cameras as New York has.

That's why alarm bells sounded inside my head when Ida rang in to tell me a city prosecutor had come to see me. Albert Blanton, a guy my old partner on the force, Matt Jacobs, had introduced me to. Well, at least it wouldn't be an anonymous executioner who pinned me to the wall.

"Send him in," I told Ida. Better now than later, I thought. Might as well get it out of the way. You can find something positive in any experience. The ability to adapt to circumstances, for instance.

But the blade hadn't dropped on my neck after all. Blanton strode up to my desk with a jaunty air, and flipped a manila folder onto it. "One of those pushed-or-fallen cases, Turley" he said, taking a seat. "I'm trying to bulletproof it."

The shock of getting a free roll of the dice was too much for me. I stood up, took a deep breath, shook the back of my chair, and sat back down. "Excuse me," I said. "Sometimes it gets stuck on the carpet."

"N.Y.P.D. have done their job," Blanton went on. "They ran the perp down and locked him up. Now it's my job to get a conviction."

"What do you want me to do, Mr. Blanton?" I asked him, picking up the folder.

"A little legwork," Blanton answered. "It's an open and shut case. Almost, that is."

"What's missing?" I asked. I wasn't inclined to look through the folder just then. Keyed up as I was, the words wouldn't have meant a thing to me.

"My witnesses were observant," Blanton answered, "but not very precise."

"Do their testimonies conflict?" I asked.

"No," Blanton replied, "but it's kind of a mosaic."

"What happened, in a nutshell?" I asked.

"The victim, Miguel Alvarez," Blanton answered, "was returning to his apartment. A luxury high rise, downtown. He passed the suspect, Galen Galton, on the way, just before he got there. Galton hit him up for a handout. Alvarez gave Galton a card good for food at a downtown eatery. Galton got mad, tore the card up, and threw it into a trash can. Alvarez walked away. Galton followed him into the apartment building, and up to the tenth floor. Somehow, he got into Alvarez's apartment. He threw Alvarez over the balcony of his terrace, and ran off with his wallet and his hat."

It was an impressive summation. Small wonder Matt Jacobs had described Blanton as a man on his way up in the D.A.'s office. The one-paragraph sketch of events Blanton had just tossed off indeed seemed enough to convict. Except for one little detail that didn't fit.

"His hat?" I asked.

"That's right," Blanton answered.

"So, no one saw the whole sequence of events as they happened?" I asked.

"Of course not," Blanton replied. "No one could have, unless they were following them around to make a cinema vérité film.

Witnesses saw Galton stop Alvarez outside, follow him up, and run from the building."

"But did they see the suspect push Alvarez off the balcony?" I asked. That reference to film had made me remember the punch in the gut I had felt a moment ago when Ida informed me Blanton had come to call.

"One sure did," Blanton answered. "A bag lady who was sitting in the plaza. She got very upset, walking around yelling 'Murder, Murder!' Says she saw the whole thing. And she knew Galton by name."

"There's your case," I told him.

"But she disappeared before the cops could buttonhole her," Blanton said. "Nobody got her name."

"How'd that happen?" I asked.

"Well," Blanton replied, "it was a continuity chase. A foot-race. But they got him."

"She'll probably turn up," I said.

"Yeah, I imagine," Blanton replied. "But that's on your list of things to do."

"If I take the job," I said. It would have been a relief to get Blanton out of the office at that point, but the business about the hat was bothering me. This Galton guy just might be getting a raw deal.

"Something about it you don't like?" Blanton asked.

"I don't know yet," I told him. "Go on."

"Fair enough," Blanton replied. "Witnesses saw bits and pieces. Plenty of witnesses, though."

"Let's hear about it," I said.

"The evidence is strong," Blanton continued. "They found the victim's wallet in Galton's pocket. He'd ditched the money somewhere, though."

"That doesn't make any sense," I said. "Why didn't he ditch the wallet and keep the money?"

"Go figure criminals," Blanton replied. "Of course, Galton claims that the victim threw away his wallet, credit cards and all. It's a lucky thing it happened so fast. There were still people hanging around from offices, taking a smoking break, who'd seen Galton flare up and shred the food card Alvarez gave him."

"Looks like the cards are stacked against this guy," I said.

"You bet," Blanton replied. "The guards at the apartment building are going to be good witnesses. They saw Galton go after Alvarez, but they weren't quick enough to stop him. Galton ran right through the front door, as another resident was going out. There are two elevators in the lobby. He saw what floor Alvarez had punched. He got into the other elevator. Beat the security guy to it."

"Not very good security," I remarked.

"There were two guys on duty," Blanton replied. "One of them started up the stairs, and one stayed in the lobby. The guy on the stairs had made it almost to the tenth floor, when Galton broke by him on the way down. The security man was winded by that time, so Galton got by him. He was wearing the victim's hat at the time."

"Did anyone see Galton on Alvarez's floor?" I asked.

"They sure did," Blanton answered. "Alvarez's ninety-year-old neighbor was coming out of his apartment just as Galton got out of the elevator on the tenth floor. The old man saw Galton lose the hat coming out of the elevator, hurry past him, and go into Alvarez's apartment. The neighbor picked up the hat, heard an argument taking place in Alvarez's apartment, and saw Galton come back out. Then Galton went back in again for a few seconds and came back out running. And finally, Galton grabbed the hat out of the old man's hands as Galton ran by him toward the stairs."

"Did the old man hear what they said?" I asked.

"No, he's hard of hearing," Blanton answered, "but he could tell they were arguing by the tone."

The evidence was mounting. "Did Galton pass anybody else on the stairs?" I asked.

"A couple of residents," Blanton answered, "but nobody seemed to want a piece of him. He made it outside, but a cop saw him run out and took after him. Never lost sight of him. They finally caught up with him. And that's where you come in."

"To do what?" I asked.

"Cops stay busy," Blanton replied. "They can only get so much done. I want you to talk to the witnesses who saw Galton hit the victim up for a handout. And talk to the residents who saw Galton on the stairs. See what else you can get out of those witnesses."

"That's simple enough," I said.

"Like I said," Blanton told me, "some of the testimony is in bits and pieces. One witness was walking past her window and saw Alvarez halfway over the balcony. She walked back to make sure what she'd seen, and saw Galton looking over the balcony at the scene below. She's willing to identify Galton. That's not bulletproof against a good defender, though. It's too fragmentary."

"Anything else?" I asked

"Yes," Blanton answered. "Another witness saw Alvarez go over, and he saw a man behind him who could have, he said, pushed him off. He's playing it safe. You might be able to firm up some of this stuff."

"Firm it up?" I asked.

"This is the kind of case a prosecutor likes," Blanton said. "The kind that gets noticed. People want to be safe on the street, and they want to be safe in their own homes. This hits them from two directions. Sew this guy up, Turley. Sew him up seven ways from Sunday."

It seemed like easy money, but it just didn't feel right. I liked looking out the window at that cityscape, but sometimes I could see my reflection in it as well. I had shot five people in the head to set up this business. Was it worth it? Was I doing the kind of work that would justify an act like that?

"I see," I told Blanton. "The plan is to give him a fair trial and then hang him."

Blanton's face turned red. "What?" he shot back. "Hey! I don't think I like your attitude, Turley."

"Then I guess we'll just part company here," I replied.

"We won't part friends," Blanton said, "but we'll certainly part. Thanks for nothing!"

Blanton stormed out. I never think of the right word when I'm arguing with someone. I should have said "I've got news

for you: Bernstein's dead." That would have let him know I
thought he was trying to get me to coordinate the testimony of
those witnesses the way a conductor would. Instead, all I could
come up with was that dimwit remark about hanging.

It didn't matter, though. What was clear was that this guy
Galton was getting set up for a fall regardless of whatever the
true circumstances of Alvarez's death might have been. I
headed to the lockup for a visit.

I needed the exercise after that emotional meeting with
Blanton. First, I'd expected the feel of handcuffs snapping onto
my wrists. Then I'd almost licked his hand in relief. And after
all that I'd ended up practically throwing him out of my office.

At the lockup Galen Galton shuffled in, uncomfortable in his
over-starched jail scrubs. "Are you a cop?" he asked me through
the visitors' window. "They couldn't have given me my
defender already."

"I'm a private investigator," I told him. "I'm here to help
you, Galton."

"Help me onto a gurney, you mean," Galton replied. "So, I
can get a needle in my arm. I don't think I want to talk to you."

"It's up to you, Galton," I told him. "If you don't want any
help, I'll leave."

"Who sent you?" Galton asked.

"Nobody," I answered. "I just had a hunch about your case. I
think you're getting a raw deal."

"I don't have any money," Galton told me. "Why are you
here?"

"To tell you the brutal truth," I answered, "somebody just
rubbed me the wrong way, and I wanted to teach him a lesson."

"By getting me out from behind the eight ball, eh?" Galton
asked. "Some kind of bet?"

"Something like that," I told him. "What happened with
Alvarez? Better get to it. We don't have much time."

"All right," Galton said. "Here it is. I didn't push Alvarez.
He jumped."

"Tell me about it," I said, "from the beginning."

"Alvarez used to give me something every time he passed,"
Galton replied. "I was in a bad mood that day, because I had a

hangover. A couple of beers would have made a world of difference. I could feel them going down my throat as Alvarez came down the street. And then he didn't give me nothing but a card for food at a burger joint. I was disappointed, so I got snippy. I tore the card up and slung the pieces into a trash can."

"Then what happened?" I pursued.

"Then Alvarez walked to a trash can himself," Galton continued. "The next one down the line. He threw something in. I could tell it was a wallet. He moved on out of sight. Around this big planter thing in the plaza. I followed him around and picked up the wallet. I opened it and saw that it didn't have any money in it. I realized Alvarez hadn't been holding out on me. He just didn't have any cash with him."

"Keep going," I told him.

"But the wallet did have credit cards in it," Galton went on. "There were several. Expensive-looking types. I had a record. I wasn't about to try and run up a tab on those cards. It would be skating on thin ice, just for a fling. I also didn't want to just ditch them. Some rat would have a party with them, and it would be sort of like I was paying the tab, not Alvarez. I figured he'd made some kind of mistake. Like maybe he'd got a new wallet, switched everything to it and then took the wrong wallet with him. Then he threw the old one away, but he forgot he hadn't taken them credit cards out."

"Go on," I prompted.

"Then I saw his hat sitting on the plaza," Galton said. "Upside down. Full of water."

"Water?" I repeated.

"Yeah," Galton replied. "I didn't know what to think. I didn't see Alvarez, but there was the hat he'd just had on."

"How'd you know the hat was his?" I asked.

"It was a big wide-brimmed fedora," Galton answered. "Like the one Indiana Jones wears."

"And full of water?" I asked.

"That's right," Galton replied. "It looked like it would fit me. I picked it up and emptied it out into that big planter thing, before the water could soak into it and ruin it."

"Then what happened?" I asked.

"I saw Alvarez again," Galton answered. "I followed him. I was going to give him the credit cards back. I figured if I could get past the security in that apartment building, he'd give me a reward. Maybe for the hat, too, although I couldn't figure out how he had lost it. I figured he'd smooth things out with the doorman and anybody else who saw me go in, and he'd give me a reward. He was rich as Croesus, after all. Call it stupid, it was just a snap decision."

"And then?" I asked.

"Upstairs, Alvarez left the door wide open," Galton continued. "It was one of those apartments that went straight through. I could see to the balcony where Alvarez was. He got up on the balcony rail. I thought he was going to jump off. Then he climbed back down. But he immediately got right back up there. I could tell what was going on. It was like hesitation marks, when you're about to commit suicide. I know, because I tried it once. I was sure I was ready to do it. I took a swipe at my wrist with a knife, and I was surprised to see that I'd made only a tiny scratch. Hesitation marks. After I did that twice it brought me around. I realized I didn't really want to do it. The same was true for Mr. Alvarez. I knew he'd come around if I could just get him away from that balcony. He'd change his mind."

"Then what happened?" I asked.

"Alvarez looked over the edge," Galton answered, "and then sort of stepped back like he was getting ready to take a running jump. That was all I could take. I ran through the apartment and grabbed him."

"'What do you think you're doing?' Alvarez asked me."

"'Trying to keep you from committing suicide,' I said to him."

"'Do I look crazy?' Alvarez asked. 'Get out of here'"

"'Don't do it,' I said. 'You'll feel better about it later.'"

"'Get out before I call the police,' Alvarez said"

"'I don't care,' I told him. 'I can't stand here and watch you take a dive like that. It ain't right to do that.'"

"'For your information, I'm a writer,' Alvarez told me. 'I'm just working out a piece of action for a script.'"

"Well you could have lit a cigar on my face, I was that embarrassed," Galton went on. "I backed up out of there, afraid to say another word, because Alvarez had just said he was going to call the police and I didn't have a thing to say to them. I was still looking at him when I got to the door and he went over. Graceful. Just swung a leg over and went down."

"Then what happened?" I asked.

"I found myself at the edge of the balcony, looking down," Galton replied. "It was pretty gruesome. Then I got out of there fast."

"You took the wallet and hat with you?" I asked.

"I didn't realize I still had the wallet," Galton answered. "And an old man was standing in the hall holding the hat. It must have come off my head as I came out of the elevator. I grabbed it out of his hands as I walked by and jammed it down over my eyes, hoping it would keep anybody from recognizing me on the way down."

"Time's up," said the voice of the guard behind me.

"Just a second, officer," I said. "What happened to the hat, Galton?"

"It came off my head while the cops were chasing me," Galton answered. "It blew down the street. I was too busy to see where it went."

"Let's go," said the guard.

"Okay, Officer," I replied. "I guess that'll have to do, Galton."

A quick look at Google gave me Alvarez's name in connection with a firm run by Garland Zale. Zale agreed to talk with me as soon as I mentioned Alvarez. I headed straight for Zale's downtown office.

"I'll be glad to talk to you about Miguel Alvarez, Mr. Turley," Zale told me.

"Thanks, Mr. Zale," I said. "That would be helpful."

"Miguel was one of the most fascinating people I ever met," Zale said. "His story is the American dream and nightmare rolled into one."

"How long had you known him?" I asked.

"Since he came to work for me," Zale answered, "in the fall of two thousand ten. I called it Jack Zale Productions then. Now we call it LaffCo, since the partnership."

"Alvarez was your partner?" I asked.

"Oh, no," Zale replied, "just an employee. But that's part of the story. Miguel came up from crushing poverty. His mother literally carried him on her back over the Rio Grande."

"That so?" I asked.

"Miguel worked hard," Zale said. "He saved his money. Tried a stint as a comedian. He was a terribly inadequate performer. But what a quick mind he had! When he came in to interview, I gave him a test. 'Give me a joke,' I said, 'that has sex, race, politics, controversy, and physical deformity in it. I'll give you half an hour and then. . .' But Alvarez fired back immediately with 'Geisha girl recaptured after short foot chase.' He'd done it with seven words."

Zale stopped and pretended to look for something on his desk, waiting for me to get the joke. I finally did, and laughed. Then he went on.

"Miguel's writing was good," Zale continued. "So, we hired him on here as a gag writer for cartoons. He was good. He was in such high demand that we couldn't keep an exclusive on him. Then he dried up. Whatever vein writers dig into just played out."

"Too bad," I said.

"Damned tragic," Zale replied. "But he'd saved his money, and asked me to introduce him to my broker. He took a fling on the stock market with his savings. He hit, big time. He was a brilliant investor. He outguessed the market time after time. He made millions. He doubled and redoubled his investments. Then he took a fling in oil futures. Bam!"

"Was that a good or bad Bam?" I asked.

"Very bad," Zale answered. "Miguel went in the hole last week, for forty million dollars."

"Thanks," I said, and left.

Miguel Alvarez had walked home to his apartment from the south the day he died, and that's the territory I covered. It didn't take long. What I was looking for turned up at the second clothing store down from his residence.

"A fedora?" the clerk asked. "A guy in a blue silk suit? Yeah. He bought a hat here. A big fedora. Wide brimmed, heavy felt. I know the guy. Can't remember his name, but he bought a few gag hats here from time to time. Some kind of writer, into comedy."

"Anything stand out about the sale?" I asked.

"Yeah," the clerk answered. "A big tip. The hat was seventy dollars. He plunked a hundred-dollar bill down on the counter and told me to keep the change. Then he opened the wallet to show that there was no more money in it, and blew into it, like he was trying to chase moths out of it or something."

"And then?" I asked.

"He put the hat on and snapped down the brim," replied the clerk. "He gave a big smile, and walked out like he'd just won the lottery."

I walked northward from the clothing store, planning to see what might turn up in the plaza in front of Alvarez's apartment building.

"Hey Gumshoe!" a voice behind me shouted, "Hey Turley, I . . . Holy Crap! Put that gun away!"

"Blanton," I told him, "don't sneak up on me like that. I thought it was a drive-by . . ."

That's as far as I got before I was interrupted by the burst of a siren. Thirty seconds later I found myself leaning over the hood of a squad car. The cops were inspecting the three firearms I was carrying and asking me why I happened to be wearing a bullet-proof suit.

"Ease up," I heard Blanton tell them. He was showing them a card that identified him as a highly-placed attorney from the D.A.s office.

"He's a friendly?" the cop asked Blanton.

"Yes, let him go," Blanton told them. "I need him for some important business down the street."

That's all it took. A minute later Blanton and I were standing on the sidewalk alone. I had to admit the guy had some pull.

"Now," said Blanton, "I believe that before the heat got here you were about to tell me you were afraid you were getting hit by a drive-by shooting. It isn't; it's a drive-by object lesson. I just saw the bag lady who's going to testify against Galton, down the street."

"That so?" I asked.

"Yeah," Blanton replied, "I thought you'd benefit from hearing what she has to say. You've been so eager to be a wart on my hind end that I thought I'd show you how wrong you are about this case; rub your nose in it."

"It could go the other way, Blanton," I told him.

"I know better," Blanton replied, "and you soon will." He motioned to his Lexus, which had been double-parked while the cops were there, and apparently was invisible to them. "Get in," he said.

I climbed into the car and we got underway. "So, you think this woman stayed put?" I asked Blanton.

"I don't think," Blanton answered, "I know. There she is now. Go on, get out. We can leave the car right here."

"It's up to you," I replied, "if you want to pay the tow."

"Won't happen," Blanton replied. Evidently, he could park anywhere he pleased. I got out of the car and approached the woman Blanton had pointed out.

Blanton's star witness was a short but sturdy-looking woman of about seventy, seated on the end of a bench eating from a large Whitman's Sampler. Next to her was a small blue shopping cart with bags arranged neatly in it.

Another shopping cart, I thought. It seemed I'd be stuck with that image forever. This woman would be hard to mistake for Samantha Dale, though. She wore a flowered dress that extended just past her knees, gray yoga pants, and short vinyl boots with ruffles above them, a white turtleneck, a beige crewneck and a charcoal cardigan. Around her neck hung a hand mirror on a chain that looked like a rosary. She smelled of vanilla, but that may have been the candy.

More to the point, above a long blonde wig that spilled over her shoulders and a curly red one that flared from the top of her head she wore Alvarez's missing Indiana Jones hat.

"Excuse me, Ma'am," I said.

"Who is this?" she asked Blanton. "I thought you'd bring the thief."

"My name is Hugh Turley," I told her. "Where did you get the hat?"

She turned to me, squinting in evident pain from a cavity the candy had gotten into. "A murderer lost it, that's how," she answered, rubbing her jaw. "A thief murderer!"

"How's that for openers, Turley?" Blanton asked over my shoulder.

"May I see the hat?" I asked her.

She obliged. "No, don't hand it over," I cautioned. "Don't let either one of us handle it for just a moment. Turn it over, so we can look inside."

The woman held out the hat like a serving tray.

"What the hell are you getting at, Turley?" Blanton asked.

"Just as I suspected, Blanton," I told him. "Take a look."

Blanton bent and peered into the hat. "There's something folded inside," he said, "tucked under the band. It's a note. Let's . . ."

"Just a minute," I cautioned him. "Put these gloves on, Blanton."

"Gloves for both of us?" he asked. "You come prepared."

"I took a correspondence course," I replied. "You want to read the note, Blanton, or shall I?"

"Uh . . . I guess you'd better, Turley," Blanton answered.

I opened the note carefully. "It hasn't smeared," I told him. "That's good."

"Uh, yeah," Blanton answered.

"It's addressed to Garland Zale," I continued. I read it aloud: "Dear Garland. You may wonder why I'm doing this. And you may wonder why I'm writing to you, instead of somebody else. Well, my Mom's dead, and I pushed the rest of my family away years ago. The national debt has just come due on me, and I'm taking the easy way out. The other way, back to the groaning belly and the dirt floors, is a longer fall than this.'"

"Uh, Turley," Blanton said. "I guess I kind of owe you an apology. I mean, uh . . ."

"Wait a minute, Blanton," I said. "You haven't heard the end of it. There's more. Listen."

The note concluded: "I'm writing to you because you're the only one who'll be able to fully appreciate this way of bowing out. My best gag. The hat trick."

"You guys ready for my testimony?" the woman asked. "I seen the whole thing! Mr. Alvarez filled his hat up and put it right there under the balcony. He checked real careful up and down. He got it just right, 'cause he hit exactly where it woulda been if it hadn't been for Galen Galton. The murderin' thief!"

CHAPTER SEVEN:

THE RUNAWAY BRIDE

"JUST DIRECT YOUR FEET . . . ," Temple Worthington sang, "to the sunny side of the . . . SOB!" Worthington had choked up again, and on lyrics that weren't usually considered sad.

"Just sing it straight," bellowed a man in a bright green jacket, "Johnny Ray you ain't."

"Who is Johnny Ray?" the woman with him asked.

Worthington paused. It wasn't Saint Patrick's Day, he reflected, so it stood to reason the guy was somebody important in the golf world.

"Danny Kaye?" Worthington replied, attempting to salvage his dignity by pretending to hear incorrectly. "Life could not better be. . ." he sang.

Worthington's engagement at the hotel museum hadn't been the same since the moment he'd realized the young man who had blown his brains out hadn't been trying to pull off some kind of a tricky happening. And Worthington himself had looked bad in the process. He had continued to play as everyone in the room looked around uncertainly. Worthington had decided to be the cool one who wasn't fooled by the act at all. Not until the arrival of a naked woman with a goldfish bowl/space helmet on her head had the crowd caught on to the reality of the situation. The woman had fainted and was only saved from drowning because the glass broke when she fell. Yes, this gig was becoming a drag

"I NEED HELP to find the woman who just ran off in the

middle of our wedding ceremony," Burlin Fredericks told me. "The whole thing will seem crazy to you."

Fredericks was still a little wild-eyed about the situation he had come to me for, so I figured I'd better help him concentrate on the essentials.

"What's her name?" I asked.

"Denise Black," Fredericks answered.

"Do you think Denise is in danger?" I asked.

"Yes, I do," Fredericks replied. "Right now, her husband is watching out for her at their house, but . . ."

Only in New York, I thought. One screwed-up guy in love with another man's wife trying to help a second guy in the same fix. "Okay, so where else might she be right now?" I interrupted. This was obviously going to be a tangled mess of a case, so I steered Fredericks back to the main concern, the woman's safety.

"She ran out of a church in the upper west side two hours ago," Fredericks answered, "and she had cut herself. I don't know how badly, but her blood is on my suit, as you can see."

"Have you told the police?" I asked.

"Yes, of course," Fredericks answered, "but it's just one more task among a million for them. I came to you so I could do something more specifically directed toward helping her."

"I see," I told him. "Do you have a photograph of her?"

"Yes," he answered, taking out a very expensive cell phone. "Hundreds of them, video and still." He thumbed through the images, showing photos of Denise Black as he continued to talk.

"I fell in love with her at long range," Fredericks told me. "I own an international hardware chain headquartered in Vancouver. It keeps me in one place. It's not a business where you tour and shake hands. You just stay in one place and organize."

I watched him run through the photos. "This one will help," I told him. "And the one before. Let's go see Ida." Fredericks followed me into the outer office and we sat down by my secretary, Ida.

"Hook into this thing and print a half-dozen eight-by-tens, would you Ida," I requested. She plucked the appropriate connector from a drawer and started the job without a word. While she worked, I continued to talk.

"How many agents do we have in Manhattan or within an hour's distance who can be freed up for a search?" I asked her.

Ida calculated silently for a moment. "Two are tagging along after errant husbands, five are working undercover in theft detection, six are on-call, and two are doing ride-along with the police."

"Okay," I replied. "Leave the theft-detection people alone, out of concern for their safety. Alert the on-calls and the two who are tailing the husbands to look for this woman. Let the ride-alongs in on it, too, in case they can turn up anything in the course of routine. Got that?"

"Sure do," Ida returned.

"Now let's sit here and get some details on the case while Ida is listening," I proposed. "She'll catch enough of it while she is working to get the general idea of what's going on. She can be counted on to be discreet as well. What do you say?"

"I'll go along with that idea," Fredericks replied.

"First," I asked, "Can you elaborate on that statement that Denise's husband is watching out for her at home?"

"It's a computer romance that caught fire," Fredericks said. "I thought I was the one who had money. I didn't realize that Denise was rich. Oh, I was aware that she was moderately well-off. I knew she was married, but that was emphatically in name only, she told me. She wanted a divorce and a new life. She was only staying in the house with her husband because it was the home she had grown up in. She considered him a weakling and was allowing him to stay in the top floor of her residence while he got used to the idea of taking care of himself. Until he figured out what to do with the settlement she planned to give him. The divorce was underway, but not final yet."

It sounded kind of awkward to me, but perhaps they had a more continental outlook in Vancouver than here.

"You didn't consider that an unusual circumstance?" I asked him."

"Not at all," Fredericks answered. "I felt I knew her through and through from our exchanges on the internet. It's funny, the power such a connection can make. The person I talked to on the computer seems much more real to me than the flesh and blood Denise."

"In what way?" I asked.

"When I met her," Fredericks answered, "I found that she was even better-looking than on the computer. She seemed more animated, too, as she revisited some of our better exchanges over the computer. She knew them by heart. But there was an animal vitality to her physical presence that I would never have expected. We hadn't talked ten minutes before she grabbed me by the hand and took me up to her bedroom." He stopped and looked at Ida, apparently concerned that he might offend her.

Ida looked up from her work. "Don't worry about me," she told him. "I've heard it all."

Satisfied, Fredericks continued. "Suffice it to say that we were compatible," he said. "It was the final bond in a relationship that had become very close in spite of the miles between us. Afterwards, as soon as we could talk, Denise told me that she wanted a wedding ceremony right away, marriage license or not. Of course, it would cause complications, with me being from British Columbia and her divorce not yet final. But it was something we could take care of later, she insisted. 'It will be fun,' she told me. 'Just look at this place,' she said. 'It will make a wonderful office for your headquarters. You will move here from Vancouver, won't you? I love my family home so much, and you couldn't find a better place than New York to operate from.'"

"Was that true?" I asked.

"I loved the idea," Fredericks answered. "It seemed the perfect solution to the problem of distance. So, we acted on it at once. Denise arranged for us to meet a minister that very morning. Today, that is. Things get confusing."

Ida put down her phone. She had managed to get the agents assigned to their search for Denise without interrupting us.

"Then things went to hell," Fredericks continued. "I shouldn't have expected anything other than what happened, I guess. Our plan was stupid and compulsive, as events soon proved. At the ceremony her husband, Milburn Howard, showed up and made a fuss."

"Denise had kept her own name, then?" I asked.

"Yes," Fredericks answered. "Howard tore up the divorce agreement in front of her. This seemed to drive Denise insane. It was a side of her I never expected."

"What happened?" I asked.

"Denise pulled out a knife from nowhere, and waved it around," Fredericks answered. "'Stand back,' Howard said, 'she has hurt herself before and can be very dangerous with that knife.'"

Ida looked surprised. She hadn't seen everything after all.

Fredericks continued his narrative. "Howard made a sudden move and took the knife away from Denise," he went on. "Denise snatched it back, and cut her hands badly in the process. Blood went all over the place. It happened at lightning speed, so fast I couldn't begin to do anything about it. I mean, after all, it was completely unexpected," he said, looking at me like a kid who has just been called back to the bench looks at his coach.

"Sure," I replied. "Anyone would have been thrown off."

Fredericks continued: "'Yes, he will have his say, won't he?' Denise said, and then. . . 'Well, Burlin, he has given away my little secret. I have moods, you see. Here, have a souvenir,'" and with that she snatched out the handkerchief from my breast pocket and wiped blood on it. Then she broke away and ran out of the church."

"What did you do?" Ida asked.

"I tried to follow," Fredericks answered, "but somehow my feet got tangled up in Milburn Howard's. By the time I recovered, Denise was out of the church. She was very fast. She had disappeared, probably into one of the neighboring buildings."

"And then?" Ida asked, looking at Fredericks intently.

"I was very confused," Fredericks replied. "This didn't seem like the woman I met on the internet. And I had come to feel that I knew her very well."

"But as for the direction she went," I prompted.

"I enlisted the help of everyone in the vicinity," Fredericks replied. "Nobody could find her. Then I came to you."

I left the office with Fredericks and we split up and did our best to find the missing woman. I left the office with Fredericks and we split up and did our best to find the missing woman. All I found was a giant water balloon hurled at me from a rooftop by laughing teenagers.

Only in New York could you experience a sense of relief by getting scored on that way. For a second, I'd thought I had become another Crankpot sniper victim.

Discouraged, I called Ida and had her assign a couple more agents from Word to the Wise Investigations to make the evening rounds looking for Denise. They were used to that kind of schedule, and I function a lot better during the day than at night.

CHAPTER EIGHT:

HOMECOMING

I WENT HOME. SHELTERED within my tiny portico I saw, as usual, the vision of Samantha Dale standing there waiting for me. I knew it wasn't real, but just the after-image of her that had burned itself into my retina. Not to get maudlin about it, but I saw her often that way. At the rail of the fence overlooking the river as I jogged, or in the back of an elevator, obscured by the other occupants.

Upstairs, on the way down the hall to my bedroom for a change of clothes I went on the alert. There's a certain sense that kicks in as you're ascending in a plane. Your body knows that something's not right, even though your mind says it is.

I stopped outside my bedroom door, gun in hand. "Come on out, slowly," I said.

The door opened and Haldis Pike stepped out, an unexpectedly voluptuous Haldis Pike. She'd liberated her hair from that tight bun, lost the glasses, and removed the modestly-tailored suit. She struck a pose, placing her weight on one leg, like a Greek statue. Six feet of Haldis Pike, totally nude.

"Don't tell me," I said. "You're good with locks."

"Well, I didn't bribe the janitor," she replied in a surprisingly husky voice, and stuck a package of condoms into my shirt pocket. "You won't need these unless you don't trust me," she said.

For some reason I remembered the first time I'd seen stewardesses pantomime the safety instructions for a plane full of passengers. Those women had suddenly come to life in that moment in the same way that Haldis Pike had transformed herself from a conservative cliché to a living doll.

I'm no delicate flower, but losing Samantha Dale had pretty much taken the starch out of me. I'd started measuring other women against her, and nobody came close. Haldis Pike was no exception, but there's a big difference between looking through a butcher shop window and having someone stick a sizzling New York steak under your nose. Her little ambush had stripped away my psychological neutrality and replaced it with a full head of steam.

I opened the top of my shirt and was reminded that I'd recently been scored on in a game of Pop the Sucker. It might have been my imagination, but I suspected the water that hit me hadn't been pure NYC tap. "I'd better clean up first," I told her.

"Me, too," Haldis replied. She headed for the shower in the tiny excuse for a bathroom connected to my bedroom, looking back at me invitingly. I didn't join her, because Haldis was a big woman and the shower was barely large enough to accommodate me alone. Besides, the gesture seemed too cute. I wasn't looking to establish a relationship, but just give her what she came for as a reward for her industriousness in getting through my security system. I retired to the big cast iron tub in the bathroom at the end of the upstairs hall.

I began filling the tub, but when I heard the shower stop running back in the bedroom, I changed my mind and did a quick wash up in the sink. Haldis Pike met me in the hallway and we went back into the bedroom. What can I say? Sometimes you just follow your instincts.

To continue with the airline analogy, we had a smooth trip until we leveled out. Then, just as you'd expect the seat belt light to go off, she grabbed the wheel out of my hands and headed the plane directly at a mountain top. We hit a big pocket of turbulence and finally made it to the ground in one piece.

To top it all, it turned out Haldis was a first-timer. Scratch one set of Egyptian cotton sheets.

"That didn't hurt at all," Haldis breathed. "Let's do it again."

"We'd better take a break," I told her. "I started filling the tub in my front bathroom. Would you like to use it to take a nice soaking bath?"

"No, you go do that yourself," she told me, inspecting the stains on her hands. "I like your shower."

That was a relief, since it would give me time to rest up from that strenuous flight. I left Haldis to her shower and walked back down the hall to the bathroom again.

This time I would run a full bath. I sank back with my ear next to the rushing water, listening to the churning coils as they surged against the tiny ripples in the enamel at the bottom of the tub. I had things to think about. Not only had I breached my own rule about sleeping with a client, but you don't usually expect to encounter a thirty-some-odd-year-old virgin.

I tried not to think about conflict, loss, or debauchery. There was no oblivion to be found in my soapy refuge though. No sunken grotto and no hidden robber's cave behind the waterfall that appears in a hundred movies because you can't prove it's not there. Instead, I heard the sounds of battle in the ancient Gobi, the fists of drunken fishwives on the tenement stairs, the thunder of dinosaurs across the mudflats. The brain can rest, but the mind can't.

I tried not to envision the face of the man I had killed in that tub a few months ago. Some people would never have gone back into that bathroom after nearly getting drowned there by a crew of assailants. They'd have moved out of the house. But I wasn't going to let my own bathroom scare me away. I'd probably never have another group of thugs in there, repeatedly forcing my head under water. It isn't that common an occurrence.

The water, or maybe just the time out, revived my libido. Plus, my back itched from the healed scars of the whipping I had received in Riyadh. I was leaning back in the tub, splashing up and down with the loofa pinned behind me and letting it scratch my back. Bare feet pattered to the edge of the tub. I looked up.

Surprise. Instead of Haldis Pike looking back at me there was Samantha Dale. Not Haldis with the imaginary head of

Samantha, but the real Sam. A nude Samantha Dale, standing at the side of the tub, regarding me with a look of disapproval. Her hair was mussed up and there was a welt under her eye that would probably turn purple.

I'd recovered from the recent activity. The thought of Haldis Pike waiting for me down the hall, in combination with the hot soapy water, had produced an effect that gave evidence of the fact that I wasn't the pining, one-woman-only recluse that Samantha might have envisioned in her absence.

Samantha was glowing. You'd think she was the one in the tub, from the sheen of her body. Radiant would have about half described it. She kept looking at me without change of expression.

It's kind of disorienting to expect one naked woman to appear, and then have her replaced by another one. "Say, didn't you run into somebody out there?" I asked her.

"Yes," Samantha answered. "I just booted a giant pear tree named Haldis Pike out of this little bawdy house, and I'm marking my territory." Her voice was a little husky, too, but I seemed to detect a mixture of emotions in it.

"You weren't too rough on her, I hope," I remarked.

"I didn't deal with her harshly at all," Samantha replied. "I told her she could sit in the bedroom and take notes if she wanted to, as long as she stayed out of the way."

Her answer rendered me speechless for a moment. This was a Samantha Dale I hadn't seen before.

Samantha paused to take a deep breath. Not to expand her bust line, which it did very nicely, but in preparation to give me a piece of her mind.

"I know what you thought," Samantha told me. "But I didn't sign on with Charles Ogden for the money. And I bailed for the same reason you did when you pushed me away in your office that day. Because I know myself and I knew I couldn't raise a baby I constantly wanted to throw out the window. I know better than to get into a trap like that. I knew what Charles Ogden needed, too, and it wasn't another high-priced call girl. We both got what we wanted out of the relationship. He got his son back, with a second chance to raise him properly, or at least the illusion of that. I got a way to resolve the matter, as well as a big settlement. There's nothing wrong with that. I had it coming to me."

I had no comeback for that lecture, and waited for her to haul in another big breath.

"Does the fact that I've stayed a wife in name only to an attractive billionaire for your sake get to you?" she asked. "You've had sufficient recovery time, so if you still feel the way about me that I feel about you,--warts and all--, get up and welcome me back."

It was an interesting speech from a woman I hadn't expected to see again, except possibly from a distance. A woman who had recently given birth to another man's child. A woman I'd been thinking about night and day since the three months we had lived together, and who had now shown up at the ultimate wrong moment.

"I'm a little confused," I told her. "A guy proposes to you, you accept, and then you go to live with another man a couple of months after your child is born?"

"Charles Ogden doesn't want me around now that the baby has been delivered," Samantha explained. "As a matter of fact, we lived on separate floors right up to the delivery. He felt it would be just too creepy, watching his wife's body expand with the development of his grandson."

"That sounds like him," I conceded.

"What's the matter, Turley?" she asked me. "Don't you want the company?"

"I think you used the word 'creepy'," I answered.

"I didn't exactly quote him," Samantha answered. "And at the price he paid, naturally you and I will avoid making a display of ourselves for the next few months. But you're a private kind of guy, anyway."

I still wasn't willing to let it go. "Couldn't we have been working around that expanding and developing problem ourselves?" I asked. Her departure had been pretty abrupt. It was hard to accept getting your guts torn out and then having to drag them around between your legs for six months.

Samantha laughed, but not with the true ring of enjoyment. "You seem to have done all right," she said. "Yes, I wasn't all that far along when I left. We could have had our long goodbye, but with the knowledge that in a few months I'd be the wife of Charles Ogden, I'm not sure things would have gone all that pleasantly."

Samantha was right again. A real man will accept his limitations, if he's blessed with enough insight to realize what they are.

"Only because I have such a hard head," I finally admitted.

I got up out of the tub, splashing water everywhere. I wanted to pull Samantha into it with me, but cast iron is unforgiving, even to the most ardent lovers. We went down the hall to the bedroom. We were alone, but I hadn't expected anyone else to be there. Samantha had made sure of that.

The bedroom was unexpectedly neat. Haldis, or at least I hoped it was Haldis, had changed the bedclothes and removed the signs of our recent encounter.

Samantha suddenly applied herself to my body like a coat of paint. I'd thought perhaps she'd want to hover around the edge of things for a while, but she was going straight to the heart of the matter. It reminded me of the time I had been attacked by a horny otter when I went camping as a teenager. The thing had almost humped a hole in my leg. Otters are strong, and they have claws. The same thing was true for Samantha. She was just as determined, and her most recent manicure must not have taken.

Haldis Pike had taken the sheets with her, along with the mattress pad. I looked for them the next morning while I made breakfast in bed for Sam, but they weren't anywhere in the house. It had either been an extremely tactful gesture on the part of Haldis, or a reversal to the kind of tight-bun behavior she'd shown at the office.

In any case I was glad that Samantha had missed adding defloration to the offence of failing to wait for her return like a dog at the tomb of its master.

About the way Samantha had left, though, I realized she had been right all the way in the approach she'd taken. I had let emotion completely overwhelm me after finding that Ogden had proposed to her. Explaining the subtleties of the transfer of an unborn kid would have been a little too abstract for me.

Then Samantha had just narrowly missed catching me between the sheets with Haldis Pike. Worse than that, between sets of sheets. So, for Samantha's sake if not mine, I wanted to keep it that way. Short one set of sheets, I'd have to squeeze in a shopping trip sometime in the day.

Plus, there was Haldis Pike to think of. I skipped my morning run and stopped at a florist's shop. I sent Haldis a bouquet of sweet alyssum, along with a note of apology. It was the closest I could come in the language of flower symbolism to "you're dynamite, kid, but please stay away."

CHAPTER NINE:

A FACE IN THE MISTY BLUE

IN SPITE OF THE COMPLICATIONS of the previous night's bedroom farce, I made it to the office on time. There I found that the search for Denise Black had failed.

Denise had turned up dead in an ice cream locker inside a storage warehouse. She had the knife with her. She had evidently used it on herself somewhere along the way, and had staggered into the seclusion of that cooler to expire like a sick dog.

"Who found her?" I asked the agent who had called me, Bettina Herbert.

"The owner of the cold storage warehouse found her," Bettina answered, "after an inspection following a robbery. The watchman was killed, but not by Denise Black."

Burlin Fredericks had been sitting in my inner office beside my desk, and he knew what the call was about. "I want to see her body in the morgue," Fredericks told me.

We went straight over. Denise's husband, Milburn Howard, had already been there and left. Fingerprints and dental records had already identified the body as that of Denise Black, but I wanted Fredricks' impression of whether this was the same woman who had blown up in the church.

"She looks different," Fredericks said, looking down at the body on the gurney. "But of course that's because she's . . ."

Fredericks wiped a tear from the edge of his eye, but not because he was overcome by grief. I was tearing up as well, from the acrid odor of the examination room. I had never gotten used to it, even though I had been there many times.

Fredericks gave a sigh, and went on in a resigned tone. "But it's her, of course," he concluded. "The wounds on her hands are the same as those she inflicted upon herself at the church." He gave me a look that probably meant "you did your best," and turned away from the gurney. Trailing his hand along the sheet with a gesture I found more expressive than if he had actually broken into tears, he headed out for fresh air.

"Were you the Medical Examiner who went out to the ice cream cooler?" I asked the man who had brought out the gurney. He looked older than the attendants who usually staffed the morgue.

"Yes," the M.E. answered. "It was a pretty routine call."

A stroke of luck. There are 31 M.E.s in the Office of Chief Medical Examiner, less than one for each of the 77 N.Y.P.D. police precincts.

"Did the time of death match up with what seems to be the facts of the case?" I asked.

"Yes," he replied. "The body hadn't reached the ambient temperature of the freezer yet. If she had gone there pretty much directly from the interrupted wedding, the timing would check out."

"Was there enough blood?" I asked.

"Counting what was on the floor," he answered, "She would have had to have lost a pint to a quart on the way."

"Close, then," I answered.

"Yeah," he answered.

"Were the knife wounds fatal?" I asked.

"The stab wound to the heart would have killed her without treatment," the M.E. replied. "But she hadn't dissected the aorta. Still, I'd say the wound killed her before the hypothermia could."

"Did the evaporation rate look right?" I asked.

"Yes, he answered. "The standard blue haze you would expect to see in the air of a freezer, if she had bled out there."

Something bothered me about the case, but I didn't have the vaguest idea what it was. "What if somebody had squirted the blood in there with a squeeze bottle afterwards?" I asked. And I got a mental image of Haldis Pike and those polka dot sheets as

I did so. No reason I should have, though. Conscience will do that to you.

"Maybe," the M.E. answered. "But that would be pure speculation, wouldn't it?"

I had to agree. He'd caught me constructing fanciful explanations for an event that seemed pretty cut-and-dried. Still, just to be sure, I arranged for an expedited DNA test to be done on the blood Denise had left at that interrupted wedding ceremony.

Then I went shopping for a new set of sheets. Samantha had liked the old ones with the polka dots. I found some, but after I bought them, I wasn't completely satisfied. Somehow, the polka dots didn't look exactly like the ones on the set of sheets that had disappeared with Haldis Pike.

I returned to the offices of Word to the Wise to find Samantha waiting there, chatting with Ida. "I've had an inspiration," Samantha told me. "Granted, you can't participate in my work, but I can legitimately be part of yours by getting you to solve my problem. It seems that my boyfriend is on the way to getting himself killed by remaining in a line of work that has proven dangerous to him time and time again."

I suddenly felt like a chicken bone with dog teeth affixed to either end. Samantha had come into a lot of money. The prospect of helping her spend it would have appealed to a great many men. The type of man who . . . I suddenly had the mental image of George Raft, dancing Samantha across a ballroom floor.

"Wouldn't that be a little like, uh . . . kind of being a . . ." I fumbled.

"It would be legitimate work," Samantha interrupted. "It's work that you would do for anyone else. And I've already determined that your personal case load is light right now."

I looked at Ida. She seemed embarrassed. "It appears a psychiatrist has the ability to get information out of people more easily than the average person can," she answered.

"Don't be so hard on yourself, Ida," Samantha replied. "You proceeded with the full determination that the information you were divulging was in the best interest of your employer. And nobody but you would be in a better position to know that."

"Very clever," I thought. Samantha had me caught directly between the alternatives of making Ida feel like a fool, or accepting the proposition Samantha had laid out for me. Deep down I knew I didn't have a chance in Hades of outwitting Samantha Dale, but I took the challenge anyway.

"I'll take the case" I told her. "What would you like me to do for you?" That should slow her down. She couldn't very well come right out and tell me she wanted to convert me to a kept man, living on the money Charles Ogden had given her for handing over his grandson.

Samantha looked at Ida to assure her that she was still a part of Sam's project to do what was best for her employer. "Very simple," Samantha answered. "Your job is to persuade my boyfriend to narrate the events of his life and career that might allow me to identify possible elements of remediable pathology."

"You mean get the guy to tell his life story, so that you can . . ." I began, realizing only then that she had me cold. I'd have to let her psychoanalyze me, with the risk that at the end of it all she'd convert me into a house pet. And at the very least, giving her what she asked for would take a lot of time, keeping me safely off the streets. She'd win either way.

"Correct," Samantha answered.

"With the proviso that I continue with the current cases I'm working on," I stipulated.

"Absolutely," Samantha agreed. "And at the moment that includes only two cases. The matter of the missing Denise Howard, and the disappearance and possible continuing threat of the killer of Haldis Pike's father."

No doubt about it, Samantha had me sewn up.

Ida interrupted to tell me that the blood test results on Denise Howard had just come in. The samples we sent over had proven to be Denise Black's blood. They matched with all her previous records. And it was the same as that of the body in the morgue.

So, all that remained was to write up a bill for services, keeping it down to bare expenses for the sake of decency. Or that would have been all that remained in the normal course of events. Except that I didn't like the look of the case, and I could tell that Ida didn't either. I gave Samantha the "timeout" sign.

"What do you think?" I asked Ida.

"It's a setup," Ida replied. "The wording of that argument in the church sounded like an old Vaudeville skit. And I don't believe the woman Fredericks met at her house was Denise Black. It's much easier to fool someone two thousand miles away than at close range. Plus, the impostor would have had all those computer records, old files of exchanges between the two of them, to study up on."

I glanced at Samantha, who was watching with interest. This was Ida's chance to recover the self-esteem she'd lost by letting Samantha pump her for information, and Samantha was pleased about that.

"It would still take an extremely good actress," I said to Ida. "And one who wasn't concerned about being identified while working in the New York area."

"Right," Ida agreed. "And she'd have to know she was getting into something risky."

"So, I guess the place to start," I told Ida, "is to send out photos of Denise Black to talent agencies, starting at places like Chicago and Los Angeles. Go through the pictures Fredericks gave us and use the one that looks the most like an agency face shot.

"Got it," Ida replied.

"Time for me to move," I told Samantha. "I trust I don't need to offer you cab fare?" It probably wasn't the most tactful thing to say in parting, but who wants to crab past life guarding every word? Samantha had never divulged the size of her settlement, but a hundred million would have been pocket change for Charles Ogden.

I hit the street. Having settled upon a direction of approach, I followed logic to its gruesome end. If another woman had been impersonating Denise Black, she'd been playing a dangerous game.

I checked the local morgues for a body and soon made an unwelcome discovery. The body of a young woman had been fished out of the East River, near Pier Five in Brooklyn Heights. Her face had evidently been struck by a boat propeller, but she was the same approximate age and build as the dead Denise Black.

There were no cuts on the unidentified woman's hands, but if that strangely melodramatic confrontation at the church had been staged, I wouldn't have expected any. Milburn Howard and the woman impersonating Denise Black would have used the kind of phony razor device with a bulb that wrestlers use to fake cutting each other in the ring.

Next, I had a chemical analysis made of the remaining blood on the handkerchief Burlin Fredericks had provided. It turned out that the blood contained a clotting inhibitor.

"Is it the same thing they put into blood at the blood bank to preserve it?" I asked.

"No, that's acid citrate dextrose," the lab man answered. "This was Warfarin."

"Isn't that rat poison?" I asked.

"That's what it was developed for," the lab man answered, "but doctors found a new use for it in medicine, as a blood-thinner."

"Could it be used to preserve blood?" I asked. "And conversely, is this acid citrate stuff used as medicine?"

"Warfarin would preserve blood, yes," the lab man answered. "But it's not a good choice. As for acid citrate dextrose, it's strictly extracorporeal."

"Meaning?" I asked.

"For use outside the body," he answered. "I see what you're getting at, but you're trying to prove a negative."

"Yeah," I agreed. "But thanks anyway."

I got on the phone with Denise Black's physician and found him eager to help. There was no reason Denise would have been using a blood thinner, he told me.

Ida rang in with an alert. She had come up with a picture of an actress named Deborah Lancaster of Chicago, present whereabouts unknown. She sent it to my phone. Ms. Lancaster bore an uncanny resemblance to Denise Black, and was younger by only two years.

I called the head of the talent agency in Chicago that represented Ms. Lancaster. As he picked up the phone he said "Wait just a minute, please," and paused. "Here's an ontological acting tip for you," he said to someone at the other end of the line, evidently finishing an important thought I'd interrupted with the call. "Don't break the 'Just Rule.' It is 'don't just;' not 'just don't.' Define your universe first, and then assign particulars to it." Evidently, I had caught him in the middle of a conversation he couldn't break away from without making a final point.

"Granger Talent Pool, Mosby Granger speaking," he said.

I identified myself to him and asked if he could obtain a DNA sample for me in order to determine whether a body found in New York was that of Deborah Lancaster.

"I'll save you the trouble," Granger told me. "If the body in question has a tramp stamp of a butterfly that's been halfway erased, that's Deborah."

The coroner had already noted the tattoo; small and only partially visible. The killer had made a mistake: he or she hadn't checked for it.

As a precaution I went to a judge with my suspicions, taking a cop friend with me. I was able to block any proposed attempt by Milburn Howard to have Denise's body cremated. After we got that done, I decided I'd put in enough work for the day and went home.

CHAPTER TEN:

TROUBLEMAKER

TEMPLE WORTHINGTON STOOD at the back of a crowd of onlookers watching a chimpanzee smear paint on a stretched canvas. Worthington didn't know why he had come to the zoo, except that he'd felt vaguely discontented when he got up, and something had drawn him there.

Worthington's gig at the hotel museum was causing him to get up earlier every day. It was throwing off his bio-rhythms. Plus, he was getting tired of the kind of songs people requested during the daytime.

A ripple went through the crowd as the attendant proudly displayed the completed masterpiece. Behind him the chimpanzee continued to play with the paint, rubbing its fingers across the wells of it that were still attached to the easel

In front of Worthington the crowd oohed and aahed at the results of the session. "There may be something in this for me," Worthington thought. Of course, chimpanzees were out of the question. They looked cute on TV, but if they caught you looking at them the wrong way, they'd rip your face off. There were plenty of other choices, though, he said to himself

"THE TIME HAS COME," Samantha told me in the morning, "to begin your story." She rolled on top of me to make sure I was paying attention. "You told me a story before I left, Turley, so I know you're good at it," she continued. "I want to hear your life's story. Or at least the part that starts when you decided to be a private eye."

"Do you think maybe we should wait on this?" I asked her, looking at the clock on the nightstand. "After all, Ida may call me at any moment with a report on developments in a case."

"I trust you to keep your place if we're interrupted," Samantha insisted. "Besides, it's early." She fixed me with a level gaze, as if to emphasize the importance of what she was about to tell me. "You were my one girlhood romance, Turley," she continued, "before I became a mother. I went straight from school to this juncture, you know. Except for that rather unfortunate stint at the drop house. You're my entire excuse for a sex life, because I don't count anything that happened to me there. I'd find it a great comfort if you'd fill in some of the blanks about yourself. About what made you the way you are."

"And I guess this doesn't have anything to do with your profession, right?" I answered suspiciously. "I think you miss going to the office and psychoanalyzing people more than you know." We hadn't talked much at the ranch we'd bought, moved out to, and sold within the span of a month. We'd been so sure we'd like the outdoor stuff that we had exhausted ourselves finding out that we didn't.

"It seems to me that our major conflict before was the fact that neither of us wanted to give up our profession for the other," Samantha answered. "Okay, I've done it. Oh, I haven't sold the practice yet, but that's because it makes me feel good to continue to view myself as Dr. Dale. I put in a lot of study to get to be her. And I need this. When somebody comes to you for help do you turn them down just because they're multi-millionaires?"

I was steering the conversation about as effectively as a sheep steers a border collie. "Okay," I replied. "If you'll agree to stop at just one. All right?"

"It's a deal," Samantha agreed. Even as she spoke, I knew she was accepting that condition temporarily, and that she would angle to draw me out once again at her first opportunity. Too bad I couldn't come right out and explain that certain details I might drop here and there could land me in the slammer if anybody found out about them. That wouldn't have been a very diplomatic thing to say to her.

"But bear in in mind that some of it is not going to be exactly 'G' rated," I cautioned, hoping that this might discourage her.

"Do your best," Samantha dared me. "Don't you suppose I've heard just about all of it sitting next to a psychiatrist's couch?"

This side of Samantha reminded me a lot of her sister Penelope, and indulging it was a little like getting a two-for-one deal.

I started with the story of how Arnold Gassner and I had sneaked into the Haj as non-Muslims. Samantha had only heard the basic details of it before. This time I showed her the network of scars from the whipping I'd received when the religious police caught us.

"I'm surprised I didn't notice them before," Samantha said. "I can't even feel them, though, and they're only visible in raking light. The doctors did a good job patching you up."

"Yes," I agreed, "but they almost nailed me another way. Luckily, by day three I caught onto the fact that they were giving me an opiate drip in that dispenser I was tapping into on demand. From the time I saw my dad get killed by a car as he came out of a liquor store, I had never taken a drink in my life. I wasn't about to start . . . ."

"Wait a minute," Samantha interrupted. "Tell me about that."

It was the psychiatrist popping out in her, but I didn't argue. "Well, funny thing," I replied. "I mean ironic, I suppose. Dad had been a fanatic about smoking, from the time I was able to remember anything. But at the same time, he was an alcoholic."

"And as a result, you grew up with an aversion to both those vices?" she asked. "In New York that must have made you a target."

"I suppose so, yes," I admitted.

"So, you grew up with a strong healthy body, and you learned to fight as well," she concluded.

"Say, maybe we could both get back on the force, and you could be a police interrogator," I told her.

"Get back to the story," she laughed.

"After firmly rejecting booze I wasn't going to accept any substitutes," I began. "Pain or no pain, I quit the drip regulator in time to save myself from total disaster. Because when I woke on the fifteenth day the ideas that had been running through my head about working for the good of my fellow man disappeared and I suddenly found myself thinking about nobody but number one, with cold clarity."

Samantha saw that I was wrapped up in the story. She settled back and let me go on, without another word. Maybe Dr. Samantha Dale, Psychiatrist, had done it with her prompting, but I continued as if she weren't there.

It had been a wrenching experience, leaving that hospital in Riyadh. It was a little like falling through the ice on a pond you didn't know you were walking over. Except that you were going from cold to hot. An orderly who had been friendly for the last two weeks came in to crisply inform me that I was ready to be dismissed from the hospital. The bill had been settled up and I was being told to leave.

The filthy rags I'd come there in were hanging neatly in the locker, clean rags now. I put them on and the orderly handed me a clear plastic card of pain meds with two pills on it and ushered me into the hall. I dropped the pills into the nearest trashcan to let him know they hadn't hooked me on the stuff, and went along as if I were delighted at the prospect of leaving the place.

Two men escorted me out to the street without a word, and one of them handed me my passport. The street was like a blast furnace after the air conditioning of the hospital, and I paused a moment to orient myself.

With no map I headed in the direction where the palms started to thin out, which meant toward the center of town. Nothing seemed to grow there except stunted bushes and those palm trees. The city fathers in Riyadh have a fetish for them, and as you head out in any direction, you'll find a million of them almost touching each other, all in a single line close to the road. After a while I found a man leaning against one of them who spoke English and he directed me to the U.S. Embassy.

With this landmark as a reference I found the planter where Jason and I had cached our passports. Jason had paid for the full treatment, not the cheapo documents that were cranked out all day for illegal immigrants on Forty-Second Street. I burned the one I had, and said goodbye to John Williams, my fake name on the passport, forever.

It was supposed to be easy from that point on, but it wasn't. The guards outside the embassy told me I wouldn't be admitted unless I was seeking asylum. Hit the road, their look said.

Then I got stopped by a confidential "psst" through the corner of the embassy fence. A Marine who wasn't being watched gave me a tip: a shipping company was looking for exchange labor. He stuck a bus schedule with the route circled on it through the fence, along with a Saudi coin for the bus fare.

At the shipping company came a lengthy interview during which I lied my head off. Then the company recruiter gave me a bus ticket, Saudi Arabian Public Transit, to Jeddah and a bag lunch. Dates.

S.A.P.T busses are luxurious affairs, tall boxy coaches with heavy curtains over the windows. I settled back and relaxed on the way to Jeddah, suspecting that the wait for the ship I'd been assigned to was going to be anything but comfortable.

I was right. The ship had been held up at a port to the south. I ate out of garbage cans and slept in a dark alley for a week, huddled under a rug at night. The tramp freighter I'd been waiting for slid into its berth while I was eating a chicken leg I'd stolen from a cat. At least I hoped it was chicken.

At the gangplank of the freighter I introduced myself to a man named Padmesh Nara and was immediately assigned to stow bags of dried dates into the dusty hold.

Meanwhile the experienced hands were offloading boxes of machinery to make room on the deck for a consignment of second-hand Lincoln Continentals being shipped north.

We were outward bound within hours. Casper Stoups was the name of the captain. Laughing Dove was the name of the tramp freighter; tramp, because it wasn't a ship with a set route. It took whatever freight was assigned it at a given port and headed for the next job.

That irregular scheduling meant that sometimes the cargo got stowed in a way that left the vessel poorly balanced. With dates in the hold and Lincolns on the deck the Laughing Dove was unstable from the beginning. I detected vomit in the scuppers several times as I was scrubbing the deck; a sure tip-off that the lading on this voyage was not riding the way it usually did.

The captain had done his research. He had accepted an inexperienced hand because he wanted to have someone around who could play chess while standing at the console beside him.

It was unfair. Stoups drubbed me at chess all through the voyage, but only because I was exhausted from work. I found I'd landed a job that amounted to full-time deck hand and part-time cabin boy.

The big scare I went through on the way back to New York began as I stood next to the captain at the console, half way between Jeddah and the Suez Canal.

"Listen to my stomach growl, Troublemaker," Stoups said. "You've got the advantage on me, I'm so hungry."

Troublemaker was my name on board the Laughing Dove because of the fact that I'd been caught participating in the Haj as a non-Muslim. A Muslim crew member had seen my scars and spread the word.

Distracted by hunger, eh? It wasn't enough that the captain was taking advantage of my fatigue to beat me at chess; he had to make excuses for not beating me worse.

As Captain Stoups finished that hypocritical remark First Mate Nara came up and set a tray beside him.

"Why are you here, Nara, instead of an orderly?" asked the captain.

"To introduce the work of the new cook," Nara answered. "He is a countryman of mine."

"I suppose that's why you let him stow all those bags and boxes in his cabin without charging him for freight?" the captain inquired. "Troublemaker here was whining about how they made him sneeze."

Maybe someone else had said it, but I hadn't. Stoups was probably using that irritating name to break my concentration. I was ahead two pawns in the game.

"Precious spices are the ingredients of his work, the tools of his trade, Captain Sir," Nara replied. "You will be glad of that

decision when you partake of the delicacy he has sent you."
Nara gestured elegantly toward the tray.

"What's this?" Captain Stoups asked him.

"Blintzes, sir," Nara replied. "Ajay wanted to show you his specialty to start off with."

"A.J.?" Stoups grumbled, and poked one of the blintzes with his finger. The smell wasn't very appealing, but the captain was hungry.

Stoups dismissed the mate and held one of the blintzes up to look at it. "Jewish food combined with Indian spices," he said. "This could be very good or very bad."

The captain handed the blintz to me. "Take a bite of this, Troublemaker," he told me. "You can be my court taster."

I was glad for the opportunity. Mess for the crew consisted largely of dates and tiny black beans about the size of lentils. Along with rice, of course.

I took a bite. The sensations, in order, were of curry, cumin, turmeric, red pepper and great pain. Was that a piece of thin pancake I was feeling with my tongue, or had the roof of my mouth come loose?

Stoups watched. "Hot?" he asked.

"Mummmph," I replied, unable to answer.

"Aw, you're just a baby," Stoups told me, and took a big bite of one of the blintzes. He chewed reflectively for a few seconds, then bent and spewed the mouthful of blintz into the waste can with a loud sputtering noise.

"Eeeeaugh!" he said. "Milk! I've heard that milk will help. Get down to the galley quick and get me some milk. A quart of it."

I started to obey the order, but the captain stopped me before I had even stowed away the chess set. "Never mind," he said, "I've got something here."

Stoups produced a bottle of coconut cordial from under the counter. "I can't wait for the milk," he said between gulps.

It was bad news for me. I'd planned to get some of that milk myself, even if I had to drink half of it and replace it with water.

Stoups finished the bottle and tossed it into the trash. He hadn't offered me any, and he'd drunk it down to the last drop.

The captain tried to speak three times before he was able to enunciate clearly. "I'll just have to wait for something more nearly edible than this," he finally managed to say. He pushed the tray aside just as Nara rushed back in.

"Captain," cried the frightened man, "disaster has befallen us." Nara looked as if a tsunami was about to engulf the ship.

"What is it?" the captain asked.

"The watch has spotted a cloud of locusts, miles wide and as high as the sky," Nara answered.

Disaster indeed. Even I knew that there had been reports of locusts sinking whole ships, and that the Laughing Dove was in exactly the wrong place. This far from land the locusts would be exhausted, and would pile up on the ship. Hundreds of tons of them. If they were already in sight, then the Laughing Dove could not turn quickly enough to avoid them.

Stoups slammed his free hand down on the console. "Schedule or no," he roared, "I'll never leave port again with a trim like this. In our condition it would take about half of that swarm to sink us."

Nara lowered his eyes as if he might have had something to do with the captain's decision to leave port prematurely. "I'll order a crew to man the hoses," Captain Stoups told the mate. "We'll blast them away."

A cluster of insects smacked into the window in front of us as if in resentment of the order Stoups was about to issue. The three of us shrank away from the unexpected noise.

"Oh, Sir," Nara answered, "it has been tried before to no effect. We are doomed."

"None of that weasel talk," Stoups ordered through the growing roar of the locusts. "We have six pallets of light oil on the deck. I'll have the men divert the hoses and blast them with that."

"Oil, too, has been tried," Nara answered. "It only adds to the weight and sends the ship down more quickly. I have seen it happen from the air." Nara was almost shouting, and yet the main body of the swarm was still far ahead of us. We were getting random outriders at this point.

"The oil is our best bet anyway," Stoups replied. He switched the shipboard announcing system to maximum volume and hailed the bosun.

"Tipton, break open a drum of that oil on deck and get the deck wash pump hose in it," Stoups ordered. "Two teams, four men each."

"If we got 'em Sir, after the deserters finish taking off," came the faint reply from the bosun's group system mike.

"I saw them from the bridge," Stoups replied. "The cook and three non-essentials. Let them go."

The bosun gave an answer I couldn't hear and rang off.

The departure of the deserters was another blow to Nara's morale. He was from Rangoon, and he knew this track of the Red Sea well. No wonder his face was ashen as he glanced from the captain to the sky and back again.

"They are dead men," Nara intoned. "To abandon ship is useless, because the locusts will drag the lifeboat down as well."

The roar of the swarm was increasing. My back teeth were rattling and something inside my head was about to break. I wondered if sound alone could kill.

A weathered hand floated past my face and back the other way, breaking the trance I had fallen into. Stoups motioned for me to put the chess set away and beckoned the mate toward him. I'd been clutching the set all the time.

"Stand by the helm, Nara" Stoups shouted. "Troublemaker, you stand here beside me as well, in case I need you for a runner. The loudspeaker is useless."

Nara and I did as we were ordered. Until a cluster of locusts shot into the cabin as if they had been dumped from a bucket.

That was enough for me. I left the bridge.

Behind me I heard the captain shouting, but I couldn't understand what he was saying. I kept walking. An idea had come to me, but there was no time to debate it with him.

Reaching the deck, I glanced at the immense swarm of locusts that were rapidly closing in on the Laughing Dove. So many, and though they still had not reached us I could feel my bones vibrating.

The strays alone, the ones that had been blown ahead by random gusts, had already covered the deck. Behind them were tens of millions that would desperately cling to the same refuge. Only duty kept the captain's hand on the wheel and the nine crew members up ahead of me manning the deck wash pump. I crunched my way through the tired locusts to the bosun's detail on the deck and his command of eight.

Clarence Tipton was the bosun's name, and we'd had a run-in. "Captain's orders," I shouted to him as I approached. Tipton turned to me with wild eyes that narrowed to a focused stream of hatred. "You," the look seemed to say, "First a swarm of locusts and now I have to deal with you."

"Captain's got a plan," I yelled. "Sent me to show you."

"Don't show me," Tipton snapped, "just relay the order."

"To complicated," I answered. "Got to walk you through it."

That got me a wolf smile. Small wonder Tipton didn't like me. He'd been used to pushing people around, and when he'd found out about my trouble with the Saudis, he'd made a point of slapping me on my injured back every time I passed by him.

Tipton had done it once too often. Waking up in sickbay a day later he'd realized his reputation as a tough guy had been ruined. The crew had been ribbing him ever since, and he couldn't respond appropriately because he had to watch out for further injury after the concussion I had given him.

Now on the deck with hungry locusts clothing us like bows on a Sunday frock, Tipton knew damned well the Captain had granted me no such latitude. Stoups would hardly even have attached me to the critically important pump detail, much less given me instructions to command it. Tipton knew this, and he knew as well that I had condemned myself with the lie.

Tipton smiled, only the second time I had seen him do it. He knew that whatever cockeyed scheme I had in mind would be on my own head. With a sneer, he accepted my statement. My claim had given him free reign to blame everything that happened next on me, should we survive the crisis.

"To the galley," I told Tipton. "Bring four men."

I didn't wait. I'd gambled that Tipton would follow with the four men.

I slid down the ladder to the galley, a hand on each rail. By the time Tipton got there with the detail I had the logistics of my plan figured out.

"Throw the eggs into that big cooking pot," I ordered, as soon as the men were in position.

"The Captain told you to break a gross of eggs?" Tipton asked.

"Yes," I answered, and pointed to a four-foot wooden cooking spoon. "Stir them up with that paddle," I told the men, and two of them complied.

I pointed to a rack with a half-dozen gallon jugs of olive oil on it. "Hold them over the vat," I told them. I ripped the jugs open with a butcher knife so we wouldn't waste time pouring them out.

I threw in a two-gallon pan of chicken broth. "To the deck," I commanded. The men looked at Tipton. The bosun waved his hand to them with a sarcastic flourish of invitation. "Give him all the rope he needs," Tipton said with a sneer.

We fought our way topside through the cloud of locusts that were fluttering down the ladder. The insects were bouncing from bulkhead to bulkhead, but they weren't too confused to bite when they got a chance.

On deck the locusts were ankle deep. The two biggest men were carrying the vat. I flailed at them with a handful of bundled aprons to keep the locusts off them. We were getting bitten everywhere the skin showed.

"Set it down," I shouted through the drone of the swarm. We were wading through locusts now, and they had already stripped away our trouser cuffs and were working on our ankles. We were stomping to dislodge them; almost running in place.

"Break it down," I ordered, pointing to a locked cabin door. Tipton himself obliged with a fire axe, fixing me with that wicked smile as he did so.

"Bring the sacks," I shouted, pointing inside the cabin. The other two members of the detail obeyed, and we fought our way forward.

We reached the spot where the men were spraying the insects with oil from the drum. "Get the lid off that barrel," I told one of the men.

He turned and looked at me with eyes dulled from pain. The locusts had chewed him up so badly that a flap of his scalp was hanging over the side of his face. Bright green insects were clinging to its borders. It looked like a strange jeweled headband. He was still game, though, and he slapped a wrench on the barrel head at once.

When the drum was open, I had the two big guys pour the contents of the cooking pot in on top of the small amount of light machine oil that was still in it.

"Hold those bags over it, one by one," I yelled. I split open the bags with the butcher knife and let the contents spill in. The men took turns stirring, because each man could only stand to twist the cooking paddle two or three times before being seized by a coughing fit.

"Get the hose in there now," I shouted, and half choked on a huge locust that had pried itself into my open mouth.

The crew began to pump as Tipton and I swatted locusts away from them. The ship was beginning to list, because the locusts had eaten through some of the ropes securing the cargo on the deck. A Lincoln rolled by and Tipton signaled six of the men to go secure the cargo.

That left only four of us to man the deck wash pump. We were all coughing and rubbing our eyes, but not from inhaling locust parts. That pumping job was a gruesome detail, worse than any truck I ever unloaded on a summer day in the Bronx.

The locusts were soon getting the worst of it, though. The deck began to clear in front of us. The locusts were fleeing from the fine spray the men were pumping into the air from the oil drum.

Ahead of us the cloud of locusts began to split into a massive wake in mid-air, as thickly packed as a stone wall. The terrifying roar slowly died away. After what seemed an eternity the Laughing Dove had passed through the cloud and I was working with the rest of the crew, sweeping the last of the dead locusts off the deck.

Stoups and Nara were leaning against the console, exhausted from the tension, as I returned to the bridge.

"It's a miracle," First Mate Nara gasped, "a miracle. Please tell me, Troubled One, what did you use to drive the demons away?"

"Yes," the captain added. "What was it you put into that drum?"

"To tell you the truth," I answered, "I don't exactly know." I saw the puzzled looks on their faces. "Other than the eggs I used as an emulsifier," I continued. "I just ordered the men to fill the drum with whatever it was the cook used to make those blintzes."

That shut them up completely. The captain and mate looked at each other with blank expressions and turned back to stare across the dark water ahead.

For the first time I noticed that the sea had gone completely silent. It was a silence so profound that it seemed to occupy every sense, so comforting and luxurious that no one wanted to break it. The watch was up, so I took my leave. It had been a long day and I was ready to turn in.

It was a day of redemption, and not for just one reason. At the bottom of the ladder from the bridge I received a big surprise. Boatswain Clarence Tipton was standing there with his insect-ravaged arm stuck out, waiting to shake my hand.

CHAPTER ELEVEN:

SEE GENOA AND DIE

PLEADING HUNGER, I had retreated to the breakfast nook. Twenty minutes later Samantha corralled me again. She took the plate I'd just emptied and set it behind her on the counter without looking. While her hand was back there, she found the Pyrex coffee pot and brought it around to fill my cup without taking her eye off me. The world had lost a terrific waitress when she had become a psychiatrist.

"Let's pick up the story at the point where you had just repelled the attack by the locusts," she requested.

"Sure," I agreed. "I haven't had this much concentrated attention before, without having a light shined in my face by cops."

Samantha smiled at the remark, but wouldn't have if she'd experienced a police interrogation.

"Two days after the Laughing Dove had survived the swarm," I continued, "she cruised northward through the Suez Canal with her cargo of late-model Lincolns nearly intact on the deck. We dropped off most of them in Sicily and took on a cargo of olive oil and wine. Two more stops and we arrived in Genoa. There Captain Stoups ordered me to the bridge."

"I know you're trying to get home, Troublemaker," Stoups told me, "and I've got a little help for you."

"And what might that be, Sir?" I asked him. I knew Captain Stoups was a hard dealer, and I was a little wary of any gifts he might seem to be handing out.

"I won't lie to you," Stoups answered. "You may have saved my ship for me, but that doesn't mean you're not still a jinx. Next time it might be a rain of frogs. One of the men who got killed by the locusts when he deserted the ship had contracted with me to deliver a couple of Lincolns inland. I'm offering you the job in that man's place."

"Where to?" I asked.

"Marseille," Stoups answered. "Can't beat that, can you?"

I suspected Stoups intended to get me to deliver the cars for no fee in exchange for a means of transportation to Marseille. I'd be leaving the Laughing Dove with very little money as it was.

"Sounds like a tough job pulling one big car behind another like that," I answered.

"Look at what you get to drive through," Stoups said, waving his arm in a sweeping gesture at the city. "See Genoa and drop dead, so they say."

"I thought that was Naples," I replied.

"What's the difference?" Stoups asked. "Look at it. Great looking city, isn't it?"

I had to admit he had a point there, but I still planned to hold out for a fee.

"What's the mileage?" I asked.

"Three hundred and forty-seven miles," Stoups answered.

"How much is that in Kilometers?" I asked.

"Five hundred and fifty-eight, Troublemaker," Stoups answered. "Are you in or out?"

"You could get there yourself before I could," I told him. I knew that the company had changed its routing and that the Laughing Dove would not dock at Marseille.

"It's no more than a six-hour drive," Stoups returned. "I'll give you fifty cents a mile."

"Fifty cents a kilometer," I told him. "And a case of those protein bars."

The protein bars were part of a spoilage allowance Stoups had taken advantage of when a pallet of them had accidentally–on–purpose broken open. This had fortunately happened before the locusts touched down and ate most of the consignment.

"This is the last case of them," Stoups told me, pushing a box out from under the console with his foot. "Go on and take them."

"Then it's a deal?" I asked.

With muttered curses Stoups agreed and advanced me half payment with the rest at delivery of the Lincolns, one to eastern France and one to Marseille.

I thought I had come out ahead until I got on the road and found that the route through Genoa was more tunnel than open air. And when you did pop out of a tunnel it was only to drive between high walls in the company of motorists who were angry at you for crawling down the highway inside thirty-two feet of slow-moving steel. Thirty-six including the tow bar.

All went well until I dropped the first car off at a roadside inn a hundred miles past the French border. I had towed the Lincoln there without getting a scratch on it, and had delivered it a little before it was expected to arrive.

The Lincoln had been treated well during its year of service at a palace in Riyadh, and it still looked new. I got a tip from its new owner and prepared to head out, relieved that the driving would be easier without the heavy weight I'd been towing.

I had unkinked my back and was ready to climb back into the car when a very old woman walked her tiny white dog past me. She stopped and looked back at me, her eyes bright and burning. "Quel domage," she said, "un jeune garçon comme vous."

"What a shame; a young boy like you," she had said. The woman walked on and, perplexed, I climbed back into the car and drove away. What had she meant by that? My mind was a little dulled by watching the road for so long.

A mile later some odd facts started to add up. For one thing, the tip had been too big. And the old woman had known something I hadn't. Plus, there was the fact that a certain model of Volkswagen hatchback was much more prevalent on this road than it should be. It was the same car. I was being followed.

Then it hit me that I had been a sucker. A callow, naïve, just-off-the-boat bozo. I wasn't just delivering cars, I was running dope.

I'd have to keep playing the innocent. If the men behind me were police they would have pulled me over already. They weren't hijackers either, because they would have jumped me long ago. The conclusion had to be that they were back there to escort the dope to Marseille.

Now what? I'd already dropped off a shipment. The next step, of course, was that I'd be confronted in Marseille by people who would extort me to make further deliveries for them. Unless the police picked me up before I got there, that is. The car tailing me was there to make sure nothing short of a police dog interfered with the delivery, while allowing the watchers to hang back and avoid arrest themselves.

But maybe the inexperience they had relied upon to rope me in could be used as a tool to get me out. What if, encouraged by the success of my mission so far, I chose to reward myself by taking the scenic route to Marseille? I'd take the coastal route along the Mediterranean to enjoy the view of southern France. At least I'd get a chance to check the Lincoln and make sure my imagination wasn't getting the better of me.

At the first opportunity I left the main road. My escort wasn't expecting that, and went on by. By the time they caught up I had stopped to check one of the rocker panels. Just as I feared, it was stuffed with bags of white powder.

I was on the road sight-seeing again before the escort picked me up, but the plan wasn't going so well otherwise. The ocean was hidden behind a stretch of terrain you could only get to by boat.

I had left the main road thirty miles or so east of Marseille. The road I took was bearing away from the ocean, so I took another side road leading back toward the water. I gawked at the terrain as I drove, hoping to look convincingly like a sight-seer.

Soon the road began to bend into hairpin turns that devolved into right angles with cars parked on the shoulders in front of houses. I kept thinking I would hit a clear stretch again, but the going got increasingly worse.

The road had completely changed into a series of short zig-zags that served one or two big houses as a system of communal driveways. It became clear that I wouldn't get to Marseille that way. I had entered a region of giant outcroppings of weathered limestone I later found were called the Calanques. Or at least the little inlets along the coast that splashed in between them were called that.

The whole area became a national park a few years later. And it was no place to build a road, unless you had about a million tons of concrete to put down on it per mile. Every place that wasn't a big spur of rock was a pile of gravel with the soil washed off it.

The men tailing me had to know by this time that I wasn't trying to run off with the dope. But how long did I have before they decided their most expedient course of action was to shoot me and drive the Lincoln to Marseille themselves? All that was saving me now was the fact that neither of the dopers wanted to risk arrest driving it.

The four or five miles I'd traveled on that side road was obviously the limit. Finding myself overlooking the ocean from a broad limestone bluff that wasn't even a road, I turned around.

Mistaking that stretch of weathered limestone for a road had been a bad mistake; a disastrous one. My pursuers hadn't been confused by it at all. That probably meant that the men following me were familiar with the area, which was more bad news. They were blocking the pathway I'd left, pointed toward what appeared to be a tiny harbor village about two hundred yards down the sharply descending road.

I had missed an opportunity for escape. When I had driven over the hill the two dopers in the car had lost me. Seeing that the Lincoln wasn't down at the village at the end of the road they had stopped. And then I had blown it by coming back over the hill.

The dopers' car blocked the road leading back to the highway but not the one leading down to the village. That's the one I took, still playing the part of the innocent tourist. I got the Lincoln half-way down what appeared to be a service road to the place before I stopped. It proved to be more obstacle course than road. I parked the car on a patch of worn rock that served as a shoulder and walked down. Sharp spurs of limestone beneath the soles of my deck shoes made the going slow, but that was okay. Maybe if I hung out long enough down there the dopers would strip the cargo out of the Lincoln and go.

What I had taken for fishing boats were luxury sail craft. I was hungry, but nobody was selling fish. My only shot at a fish dinner was a kayak rental concession that offered fishing equipment to go with it.

Renting a kayak might have looked too much as if I'd gotten wise and was trying to escape. I settled for a bag of vegetables a woman was selling from the deck of a motor launch. Dressed like a fashion model, she was offering tomatoes, broccoli and carrots at a surprisingly low price.

I filled a bag with tomatoes and huge cone-shaped carrots. I was about to fill another when she took a good look at the patchwork assemblage of work-clothes I had bummed from crew members on the Laughing Dove. I definitely didn't qualify as a preferred customer. With a frown she started pulling the crates of produce down off the fantail. I got the impression she had carted the produce there from a market somewhere further down the coast as a means of currying favor among the well-to-do sailors whose boats had put in there.   I had given the plan long enough to work, so I moved along. I took the vegetables back to the Lincoln and turned it around.

Back on the limestone bluff at the top of the village road I regretted that trip down to the village. The Lincoln had come up with a flat and the likely cause was those sharp rocks down the primitive road I had just ascended.

I turned left, to the west, and parked parallel to the ocean, pointed away from the dopers. At least I had an excuse for stalling now. I stretched as I got out of the car, to reconnoiter. Further down the coast to the west a massive knob of limestone extended hundreds of feet into the ocean and ended in a cliff. Two hundred yards further along the shore in the same direction was a fjord-like gorge, a much rougher version of the inlet occupied by the ritzy little harbor village down the path behind me. Both inlets were calanques, but the one ahead had evidently been formed by the collapse of a limestone cave. It was lined with precariously balanced rocks like a giant mousetrap.

Speaking of traps, behind me were the dopers and to the right was a field of limestone rubble interspersed with weeds and bushes too small to hide behind. There was no avenue of escape anywhere, and not a witness in sight.

Wondering just how much patience my escort detail might have, I popped the trunk of the Lincoln. The spare was no good, but at least it wasn't packed with dope. Even checking on it had been like spinning a roulette wheel, because as soon as the dopers determined I had tumbled to them I'd probably take a bullet.

The trunk held a tool kit that a master mechanic would have been proud of and a can of compressed air that would have inflated a dirigible, but no usable spare.

I had seen a couple of rowboats stuffed full of inner tubes being rented as floatation devices at the sailing village. I'd just have to buy one of those inner tubes and put it into the defective spare. That would hold me till I got to a service station, if I lived that long.

The process would probably take hours, though, and I was tired from driving. Plus, I would only be able to walk past that car with the two thugs parked in it a certain number of times without revealing the fact that I was purposely ignoring them. They might spare a goofy kid who had the potential to be of use to them, but not a knowing witness.

In that case, I'd better play that goofy kid well. I'd pretend the flat tire had defeated me. Camping out for the night would allow the dopers to take possession of the hidden cargo at their leisure. They couldn't take the Lincoln without killing me, because they wouldn't want it reported as stolen before they got to Marseille with it. But if they would strip the dope out of the Lincoln and go, we'd all be the better for it.

I took a couple of blankets and some protein bars out of the Lincoln and headed for the gorge to the west. To keep walking along the coast and away from the dopers was no option, because I'd have to take at least a couple of gallons of water along to make it across the calanques. Sure, I could get the water down at the village, but the thought of a bullet coming from the top of that limestone incline I'd driven up stopped me.

I sat at the top of the bluff, outlined against the sky for the dopers, and watched the sunset. You never can tell which one will be your last.

Night descended as I walked back down the incline toward the gorge. A little way down it was a sign that warned of danger from falling rocks. That was far enough for me, in the dark.

There was light enough on the flat above for the watchers to see that I wasn't trying to sneak back out of the gorge past them, but it was dark a few feet down the path. A hundred feet below tiny marine organisms outlined a bowl-shaped inlet with their glow. The surf crashed in past a huge boulder that almost blocked the inlet. I didn't mind the noise, and the precarious path could be a life-saver in case there were visitors.

I rigged up a dummy under one of the overhanging rocks, on a patch of ground that had been smoothed by the passage of travelers over the years. Settling back into a strategically-located niche I rested with a rock in my hand. If one of the dopers tried to sneak down the path and pot me, I'd brain him and improve the odds. If both of them came I'd clobber one of them and go from there.

It was a good night to listen to the surf, resting deeply but certain I'd come alert at the approach of an intruder. And tomatoes don't make much noise when you eat them.

I woke with a start when the shadow of a man passed across my face. It turned out to be from one of a group of three rock climbers outlined by the sun, walking along the top of the limestone knob to the east. When they saw me, they reversed their course, looking for another venue. As noted on the warning sign, the gorge was forbidden to rock climbers and there was a heavy fine.

When I got back to the Lincoln it had been invaded, but not by the two I had expected. An entire family had moved in. Three kids were asleep in the front seat and a man and woman were asleep in the back.

Things were getting worse. The Lincoln was laden with heroin, two caffeine–deprived killers were parked about a hundred yards away, and five more potential victims had been introduced to the mixture.

There was nothing to do but play through. The five newcomers woke up when I got to the Lincoln. Their names were Arthur and Ellen, Johnny, Kenneth and Sally Wright. You couldn't imagine a more typical American middle-class family, or one more out-of-place where they were. Two boys, twelve and ten, and a girl, eight. Even the little girl was carrying a backpack. They were on their way from twenty miles east of Marseille to Rockport Maryland.

We conversed over a breakfast of the protein bars Stoups had given me when I'd taken possession of the Lincolns. They were stale, but we would all have eaten them if they had been petrified.

"We were grabbing a cat nap," Arthur told me between bites. "We stayed at a cheap hostel last night, and none of us got a wink of sleep. Bugs and suspicious-looking characters were too tough a combination."

"It was my turn to keep watch," Johnny said, "but the seats in this car are awful soft."

"To tell you the truth," Ellen said, "when we saw the expensive American car, we thought maybe it belonged to a big shot who might have some insight into a problem like ours."

"You mean being stranded travelers?" I asked.

"Being stranded sailors," Ellen answered.

"Sailors," I thought. Now their appearance made sense. Fresh off a ship, they were carrying cheap camping gear recently purchased from some European equivalent of Walmart.

"Yeah," but being stranded tourists is worse, I guess," Arthur admitted. "We weren't expert sailors by any means, but we're even worse tyros as tourists."

"We sold our house to buy a boat and sail around the world," Ellen continued. "We were deeply involved in our family voyage, what with the home schooling on board. We didn't get much practice at being tourists."

"What brought all this on?" I asked them.

"One evening Ellen was reading Joseph Conrad and I was reading Jack London," Arthur replied. "We looked up at each other and the world changed."

"Mommy reads to us all the time," Sally added.

"We were fishing to save on food," Arthur said. "Even took in a little money that way."

"And we confined our sightseeing to what we could view from on board," Ellen said, "But that was a lot in the Mediterranean."

"I saw a mermaid," Kenneth told me.

"Or maybe even a dolphin," Sally commented.

Kenneth gave Sally a sour look.

"So what happened?" I asked.

"What happened is that we got cheated out of our boat," Ellen answered.

"I'm guilty," Arthur said. "Guilty and stupid. This slick talker offered to buy our boat for cash. According to him there weren't enough boats in the area to accommodate the demand."

"Yes," Ellen added, "He didn't want to wait for one because his brother had a terminal illness and wanted to spend his last days on the water; wanted to get underway at once."

"It was much more than the Rockport was worth," Arthur continued, "so I should have been wary."

"We brought the buyer on board for a trial run," Ellen said. "His name is Pierre De Lafontaine. He offered to buy the boat on the spot. We agreed, and stopped at a small port ahead of us."

"The buyer told us that we might as well make the exchange at the tax office," Ellen continued, "because we have to go there anyway. We would have to pay the VAT tax when we sold."

"We went to a room that was supposed to be the tax office," Arthur said. "It was a small port, so we didn't think it was suspicious. We gave the official our ownership papers, surrendered our certificate of temporary import, registration, everything. The official produced form after form for us to sign."

"Arthur doesn't read French," Ellen said, "and I didn't want to show him up. So, we signed some of the forms without looking."

"We signed and De Lafontaine signed," Arthur said. "De Lafontaine took out his checkbook and started to pay. "Or would you prefer cash?" he asked. "It is just as easy. The bank is close."

Arthur continued: "at that point the official stopped the transaction. The sale must take place in my presence, the official told us. He called for an assistant named 'Henri' who was supposed to notarize the papers, but Henri was gone to lunch. The official told us we'd have to come back after lunch."

"De Lafontaine told us he was famished," Ellen added. "He offered to take us to lunch. 'It's a special day,' he said."

"And so, you left the office without the papers," I said.

"Pretty stupid, wasn't it?" Arthur asked. "The restaurant didn't have the right wine, De Lafontaine told us. 'I will bring the wine,' he told us. 'See that villa, it belongs to my father, and his cellar is first rate. I will walk up there and get a special wine and meet you at the restaurant. You order and I'll be right over.'"

"We ordered and we waited," Ellen said. "No De Lafontaine. We went back to the office to find it was closed. We asked around and someone explained it was an empty building."

"And the boat was gone?" I asked.

"Yes, the Rockport had disappeared from the harbor," Ellen answered.

'We waited overnight and then went to see the mayor," Arthur continued. "But the mayor broke out in a shouting fit when he heard the secretary mention our names. It seems we had signed a petition to recall the mayor, and that I had signed a document declaring myself a convicted sex offender."

"You couldn't get a lawyer?" I asked.

"We were advised by an English-speaking lawyer not to pursue the case," Ellen answered.

"Because of the circumstances," Arthur finished for her. "De Lafontaine turns out to be a member of an important family in that town."

"Important but penniless," Ellen added.

"Right," Arthur confirmed. "And it's our word against his."

"Don't you have copies of those papers?" I asked.

"We sure do," Arthur answered. "Hidden aboard the Rockport. But we don't dare mention that to any of the officials around here. We can't trust them."

"We loved that boat," Ellen said. "It was the best home we've ever had, even though we only had it six months.""Ellen is still carrying our pictures of it, and the blueprints," Arthur added.

"May I see them?" I asked.

"Sure," Ellen replied, and spread the treasured keepsakes out on the hood of the Lincoln. The plans were very detailed. I looked at the specification sheets. The Rockport was low rent all the way; the minimum in engineering specs to get a boat of her class into the water. Minimal engine, minimal pumps, minimal in materials right down to the hollow ballcock inside the valve that shut the seacock in the lavatory. She was underpowered and crowded for a family of five. And yet the Wright family had clearly loved their life aboard her.

"How do you know how to read those?" Ellen asked me

"People at the model ship lake in Central Park are eager to tell you everything they know about boats," I told her.

I looked at a blueprint of the hull, and at some photos of the interior. "Who did the cabinet work in the head?" I asked.   "I did," Arthur answered. "I used to be a carpenter."

"And you haven't been to sea before, have you?" I asked.

"Well, no," he answered. "How did you know that?"

I was about to reply when Johnny came to report that he had seen the Rockport. He had been watching the sea with binoculars from somewhere close to the spot where I'd spent the night.

"You mean she's out there now?" I asked.

"Yes," Arthur replied. "We've been following our boat back and forth along the coast, hoping for a miracle. For some kind of break."

"But De Lafontaine never leaves the boat," Ellen said. "And even if he did, there's that phony official on board. He's actually De Lafontaine's brother, and in fine health."

"The Rockport is right below the cliffs, just beyond the breakers," Johnny told me. "Wanna see her?"

"It's so tantalizing, seeing her out there," Ellen said. "But of course we're just punishing ourselves doing this. We really should be trying to find some way to get back to Maryland."

I borrowed the glasses from Johnny and went with him to the lookout post. The Rockport was riding at anchor, a quarter of a mile or so from the cliffs. Two men were on the deck, fishing. They looked like a couple of tough customers. I handed the glasses to Johnny and walked back with him to the Lincoln.

"Kind of like seeing your girl walk down the street with another guy, isn't it," I asked Arthur.

Arthur sighed. "Yes," he agreed. "Bringing it out into the air with a young man who seems to be going about his business sensibly has been a big help. I guess we might as well admit it; we're whipped. No use trying to follow the boat any longer. What are the prospects of getting a ride to Marseille with you?"

Taking the Wright family along in the Lincoln was no option. The dopers would probably decide I was using them as a shield and massacre us all. But I had a solution that would take care of two problems at once. It included immobilizing the Lincoln so that the only logical course for the dopers would be to collect the hidden heroin and go away.

At the same time, I had figured out how to sabotage the Rockport so that De Lafontaine and his brother would have no recourse but to abandon her. Long enough for the Wrights to get her back, at least.

And the best part was that by giving De Lafontaine the hard time he deserved I'd be able to create enough confusion to discourage the dopers from looking for me.

"You won't need a ride," I told Arthur. "I'll get your boat back for you."

"WHAT DID YOU STOP FOR?" Samantha asked.

"Thought you might want to take a break," I answered.

"Go on," she urged. So I did.

Arthur and Ellen looked at me the way your date looks when you say something stupid at a party. Arthur had just called me sensible and here I was, fuzz on my face and in wrinkled work clothes, offering them the impossible.

Still, they were desperate enough to trust me. I borrowed Arthur's pocket knife and cut off the legs of my trousers. Then I got the tools and slid partway under the Lincoln.

"Whatcha' doin'?" Kenneth asked, peering under.

"I'm stripping out a short length of the car's brake line," I told him.

"How come?" Kenneth asked.

"It's a secret method I've invented for getting your boat back," I told him.

"How do you know how to do that?" Kenneth asked.

"In New York mechanics will show you how to do stuff," I answered.

"How come?" Kenneth pursued.

"Well, you've got to help them for free," I explained. "But you learn stuff."

"Oh," he said. "Why did you cut your pants off?"

"Because I'll have to swim out to save your boat," I answered.

"Like a pirate?" he asked.

"Yes, with a carrot between my teeth," I answered.

"Oh, okay," he replied. "So," . . . are you a kid or a grownup?"

"I'm a little bit of both," I told him. I stuck the section of brake line into the bag of vegetables. I added the can of compressed air and a screwdriver, and crawled out from under the car.

"Could I borrow that parasol from you?" I asked Ellen. "You might not get it back."

Ellen nodded in assent and gave Arthur the parasol to hand to me.

"I see you're pretending not to notice those men who are blocking your path with their vehicle, Turley," Arthur said quietly. "Is there anything I can do to help you?"

"I'll be fine," I told him. "But for your safety, don't draw attention to yourself or your family as we walk past."

Arthur agreed under his breath, and gave Ellen the same message. Then the Wright family and I walked down to the sailboat village. I tried to rent a rowboat, but the two they had were such pieces of junk the owners wouldn't take the responsibility of renting them. I ended up buying one. They were glad to get rid of it anyway, and threw in oars and a fishing pole. Plus, it came equipped with an anchor consisting of a rope tied to a chunk of limestone, and a coffee can for bailing.

Pushing off from the coarse-grained sand I immediately got a new perspective on the Calanques. The cliffs along the shore were indented with a continuous niche cut into the limestone by the waves. Twenty feet seaward of that niche the tidal surge balanced the rebound effect from the cliffs, adding up to a pathway of relatively still water that made the rowing easier.

Until the water took on a pale glow, that is. The placid water along the shore line was a trap, hiding the fact that innumerable huge chunks of limestone lay at various depths under the surface, waiting to rip out the bottom of a boat. If you wanted to row in a straight line it had to be further away from the immense broken-radiator surface of the cliffs.

My clumsy rowboat was much slower than the kayaks flitting through the safe zone beyond the rocks, though, and they were passing me. One of them went by on the inside and an oar scraped along a submerged boulder. The kayaker cursed. "Slowpoke," he shouted.

First the Lincolns and now the rowboat; I was still holding up traffic. But at least the hazard I posed for the kayakers gave me a logical reason to drift out toward the Rockport, riding at anchor further away from the cliffs.

Taking care to look casual about it, I rowed east and began to fish fifty feet away from the Rockport. I put up the parasol and pretended to be at a loss about how to brace it. Propped against the gunnel it cut off the De Lafontaines' view of me.

So far, so good. As soon as the rowboat had stabilized against the current, I tied off the anchor and kicked off my deck shoes. Slipping over the side away from the Rockport I let the bag I was carrying pull me down.

I was suddenly reminded that the ocean is no swimming pool. A few feet under the surface the water was shockingly cold and a strong current was tugging at me. But was it moving toward or away from shore? Surrounded by a dazzling fog of shiny bubbles, I no longer knew which way was up. Drowning would be a very ineffective opener for my plan to save the day for the Wrights.

Then I saw the Rockport, a sliver of blue light that marked the surface ahead. And closer than I expected. It was almost as if she were in on the attempt to reunite with her proper family.

I swam under the little yacht and took a breath of air on the side away from her temporary new owners. Time to gear up. I jammed the section of brake line onto the nozzle of the air can, stuck the screwdriver between my teeth, and went back under.

Something cold bushed against my leg. Whatever had done it had shocked me like a live wire, but all I saw was a little jellyfish drifting away. It was tiny. I'd heard people complaining about them before, but now I realized those people hadn't been exaggerating.

The jellyfish had evidently rolled its way along my skin as it passed, because I felt a band of pin pricks that was very like a cluster of bee stings. I'd seen dozens of them in the water as I went in, and hadn't been worried about them. Now, having been educated the hard way, they were very much on my mind, and it was distracting.

I'd just started feeling along the surface of the hull for the brass strainer over the raw water intake hole of the Rockport's seacock. The plans had shown it amidships, but the bite caused me to lose track of my position along the hull. Plus, the gel coat of the fiberglass was lumpy under there and I kept mistaking the lumps for the curve of the strainer.

I had to go up for air and try it again. Things were getting complicated. One hand was stinging from contact with the little marine organisms that had wedged themselves into fissures in the fiberglass and the other was cramping from the effort of holding onto my improvised shipwrecking kit.

Jellyfish were drifting past my face now, but I wasn't going to be beaten by a creature with an IQ of zero. On the third try I found the strainer and ripped open the slots in it with the screwdriver. Shoving the metal tube of the brake line up the intake hole of the Rockport's seacock, I probed until I felt it bottom out inside the hollow ballcock. Then I triggered the air can.

A thump from inside the Rockport and a vibration down the brake line announced that I had blown out the seacock under the sink cabinet in the head. The water surging past my hand and into the hold of the yacht verified that the job was done.

Hugging the lee side of the Rockport I marked a new Plimsoll line on the hull with seawater to make sure she didn't settle too far while I was dealing with the jellyfish sting. I tried rubbing the leg with the canvas bag, and it worked. No hound dog ever got more relief from rubbing his back on a fence post.

The line I made on the hull was closer to the surface of the ocean now. I swam back to the rowboat and came up at the windward side, out of view of the men.

I struggled back over the gunnel of the bobbing rowboat to the protest of a flock of seagulls who had claimed it. Six inches of water was sloshing around in the bottom, and the parasol was gone. It was floating upside down about fifty feet away with a seagull high-stepping at the lower side to keep its feet dry.

Had the De Lafontaine brothers seen that the rowboat was empty? They were missing as well, undoubtedly below deck on the yacht. They had gone below while I was swimming back to the rowboat, because nobody had moved on the yacht while I was clinging to the side or I'd have felt it. But had the parasol blown away before or after that happened?

There was nothing to do but play it out. I fished my shoes out of the water and slipped them back on. My leg hurt like hell, so I found a carrot in the bilge and chewed it into a chisel shape. Scraping it across the leg brought instant relief, like picking out a hundred fishhooks at once. I rescued two carrots and tied them to my waist inside the canvas bag.

Whatever the De Lafontaine brothers were doing about the leak at this point it was by feel because, according to the photos Ellen had shown me, the cabinet over the seacock was improperly constructed. It was a solidly-built, homemade affair, instead of the breakaway kind you'd need if you wanted to get to the seacock in a hurry.

My assumption that the brothers would not know what to do about the problem I had given them turned out to be correct. In less than five minutes they had started shifting some of their belongings to the deck.

I fished for a while, continuing to bail as casually as possible. I pretended not to notice the commotion aboard the Rockport. "Garçon," one of the De Lafontaines called.

Pretending not to hear, I turned my head when he called a second time. "Garçon," De Lafontaine repeated, "aidez moi."

I pleaded ignorance of the language, which wasn't that difficult. "Je parle pas un peu," I said. "I mean je parle pas Français un. . . Oh forget it. Whatcha need, pal, a trip to the beach?"

"He speaks English," one of them said to the other. "Yes, friend, we need to get to shore, so how about doing us a favor and rowing over here?"

"I've been getting a bite," I told him, "so maybe it would be worth . . . say ten dollars?"

They gave each other a look that let me know what was coming, even though I would have expected it already. "Sure," the man answered. "Sounds reasonable."

I rowed to the foot of the diving ladder. The De Lafontaine I had talked to stepped down into the boat. "Keep her steady," he instructed, and he started catching and stowing items the other De Lafontaine threw down to him from the deck of the Rockport.

"Hey, this boat will only hold so much," I complained.

"Just a few more things," De Lafontaine One said. "It will be all right."

They finally finished loading, and as De Lafontaine Two stepped down I pretended to lose my balance and fall overboard. When I surfaced at the ladder of the Rockport they didn't even notice. They had planned to throw me overboard anyway, so I had saved them the trouble. They had already started rowing away. One of them said something to the other, but I couldn't make it out. All I heard was the word "idiot."

I climbed on board the Wrights' yacht, experiencing a surge of alarm as I felt my weight affect the balance of the craft. I'd miscalculated and waited too long while the water rushed in. The Rockport was near to capsizing.

The venture had seemed pretty easy in theory, but now I stood at the hatchway in near-paralysis. I could hear the hull groaning as the water that had shipped aboard was straining the Rockport's sides.

Somebody wailed below in fear and confusion. "Hold on," I shouted, "don't move!" I was committed to saving the boat now, and I didn't want anybody grabbing at me in panic while I did it.

At the bottom of the ladder to the hold the water was above my waist. The pumps were running, but they weren't making headway against the inflow of sea water gushing in through the broken seacock.

I struggled over to the area where the leak had to be. The layout inside could only correspond to the intake hole under the hull. There wouldn't be any use trying to disassemble the cabinet Wright had built around the intake; I just stuck my hand in and jammed a big carrot into the broken seacock.

There were two people inside the hold, clinging to each other. Two women, young, nude and very confused. Evidently, they had been sleeping when the De Lafontaine brothers abandoned ship.

"It's all right ladies. . ." I began.

One of the women jumped back and slipped under the water. She had tripped over something beneath the surface. She popped back up and they both yelled "key S-two."

The pumps were running, so I had assumed that the keys were in the console. How was I going to find a key marked "S-Two" in the middle of a flood?

The women had each torn half a curtain from the porthole beside the hatchway ladder before I realized they had asked me "Qui étes tu?" "Who are you?" in French.

A plastic bucket was floating by and a stainless-steel bowl was hanging on the wall. I grabbed them and followed the women up the ladder. Topside they each retrieved a towel from the floor next to the console, for cover. The women were watching the retreating rowboat with the men in it, apparently unable to comprehend the situation.

The Rockport was listing, but the pump was still running. The boat felt leaden. Twenty or so more gallons in the hold and she would go under. I handed each of the women a tool to bail with and pointed back into the hold. They got the idea and went to work, with me at the hatchway flinging the water over the side. I was keeping an eye on the men in the rowboat. So far, they were still heading away from us.

The bailing wasn't helping much, but it kept the women focused. I pulled the engine out of idle and headed the Rockport toward the calanque through which Johnny Wright had spotted her two hours ago. We were making little headway, because the pumps held priority by design.

The men in the rowboat had hesitated and were looking back. They saw that the Rockport had been stabilized, and they were turning the rowboat around. I didn't want to discourage them, so I didn't try for more speed.

The woman at the top of the ladder threw down her bucket and went to the rail. She stared at the men in the rowboat. "Quelle espèce de cochon?" she growled, roughly meaning "what kind of pig?" She turned to the other woman with her fist in the air. "Cruse de viol de date!" she yelled.

"Cruse de viol de date?" repeated the woman below. "Mon dieu!"

I had learned a new French term from context: "date rape drug."

Our miserable regatta entered the calanque, a half-foundered bargain basement yacht and a leaky old rowboat. The Rockport yawed toward a huge rock that had fallen from above. It was the one I'd seen from the cliff earlier, and beyond it there was room to turn the yacht inside the calanque. If we could get past it without breaking up, that is.

It came down to me and Arthur's boat hook, with my back against the cockpit wall. The Rockport was only thirty-five feet though, and the four previous summers I'd spent rolling sod had given me wrists like Popeye. I held her off the rock without the hull touching it once.

"Il est très fort," one of the women said, leaping to steady the tiller as I pushed the boat into the clear. "Oui." Said the other, "Très fort. Je m'apelle Georgette, Monsieur."

"Je m'apelle Marie," offered the other. Two beautiful women had agreed that I was very strong, and they were introducing themselves. That one moment of glory paid for my two semesters of struggle in high school French.

Georgette and I seemed to be communicating in spite of the difference in languages. "Bring her about," I commanded. "Keep steering."

Georgette understood my meaning from the direction I was pushing off from the rock, and she continued to steer in the right direction. We came about, pointed at the oncoming rowboat.

The De Lafontaine brothers had assumed that I was taking the Rockport into the calanque to look for a place to beach her. They had been concentrating on their rowing, and were surprised to see that they were looking at the oncoming bow of the Rockport instead of her retreating stern. They did their best to turn, but only set themselves up for a broadside impact. The Rockport hit the rowboat dead center and tore it to splinters.

While the De Lafontaines were flailing around, I selected from among the more promising cases and packages floating on the water, snagging them one by one with the boat hook.

The De Lafontaines were stronger swimmers than I had expected. Before I managed to take over the helm one of them had started to struggle aboard up the diving ladder. Thinking it would be the end of the problem, I socked him on the head with the blunt end of the boat hook. It collapsed harmlessly.

Unfortunately, I had pushed in one of the studs in the telescopic pole as I gripped it to deliver the blow. De Lafontaine wasn't discouraged at all, and ripped the boat hook out of my hand.

The effort caused him to fall back into the water, so once again I thought I'd gotten rid of him. With the boat hook gone we had salvaged all the potential evidence we could, and I relieved Georgette at the wheel.

But the De Lafontaines weren't finished. We were past the boulder and ready to steer for the dock when Marie alerted me to the fact that one of them had snagged a rung of the diving ladder with the boat hook. Georgette took over the steering again and I looked.

There he was, pulling himself along the shaft of the boat hook, impeded only by the weight of De Lafontaine Two, who was himself inching along over his brother's body toward the diving ladder.

Two for one. I leaned over the ladder with a screwdriver in my hand, planning to pry the boat hook off the rung. The Rockport was within view of the passing kayakers, and I was beginning to wonder how secure a legal footing I was on in the process of repossessing the yacht. On their home ground and in their own language the De Lafontaine brothers would be able to plead their case with the cops more effectively than I would. I would have liked to have finished this fight in privacy, but drifting back into the calanque was no option; we'd be wrecked for sure.

De Lafontaine was getting closer and the screwdriver wasn't helping. Marie handed a claw hammer down to me, and I tried to break the head of the boat hook off with it.

The hammer glanced off and De Lafontaine, with a lunge, snatched it away from me. I had leaned over too far and was off-balance. I had to grip the ladder with both hands to recover, and De Lafontaine was winding up to hit me with that hammer.

It was touch-and-go, but I hand-walked myself back up the ladder and onto the deck before De Lafontaine had a chance to hit me. He was close behind, though, and his brother had reached the bottom of the ladder as well.

Now it was De Lafontaine who was off-balance. I hit him with a good kick in the ribs. He wasn't dissuaded, though, because I was wearing deck shoes instead of boots. Fortunately, he had lost the hammer on his way up, and was also holding onto the ladder with both hands. I clocked him with a left.

That did the trick. De Lafontaine fell off the ladder, taking his brother with him on the way down. We were rid of them now, and I'd managed to do it without attracting any attention from the kayakers.

By the time we put in at the sailing village Georgette and Marie had retrieved their clothing. They had also found an official-looking state seal embossing tool in one of the cases. If the De Lafontaine brothers were dumb enough to go back home any time soon, they would find the gendarmes waiting for them, on a federal document rap in addition to the rape charges the women swore to pursue.

A crowd grew as kayakers returned from their picnics and sunbathing outings at the various calanques to the west. We had limped into the port clothed in drama. People took photos, asked for details about the downfall of the De Lafontaines, and took up a collection to aid in the refitting of the Rockport. The Wrights were scoring because of the novelty of the event. By chipping in the well-off vacationers were buying part of a story they could take home with them.

While this was going on someone circulated through the crowd to alert the owner of a Lincoln parked above the hill that the car was being towed away. It was a lucky break for me. Evidently the return of the Rockport to the little village below had caused such a commotion the dopers went ahead and took their cargo past the police behind a tow. Maybe I had inadvertently given the heroin smugglers of Marseille a new method of procedure. Or maybe I had forced them to employ a tactic that was sure to backfire. One thing for sure, after causing a rough crowd so much delay it would not be a good idea for me to be seen on the road.

The Wrights pushed off, equipped with a few more carrots to make sure that seacock stayed secure until they could get to dry dock. Monique, the well-dressed vegetable vendor with the motor launch, was basking in the attention she got for providing those championship caliber carrots. I saw a chance to get out of there. A bilingual vacationer helped me approach Monique with a request for employment, and she readily agreed.

I needed to get out of the area fast, so I couldn't be bashful about it. I ignored the knowing smiles that passed among Monique's associates as I stepped aboard the launch. She was over forty and I was twenty and lean and fit from hard work.

Let them have their fun, I thought; the important thing was that Monique was heading back east, away from Marseille, for more produce. Call it play-for-pay if you like, but the surrounding roadways held the potential to be very unhealthy for me.

I thought I was taking advantage of Monique as we began the voyage, but what really happened shows how much I had to learn.

"Just a minute," Samantha said, "I know I gave you the go-ahead, but I'm not sure I want to hear the end of that one yet. I might not want to know what happened between you and Monique in that boat while I'm still smarting from meeting your giant pear tree.'"

"You won't mind this," I told her. "It's kind of pathetic. It would be an understatement to say I was overmatched in that boat with Monique. Even though she was twice my age. She put me ashore on an abandoned jetty half way between Bandol and Toulon when I asked her to marry me. I hope you don't give me the same treatment."

Samantha tried not to laugh, but she couldn't help it.

CHAPTER TWELVE:

THE GRACE AND CUNNING OF A GREEK

"SOMEBODY TOLD ME they heard cackling in there," the landlady told Temple Worthington through the half-opened door of his tiny apartment.

"Oh, that was my Synthesizer, Ms. Arias" Worthington replied, smiling innocently. A dribble of toothpaste escaped his mouth as he spoke, and he wiped it delicately aside. Behind him the water was running in the tub, barely audible through the closed bathroom door. The towel wrapped around Worthington's waist had halted the woman's progress into his apartment.

"It's going to be a funny routine," Worthington told her, sticking the brush back into his mouth automatically and withdrawing it when he caught himself in the act. "I kind of need to hear it out loud as I'm working," he continued. "I hope you don't mind."

"Naw," I guess it's all right," Ms. Arias decided. "As long as you don't play it too loud."

"Absoloroply," Worthington replied past the toothbrush between his teeth.

THE NEXT MORNING Samantha suggested an alternate form of exercise for my morning run. I liked it a lot. Somewhat later she listened to the news while I made a phone call to Matt Jacobs.

"You messed up when you let me know you knew something about the law," I told Matt. I gave him the particulars of the Denise Black case and asked if he could tell me how to get through Milburn Howard's defenses. It burned me that Howard hadn't even made an attempt to have Denise's body cremated. He evidently considered the corpse evidence to support his story.

Samantha was lying in wait as I hung up the phone. "'If you want to get something done, ask a busy man,'" she said brightly. She had overheard enough of my conversation to know that the case I was concerned about was at a standstill.

"Meaning?" I asked.

"According to the morning news," Samantha replied, "a man I knew has been killed, and I predict that his ex-wife is going to be interested enough to hire a private investigator to make inquiries about the case. That could be you, provided that I get to go along for the ride."

"Oh, so you have an interest in the matter?" I asked.

"I do," Samantha replied, "because I know the widow, and I'm sure that an inquiry about the case will give her years' worth of things to talk about."

I agreed, because if Samantha kept dragging stories out of me, I'd eventually incriminate myself. After a short phone call by Samantha we went to see the victim's ex-wife, whom Samantha had met frequently at social events. The lady's name was Freda Lester, and she lived at the Beresford, 211 Central Park West. You've seen it in photos, and you liked it.

"I think the Greek government killed him," Ms. Lester told me, referring to the ex-husband.

Good for openers, I thought. Why would the Big Fat Greek government want to kill an art historian, I wanted to ask, but I didn't. Samantha had brought me to Ms. Lester, her big-wig society friend, on the condition that I'd behave. I complied, even though I didn't see a case in Lester's story.

Samantha was sitting next to Ms. Lester, so I'd have to listen to the suspicious woman's entire theory. Lester was eager to hire me to do a follow-up on a death investigation that had just taken place in Colorado.

The victim, Ms. Lester told me, was her ex-husband of long ago, Dr. Ethan Timmons. Ms. Lester had been following Timmons' activities for many years. While the couple had not proved compatible when married, Ms. Lester had derived a great deal of pleasure from keeping up with her ex-husband's achievements

Timmons had been a famous archaeologist and art historian, known for discovering a number of Greek vases. Timmons' exploits had made him a media phenomenon among the museum crowd; a kind of real-life combination of Indiana Jones and James Bond.

First in Timmons' discoveries had been the magnificent krater, or wine-mixing bowl, that had received his name. Reluctant to reveal the location of the site from which the Timmons Krater had come, he'd had to smuggle it out of Greece in fragments and reconstruct it back in the United States. The act had brought an indictment *in absentia* from the Greek government, and they had attempted to extradite him.

Timmons' find was an important one, the work of a previously unknown artist historians had subsequently dubbed "the Master of the Three Centaurs." After Timmons had allowed the new find to be reproduced for the Athens Museum the Greek government had permitted him to come back to the country for further studies.

Almost immediately Timmons had confounded them by sneaking away and coming up with another find, a hydria, or three-handled water jug, which was evidently by the same artist.

The hydria, too, Timmons managed to get out of the country and back to the States. That only made the Greeks more determined to get him back to their country so they could follow him to that crucially important burial site.

It hadn't worked. Timmons had no sooner made it back to Greece before he disappeared again. And for the third time he appeared back in the States with an important find, the great Timmons Amphora of the Six Warriors.

While it was true that this third breach of the Greek Antiquities Act was the final blow that had caused Timmons to be banned permanently from Greece, it was certainly not the kind of thing you'd get on a hit list for. The Greek authorities were anxious to find that burial site, so Timmons' death would be the last thing they'd want.

Ethan Timmons had died in a fire in his mountain home in Colorado. The cause was clearly arson, but the killer had died in the act as well. Timmons had made the mistake of sheltering an eccentric hermit from somewhere in the neighboring slopes. Timmons had provided the homeless man lodging in his basement in exchange for a few odd jobs.

Timmons' good deed had been punished by a fire the hermit had set while Timmons slept. The arsonist had died in the fire as well, evidently due to a miscalculation about how quickly a house made of logs can go up in flames.

For Freda Lester the death-by-crazy-hermit explanation was too matter-of-fact to accept. A man with such interesting events in his past doesn't just die in his sleep from a mistaken act of kindness, she believed. Thus, the invention of Greeks with fire.

Samantha sat close to Freda while the discussion was going on, clucking sympathetically while the bereaved woman theorized.

"While I considered my husband to be an egotist when we were married," Ms. Lester concluded, "and an adventurer in the least flattering sense of that term, I'd hate for his achievements to die along with him. I know it is a doubtful proposition, Mr. Turley, but I'd like an experienced investigator to take one more look at the ruins of the house in which my ex-husband died. To look for some indication of where in Greece Ethan's secret burial site might be. It would be a terrible loss to the academic community if the remaining artifacts there were to be lost completely."

Samantha had been listening attentively with her hands folded in her lap. "I would venture a counter theory," she told Freda. "The three vessels were demonstrably by the same artist and potter. They were made to serve three different but compatible functions: the storage of wine, the transport of water, and the mixing of the two. I think there's a good chance that the site was the home of that artist and potter, not a burial site at all."

Lester paused to consider. "But of course," she replied. "And that explains why the three were such prime examples of their type. What a wonderful idea! You're approaching the problem from a psychoanalytical point of view, as befits your profession."

"Thank you," Samantha said, and smiled modestly.

"I didn't know you were so conversant with Classical art," Freda enthused. "Have you any further insights on the subject?"

"Yes," Samantha answered. "As it was not uncommon for houses to be attached to workshops at that time, and since no amount of stealth would have allowed Dr. Timmons to probe around in what's left of the ancient Agora, I predict that his remaining discoveries will one day be unearthed in the nearby Plaka district. In the basement of a shop or restaurant perhaps."

I got it then. Samantha was angling for a vacation, to Colorado at least, and maybe even to look for the ruins of that artist and potter's home and workshop in Greece.

Once we were alone, I waited for Samantha to explain what she was up to. "Do it just to please Freda," she urged me. "She won't miss the money. She's quite wealthy. This will give her peace of mind, or at least something else to talk about at parties. A continuation of her history with a famous man."

"What about you?' I asked. "Were you a fan of this Timmons?"

"Not at all," Samantha answered. "Maybe I'm just a blue nose, but the fact is that Timmons exploited burial sites, removed artifacts from their archaeological context, and sold his finds for millions of dollars to museums in which they didn't really belong. But listening to your experiences in southern France has left me hungry for an adventure myself. One that doesn't involve danger, that is. And this project looks ideal."

What she said made sense. All we had to do was go to a burned house at the end of a steep mountain road in Colorado, and look around for clues. We wouldn't be cheating the client, because there was always the chance we would find some charred souvenir from the Plaka district the authorities in Colorado hadn't known was significant.

While Samantha and I were waiting for our flight at Kennedy I went over all the known data about the case. Timmons' house had already been examined by the fire department and ruled a straightforward case of arson, as was evident by the remains of the unidentified man found in the basement. It had been verified by witnesses that the arsonist was a local hermit who'd been hired by Timmons for occasional odd jobs. The fact was backed up by two men who lived further up the road in a house that overlooked that of Timmons. They, too had worked for Timmons at various times, and had seen the hermit on the premises. They didn't know the man's name either, but the police and fire officials were satisfied with the answer.

Our flight was delayed at Kennedy, and there were other complications as well. We arrived at Denver International Airport too late to get anything done but book into a motel. Early the next day Samantha and I rented a car and stopped in at the fire station that had taken the call to Ethan Timmons' house. According to them, Timmons had been considered a bit of a hermit himself. He lived in a remote area, liked his privacy, and never invited anyone to visit.

To get to Timmons' place, Samantha and I drove up a state highway with many switchbacks along the side of a mountain to a cut-off. We continued up a narrow lane with a dozen more switchbacks and soon lost sight of the main road. Timmons' place was nearly at the end of the lane. There was only one other house above it, a modest but nice-looking log structure overlooking Timmons' house.

Timmons' place had been a big one. Having been constructed almost entirely of wood, it had burned completely and filled the basement with burned timbers and ash. During their investigation the fire inspectors had removed all the burned rubble from the basement and piled it around the perimeter of the structure. They'd been required by regulations to do this, even though it was unlikely they'd find any other bodies after the discovery of the charred remains of the arsonist. The mounds of ash seemed surprisingly extensive, even for a log house.

The house had been long and wide, anchored by a massive chimney along the lines of a design by architect Frank Lloyd Wright. The chimney was still intact, and was buttressed in the basement by a massive extension with its own flue.

The outbuildings behind the house had escaped the fire. They were upslope and a strong wind had been blowing down from the mountain during the fire. There was a garage, a long woodshed with an overhanging roof and two separate compartments, and a large toolshed. A stepladder had been left outside, leaning against the shed.

The basement hadn't run the full length of the house, but it was still some twenty by thirty feet in extent. I stuck the ladder over the edge where the basement stair had burned away and we went down. It didn't take me long to conduct my inspection. The place had gone up like a fuel dump.

I gave the basement a onceover anyway. In one corner was the outline of a massive workbench that had burned away. In another were the warped remains of steel drums that had evidently contained potting soil, compacted now into ashes. Close to that was a drain, clogged now with burned ashes. The third corner of the room had burned so hotly that the stonework was fused in spots. Except for the huge blackened extension of the chimney base, that was all I saw. Nothing more readable than that had survived the fire. It seemed there were no clues left; certainly, no Greek skirts or empty ouzo bottles. All I could do was look at Samantha and shrug.

"There's more to this than I'd expected," Samantha told me.

I looked again. Aside from the burned rubble I saw only a chalked outline where the body of the hermit had been found, and nothing else. Timmons' outline had been chalked above, on the first floor. His remains had been found in an area that extended past the basement, near the front door. He'd almost made it outside, but from the shape of that outline I wouldn't have wanted to be him if he had. "Okay," I asked Samantha, "What are you seeing that I'm not?"

"Don't blame yourself for not seeing it," she answered, "The fire officials and police didn't see it either." She turned slowly in a circle, pointing. "There's the imported clay," she said. "There's where the firewood was kept for stoking. There's the workbench area. And that structure in front of us is not just part of the chimney; it's a kiln."

That last part wasn't just a simple statement, it was a punch in the head. A man, Ethan Timmons, who had supposedly discovered a series of priceless Greek vases. A nearly inaccessible house up a winding road. A huge kiln disguised as something else. It all added up to fraud on a very expensive scale.

Samantha pointed at the floor. "Look for potsherds in the ashes," she told me.

"You mean you think . . ." I began.

"You know very well what I think," Samantha answered. "And you're thinking it too. Our Indiana Jones was putting one over on the art world. Try not to step on anything you find."

But I already had. Something crunched under my foot. I picked it up. It was a blackened fragment of baked clay. A potsherd, just as Samantha had predicted.

I handed it to Samantha, brushed aside the ashes on the ground with my hand, and found more. Samantha spat on the one in her hand and rubbed it on her shirt cuff to clean it. My kind of investigator.

"Look at this," she told me. "Hold it against the light at an angle."

I saw nothing but a little bit of texture against a smooth piece of clay, all black. I took a stab at identifying it.

"It could be a Greek character, I guess," I told her.

"That's shorthand," Samantha answered.

"You mean some abbreviated version of Greek lettering?" I asked.

"No, English shorthand right out of the typing pool," Samantha replied.

I had no answer for that, so I could only look at her like a cow trying to read a street sign.

"Collect the rest of those shards you found and put them in here," she instructed, ripping a slit in the bottom corner of her kapok-lined jacket with her nail file. I did as she said.

While I was collecting shards, Samantha carved away the ashes from the brickwork in the area of the kiln that proved to be a doorway. She scrubbed at the shards I had collected, cleaning the smoke residue while I opened the kiln as she instructed.

"What are we doing?" I finally asked.

"We'll never be able to make out this message while the shards are all black," she answered.

She was right. Reconstructing the pot would be like putting together a three-dimensional jigsaw puzzle with all the pieces one color. But what alternative did we have?

"What alternative do we have?" I asked. Why be proud at this point? I was learning to be a detective.

"Timmons was using the ancient Greek method of producing pots," Samantha answered. "It's all done with one clay body, which he probably dug somewhere near Athens."

"One clay body," I repeated. "You mean it's not really painted?"

"Believe it or not," Samantha answered, "the ancient Greek potters could get two different consistencies of the same buff-colored clay to come out black against light red."

"But those shards are completely cooked all black, aren't they?" I asked.

"For the time being," Samantha answered. She pointed. "Open that area of bricks right there," she said. "It's the fuel chamber.

I did as instructed. "Good," Samantha said, as soon as I got the bricks out. "It's cleaned and ready to go. But first, clear that area directly above, where the flue leads into the chimney. There's some kind of damper there, because the kiln is not drawing properly."

I followed orders while Samantha arranged the shards inside the chamber around a small stack of bricks. Then she closed up the front with bricks I handed her, leaving a tiny peep hole.

"Now go ferry in some of that firewood from the woodshed," she instructed. "The part with the overhang. Bring the driest you can find."

I did as instructed, wondering why some of the wood had been stored with the seeming intention to let it get wet.

Samantha had anticipated the question. As I was loading the fuel chamber she explained. "The part of the clay that will come out black gets that way by locking in the carbon," she told me. "The wet wood is used to make lots of smoke, so the carbon goes into both clay bodies. Then the dry wood is used to drive out the carbon. The Greek potters stopped the process after the carbon had been burned out of the main part of the pot, but while it was still trapped in the marks their brushes had made."

It seemed incredible, but if Samantha was right, we'd be able to make the shards readable. I kept dumping firewood into the basement while Samantha fed the firebox. Within an hour or so she was sneaking quick peeks through the tiny hole in the front of the kiln to check on the condition of the shards. "Get a coal shovel and a hoe if you can find them," she told me.

I went to the toolshed and found what she wanted. "Make sure there's a dry area to rake the embers out on," she instructed.

I did as Samantha asked and waited. "All right, rake those embers out of the fire box," she said after a while. "Don't make any smoke in there if you can help it."

After I'd emptied the firebox Samantha directed me to break out the front of the firebox. "Be careful," she said.

She didn't have to tell me that. It was getting hot down in that basement. After I got the job done Samantha had me run the coal shovel under the cluster of shards and rest it on the pile of hot bricks outside the kiln. They were glowing, but it could easily be seen that the marks on them were now black on light red.

Samantha watched the shards carefully while I went for some clear water I'd seen in a bucket in the yard. When the fragments of pottery were ready, she let me quench them.

"All right," Samantha said, "I hope you're good at jigsaw puzzles." I arranged the shards while she made notes in the notebook I always carried for case work.

Samantha's expression changed as she worked. "Let's stop now," she told me after a half-hour. "I have the gist of it."

Her reaction surprised me. Instead of the gleam of triumph I might have expected, there were tears in her eyes. She wiped them away with her sooty cuff, then dipped her fingers in the water bucket to dissolve the soot she'd picked up from her sleeve.

I put the shards aside and waited. "The man who made the pots was Timmons' prisoner," Samantha told me. "Timmons' henchmen broke the man's' toes with a rifle butt when he tried to escape. Timmons examined the pots microscopically to make sure the prisoner hadn't tried to get some kind of message through that would save him. After the third pot the prisoner was convinced they would kill him soon. The rule of threes you know. Timmons had pressed his luck already by slipping three counterfeit pots past the experts. Four would have defied credibility."

No wonder Samantha had been so affected by what she read. The anonymous potter had been trapped by sadists who were going to kill him. It was a lot like the situation she'd been in at the house where she'd been imprisoned and raped.

Samantha continued. "Then the prisoner heard his captors arguing about whether they should cut him up and burn him in the kiln," she said, "or just kill and bury him without going to all that trouble. Looks as if he got in this one final burn before he set the place on fire and took Timmons with him."

"I've dealt with some grotesque acts in my work," I told her, "but seldom one quite so cold-blooded. I guess we'll never know who the victim was unless we find the rest of those shards."

"Oh, it could only have been one person," Samantha replied. "Panos Markopoulos."

That's what I liked: full-service detective consultancy. "How's that?" I asked.

"I think you'll remember, if you cast back about eight years to the headlines," Samantha answered. "The Greek art historian who disappeared over the Atlantic?"

"Oh yes," I said. "Passed out and then ran out of gas somewhere out there."

"Except that it had to be faked," Samantha replied. "Markopoulos was a world expert on ancient pottery and Timmons' mentor."

"A fine way to pay him back," I said. "A vampire couldn't have been more heartless."

Samantha started to reply, but before she could say anything, we were interrupted by a noise from outside the ring of rubble above us.

"What was that?' Samantha asked. Retreating footsteps came from above on the yard, a running man heading uphill.

"Of course," I said. "The men in the cabin overlooking this place. They were Timmons' assistants."

Samantha's face went pale. "That's right," she said. "They vouched for the fact that the man in the basement was a crazy hermit from nowhere."

You never need a rifle until you need one, and now I needed one badly. But all I had was the automatic in my shoulder holster. The men upslope had them, though. I had seen a bear skin and some deer antlers displayed on the wall behind the porch up there.

"We need to leave now," I told Samantha.

We made a hasty departure. But there would be no way, with those switchbacks on the road, to make it down to the highway without setting ourselves up as perfect targets. The men upslope had already started their car by the time we'd gone a quarter of a mile.

Leaving our vehicle and running away into the woods was no option. We would only be offering the men behind us some light exercise. But whatever I did, it would be better to do it before our pursuers started thinking.

I decided to face the issue at the first turn, because the cover there was good. Our pursuers would probably wait to set up to shoot at us from the switchback after this one, because there was better visibility across it. And that was the very reason I couldn't wait.

Yes, they'd be anticipating that next switchback, with its clear view along a road obscured buy only an occasional spindly aspen. At the first turn, which was heavily wooded, I swerved and put the car across the road to block it. "We get out here," I told Samantha.

She didn't argue. She just jumped out. "I've got this one," I told her, "duck soup." It sounds cocky, I know, but it was better for morale then "odds are we're going to be dead within five minutes."

Samantha was on the downhill side of me, so I switched her to my left. "Get ready to dodge," I told her as a precaution, and picked up a football-size rock from the ditch we were facing.

I heaved the rock up the slope in front of us, in the direction of a big tree about sixty feet away. The rock sailed about thirty feet, bounded back, and rolled past me to the right. It had disturbed the grass nicely.

"Oh, a false trail," Samantha said. She had seen, too, that the trees on the far side of the road offered as much cover as the ones ahead of us. "They'll see it and--"

"Zip it," I told her, and picked her up. There was no time to point out that the slightest tip-off we gave our pursuers from here on would kill us. And what I was about to do called for concentration. I carried her up the slope, moving from rock to rock, and got us behind the tree we'd been facing. It was none too soon, because the men in the car behind us were almost in sight. I sat Samantha behind the tee with her back to it and stood up leaning against the trunk.

A car slid to a stop and two men got out. They moved up the hill quickly, heading toward the tree we were behind. They had gone about thirty feet when the footsteps suddenly stopped.

"False trail," one of them said. Their boots scraped the ground, signaling that they had pivoted to walk back downhill.

I stepped out from behind the tree and yelled "Freeze." Both of them did, with a high lift of their shoulders that spoke strongly of self-disgust. They had fallen for a sucker play that probably wouldn't have fooled them any longer than it took to get down to the road.

"We don't want any trouble," one said loudly.

"We thought you were trespassers," the other said. I was a man with a woman. They were banking on my reluctance to shoot them in the back.

"Freeze," I repeated. "Last warning." I splintered the rifle stock that showed the most area, to let them know I could hit it.

That froze the one holding the damaged rifle, but the other one turned to fire. I shot him in the chest twice and once in the groin as he fell back, in case he was wearing armor.

The other man threw his arms as straight up as he could get them. I had the impression that he had been shot before.

Once the second man was tied up securely, I turned to see Samantha signal that the first man had died. She had bent over him to help. Most people would still be cowering behind the tree, but after all, she was a doctor.

We transferred the bound man into the back seat of our car and drove down the road until we picked up some bars on Samantha's cell phone. When the police arrived, they found the weapons spread out on a blanket on the roadside, bolts back, and Samantha and me with our hands resting on the car roof. I've never been one to take chances for the sake of looking cool.

We were questioned at the station, and fingerprinted to confirm our identities, but it helped to have friendly voices on the phone at N.Y.P.D. to put in a good word or two. I did most of the explaining as we went through the process of pointing out what had happened, and why it was necessary for me to brace two Coloradans on the mountain and kill one of them. Then on the way to the motel Samantha was quiet.

We got to bed right away, because we had managed to book an early flight in the morning. I wasn't sure whether Samantha was more upset about me killing a man or about me telling her to zip it, until we actually got horizontal. "That was some pretty fast thinking, Turley," she said as she hit the lights.

CHAPTER THIRTEEN:

WHISTLING IN THE DARK

BACK IN THE CITY I left it to Samantha to brief Freda Lester about the Timmons case, while I went to the office. "Word to the Wise Investigations," I told the phone a little later.

"Turley?" the voice asked. "Grant Byars here, remember me?"

"Sure, Officer Byars," I answered, "after that stunt you pulled at Renfro's house, how could I forget?"

"It's Sergeant Byars now, Turley," Byars informed me. "Plainclothes detective."

"Congratulations," I replied. "That's quick work. How can I help you, Byars?"

"Don't go professional on me, Turley," Byars returned. "This is not money talking to you. I'm calling as one cop to another. Or to an ex-cop, that is. My little brother and a friend of his are in trouble. They're accused of mugging a guy in Central Park, and killing him."

I could have told him about the agreement I'd made with Samantha not to take any more cases at the moment, but Grant Byars was drawing on a previous commitment I couldn't ignore. This guy was a cop, and he was hurting. The boy-girl stuff would have to be tabled for a while.

"Sure," I said, "I'll do some pro bono for you. The cops help me all the time. As long as you know I'm not doing it to get them off, but to get to the truth of the matter."

"I'll agree to that condition," Byars said.

"Are you officially involved in the case?" I asked him.

"I was," Byars told me. "I busted them. The two of them ran out of Central Park in my direction. I was standing there on the corner when they came along arguing about some dust-up they'd had with a guy in the park, and whether they think he's dead or not. I had to arrest them. What else could I do?"

"A tough spot to be in," I agreed.

"Steadman hadn't even noticed me," Byars continued. "The way they were going on they were sure to be connected with the case eventually. We had officers working overtime all around the area to try and spot this Crankpot killer setting up for his next shot. I'd have blown my career if I'd ignored Steadman and his pal passing by like that."

"What are the charges?" I asked Byars.

"The full boat," Byars answered. "Murder, aggravated assault, grand larceny and more. The guy died of a broken neck. I mean twisted as if someone had tried to uproot it. Plus, a concussion."

"Where in the park was it?" I asked.

"On a jogging path in the Ramble," Byars answered. "We can't exactly establish a scene. A couple of homeless guys looking for food in the trash cans found the victim. He was still alive and these idiots carried him to the station slung in a tarp. He was dead on arrival."

"After hours, eh?" I asked Byars.

"Middle of the night," Byars answered.

"The bums couldn't say where they found him?" I asked.

"They sneaked away," Byars answered. "They're probably on a train to Stillwater by now. A prime foul-up. But the victim's phone and what's on it are going to be tough evidence for those boys to overcome."

"And yet you believe them?" I asked Byars.

He paused, because he knew what he was going to say would sound sappy. "With all my heart I do, Turley," he answered.

"I'll see what I can do," I told him.

I took a cab to the lockup. Once there I talked to Steadman Byars first. The two suspects were separated, according to the usual policy, so they couldn't get together and coordinate their stories.

"We were running down a jogging path," Steadman told me, "about one-thirty in the morning, when this guy plowed into me like a rocket. Has to be dusted, I thought. Although they tell me now, he wasn't. Seemed like he weighed three hundred pounds. Took Jackson and me down at the same time. I was startled. Okay, I was scared. Jackson and I were both out of breath and dizzy from running in the first place. When somebody ties into you in the dark like that, in the middle of the night, of course I was scared. Plus, you don't know who else is with somebody like that. Maybe a whole gang."

"So. you did hit him?" I asked.

"Yeah, I hit him a couple of times," Steadman answered. "Okay, more than that, but not out of spite. I certainly didn't mean to break his neck. I didn't mean to do anything more than protect myself. I stopped once I saw the guy wasn't able to fight back."

"Where were you, exactly, when it happened?" I asked.

"We were racing," Steadman answered. "Jackson and I had just passed through some archway on the path. Don't know what it's called. That archway put us close together. I can stand inside and put a hand on each wall. And you can't see to either side coming out, so it's a natural place for an ambush. That's what made me so sure Jackson and I were about to get our butts kicked."

I knew what Steadman meant. I'd been there myself. Not symbolically, but physically. I remembered running through that archway in the Ramble myself, and the hollow sound of my footsteps as I ran through.

"The guy carried a very expensive cell phone," Steadman continued. "Top of the line. We checked it, trying to see who he was. We ran out of the park, arguing about the phone. Jackson wanted to keep the phone and not tell anyone what had happened. I wanted to report what had happened to the first cop we found, so that people wouldn't think we had killed the guy. I mean, attacked him on purpose."

The guard called time on us. I gave Steadman a thumbs up and went to see the other suspect.

Maurice Jackson, the other kid, was evasive. What he did have to say, however, matched up pretty well with Steadman's story. Either the account they gave me was true, or they were guilty. I thought about it. I thought of the park at night. I hadn't been there after hours for years, because I was strictly a morning man now.

There wasn't enough to go on yet. Newton Stamper, the victim, had lived in an apartment a few blocks from the park with his brother Drexel. I called and asked if I could come by and see him. I told him I was a detective. What kind I didn't say.

At his apartment Drexel Stamper informed me that the reason Newton had been to the park was that Newton was writing a story about fear. He'd gone into the park after closing time to experience that emotion, gambling that he could get away with it once.

"The two of us have always been timid," Drexel said. "I admit it. A life of luxury here in the Upper West Side, living on inherited money kept us from any challenge. Newton was determined to change that self-image. Who knows? Maybe he did lose his head in the park. Maybe he tried to fight back against some ruffians who were intent upon robbing him. They didn't have to kill him."

"Down at the precinct they say you have a record of Newton's walk last night," I told Drexel. "How complete is it?"

"I was communicating with Newt throughout his adventure until just before the murder," Drexel replied. "I was monitoring him with the cell phone I had here. Newton was logging his progress by means of this GPS-equipped phone." Drexel touched an area of the phone with a manicured finger. "Newton was at this point at one-fifteen, this point at one-twenty, et cetera," he continued.

"Very interesting," I replied. "Didn't the police want this phone?"

"I didn't think to offer it to them," Drexel returned. "They had the one Newton was carrying, the one they took from the killers. I suppose that was all they needed."

"I wouldn't ask to take your phone," I told him, "but would you mind if I download the record of Newton's trip into my device?"

"Certainly not, if that would help," Drexel replied. "But the police have told me that it records his position only approximately."

"It's something to start with," I told him.

After I left the Stamper residence, I examined the evidence from Drexel's phone. It consisted of a running conversation between Newton and Drexel, accompanied by an on-screen map that marked Newton's progress through the park.

Drexel was right about the GPS app part. It was pretty vague. But the most damaging evidence was the recording of the conversation. Toward the end Newton got hysterical, telling his brother that someone was pursuing him in the dark. ". . . Black man . . . after me," Newton gasped, accompanied by the sound of feet running through dry grass. The call ended with sounds of a struggle which included shrieks of terror from Newton and angry shouts from two people clearly identifiable as Steadman Byars and his friend Maurice Jackson. Evidence like that was going to be hard to refute.

And yet Sergeant Byars still believed the kids. I was at a loss.

When in doubt, stall. I knew a high-priced lawyer who owed me a favor. At least I could ask him whether that crime scene foul-up might constitute grounds to quash the indictment that was sure to come.

Soft music was playing in the elevator to the attorney's office. ". . . When you're caught between the moon and New York City" a wistful voice intoned. Next to Paris, I guess, New York has more songs written about it than any other city. I'd always considered the one playing on that elevator useless until now. I stood there as the door opened on the attorney's floor. A woman carrying two goldfish in a plastic bag stepped into the elevator. "Getting out?" she inquired politely.

"No, I've changed my mind," I told her. "I'm going back down."

I had an idea, and it was a long shot. I dropped in on a man with some pull, even though he'd be pulling the lever that slammed the door on Steadman and Jackson for life if I was wrong: Albert Blanton, high on the staff at the D.A.'s office and an up-and-comer.

Out of curiosity I suppose, Blanton told his secretary to send me right in. "Blanton, I think I can give you some info about a case coming up," I told him. "I suspect you might be the one prosecuting the case, but it's not on the docket yet. What do you say I go with you into Central Park and recreate the conditions of the case?"

"Central Park?" Blanton repeated.

"Yes, the victim's phone was equipped with a GPS positioning feature that tracked his movements through the park," I told Blanton. "I have the brother's copy of the route Newton Stamper took last night. You can see the conditions of the journey that led to the victim's death."

"What's the catch?" Blanton asked. "You know I can use anything I find out there."

"Catch? A minor thing," I told him. "We need to go after closing time."

"Why are you so interested?" Blanton asked. "Those boys don't have any money. Their case is going to be processed by a public defender."

So Blanton knew about the case already. Give the guy credit. He kept up with the flow, all right.

"Just thought I'd save the city some expense," I told him.

"And in the process try to find a way for a certain couple of serious offenders to weasel out of the charges, eh?" Blanton asked.

"Don't forget about the possibility of some public defender, low down on the chain, coming up with an overlooked detail that will make a monkey out of you," I cautioned.

"You have a way of putting an image into a guy's head, Turley," Blanton answered. "Okay, but It will come at a price. I can swear you in as a deputy to develop a case for the state. That means I'll be able to use any evidence we find against the defendant or defendants. How does that sound to you?"

"I'll take that," I told him.

"I get a bonus out of it," Blanton said. "I've only been to the park a couple of times, and only part way in. I've always wanted to see Central Park at night, but I didn't want to go to the expense of hiring an armed escort."

"That's a firm commitment, then?" I asked.

"Okay," Blanton answered. "When do we start?"

I made some preparations, and met Blanton at One-fifteen A.M. near his office. One of his staffers dropped us off at a spot on Seventy-Second Street and we started the tour from there.

"What the heck are we doing?" Blanton asked, as I directed him to climb over the railing with me at a bridge that carried Seventy-Second over a bridle path that ran through the park.

"You want the whole tour, don't you?" I asked him. I had started off with a pure fabrication. Stamper lived on the Upper West Side, yes, but he had walked to the Eaglevale Bridge that takes Seventy-Seventh Street over the bridle path to West Drive. I wanted Blanton fatigued, and I needed the extra five blocks we would walk from that dusty bridle path getting there. I wanted him disoriented as well, and the difficult descent to the bridle path over the stone railing at that point on Seventy-Second was a good start in the process.

"We'll break our necks," Blanton protested.

"No," I assured Blanton, "just grab my hand while I hold onto this bush and we'll make it just fine."

Once on the bridle path we seemed to be in a different world. It was more often used by runners than riders, but it still smelled like horses. And the ground was dusty because the path usually flooded at this point during even a moderate rain. The city had been dry for nearly a week, though, and the surface had developed a web-work of tiny fissures. The surface crackled as we walked, and the urban sounds above were muted as a result.

It was unexpectedly dark down there too, shielded from the spill-over of street lamps. Only the city's reluctance to change any detail of the original Olmstead plan kept the place the way I needed it tonight, secluded.

Blanton took in the unaccustomed sounds of crickets and tree frogs as we walked. After a while he asked "What bridge did we go over to get down here?"

"Riftstone," I answered, consulting the cell phone as if it was telling us which way to go. We were picking up the sounds of unidentified night birds as well.

A bird rose from its nest on the ground and flew away through the grass. Its wings thundered like the hooves of a horse and Blanton looked around for one, bewildered.

Our destination was five blocks to the north, but it seemed longer on the dirt. "What's that up ahead?" Blanton asked fifteen minutes later.

"Eaglevale Bridge," I told him. "It takes Seventy-Seventh Street over the bridle path to West Drive at Naturalist's Gate."

"How do you know all this?" Blanton asked.

"I've lived in New York man and boy for thirty-four years," I told him, "but I'm an outdoor guy at heart. You can find more of the great outdoors in this city than you could explore in a lifetime."

"Oh, come on," Blanton protested. "How could that be?"

"Besides Central Park," I answered, "there are another seventy-six parks in Manhattan alone. And there are bigger parks in the city than this one. There's the Staten Island Green Belt, for instance, or Pelham Bay Park. You get off the Kazimiroff trail in that one and you're in the deep woods. You've got a hundred other parks in the surrounding boroughs. You've got three zoos, the botanical gardens, thousands of acres of green space if you know where to find it."

"Is that so?'" Blanton asked. "I never thought about that."

"Come on, we're going up to Seventy-Seventh," I told him.

We made our way up a path to the right and followed Seventy-Seventh to West Drive. We came to a halt in the middle of a bridge with semicircular benches built into its sides. "What's this?" Blanton asked.

"The Balcony Bridge," I told him. "These stone benches have comforted a lot of weary travelers."

"It's a little moody at night, though," Blanton said, looking around warily. We walked on down the path and over the Bank Rock Bridge, its white oak floorboards rumbling ominously beneath our feet in the darkness. An occasional owl could be heard among the night birds. "Spooky," Blanton muttered.

"That's what I was thinking," I told him. "I'm beginning to wish I had brought my gun."

"What?" Blanton asked, "You didn't bring your gun? But you had it out and pointed at me in a wink a few days ago."

"Oh, I was on the alert for someone who was stalking me back then," I told him.

"All right," Blanton replied, looking left and right. "Well, where do we go from here?"

"Up ahead, of course," I answered.

"Up there?" Blanton inquired, looking ahead at a thirty-eight acre stretch of apparent wilderness. We had reached the Ramble. This section of the park had been planned inch-by-inch by Frederick Law Olmstead, but in the dark it looked like something Daniel Boone would be afraid to set foot in. The picturesque limbs of huge trees outlined themselves against the sky like grasping arms. The large boulders artfully scattered around looked like crouching animals. At least to first-timer Blanton, I hoped.

A huge owl flitted past us in utter silence, a foot above the ground. It disappeared into the forest.

"It caught a mouse," I whispered. "Did you hear that squeak?"

"I didn't hear anything," Blanton replied, in a tone that suggested he'd be very reluctant to testify against the owl if pressed.

We made our way forward and encountered a strange presence emerging through the darkness to our left. We had approached the Gill Bridge, spanning a small stream in that direction. It was made of wood, and the railings had been fashioned from the trunks of saplings that retained their natural curve. In the dark, and to a person who had not seen it before, it could be counted on to stimulate the imagination.

"This is the most vandalized section of the park," I told him quietly. "Every time the park board fixes that bridge, gang members come and tear it up again."

I looked around, checking the lighting conditions to make sure they matched up to those of the night before. There was a full moon and heavy clouds were passing over the face of it. My plan called for those clouds to do what I wanted them to do, and that was a tricky proposition.

Blanton watched me as I made my calculations. I hoped he was thinking I was worried about some potential threat lurking in the woods. To help him along, I produced a whistle from my pocket. "No gun," I said, "but this might help a little."

"Great," Blanton replied sarcastically, "a rape whistle."

A cloud was just about to move past the moon. "They're pretty loud," I assured him, and blew the whistle. "Let's move along," I said. "I think I hear something."

Blanton heard it too. The sound of distant footfalls that could have come from anywhere. And they were getting louder. We walked up the grade, toward another bridge.

We had almost reached the rough stone bridge ahead of us when I turned around and pointed behind us. "Look," I said.

Blanton turned around and stared. Two menacing forms stood there, as black as shadows, beside the Gill bridge.

I broke into a run up the slope we had been climbing, and Blanton didn't have to be invited to join me. He ran, too, brushing the dry grass alongside the path. I hadn't given him space to run along the path in the clear.

The dry brush rustled and cracked as we ran, but the noise was drowned out by the reverberation of the footsteps that seemed to be overtaking us. The footsteps of giants.

We had reached the edge of the bridge. "Should we jump for it?" I asked Blanton.

"No choice," he replied, and vaulted the railing toward the path twenty feet below.

He tried to, that is, because I neatly grabbed him by the back of his coat and pants and hauled him onto the path he had left.

The footsteps halted and two teenagers looked up at us from just beyond the archway of the Ramble Bridge. "Nice job, fellows," I said. They waved and ran on, just in case Blanton decided to have them cited for being in the park after hours.

But there was no chance of that happening. Blanton had decided to take the live reenactment he had just experienced like a man.

"I caught on just as I was going over, Turley," Blanton told me. "Thanks for being on guard."

"I wouldn't want to get sued for a million dollars," I replied.

"Shadows," Blanton said. "Imagine almost being scared to death by your own shadow."

"Not so hard to imagine," I replied. "It happened to Newton Stamper last night."

"Yes," Blanton agreed, glancing up at the moon and back down the trail behind us. "Let's go look at that again."

We walked back far enough to view the optical illusion that had sent Newton Stamper over the edge of Ramble Bridge the night before. The illusion that had caused him to crash into Steadman Byars and his buddy and break his neck on the pathway.

It was still there. Our shadows, big and menacing, were framed in the light of the moon from an opening through the trees behind us.

"It probably only happens a few times a year," Blanton said, "When the full moon is in a certain position."

"And even then, there's nobody to see it," I added.

"You know," said Blanton, "I wondered why you kept consulting your watch. You wanted to be sure you were recreating the conditions of the event accurately, weren't you?"

"You pick up on details pretty well," I told him.

"It's too late to salve my ego," Blanton returned. "All right, you win this round, Turley. Steadman Byars and Maurice Jackson will be out of jail as soon as I can get there to sign their releases. But if I ever get you into court on a charge that will stick, you better hang onto that rape whistle."

CHAPTER FOURTEEN:

THE WOMAN BEHIND THE MAN

I WASN'T USED TO keeping late hours, so that walk through Central Park with Albert Blanton had put me off schedule. Samantha had gone to see Ogden. It was something about the baby. I owed her some trust after she had come in and caught me practically in the act with Haldis Pike, so I didn't pout about it.

My body voted to take the usual morning run, even though it would make me late to the office. I was already over an hour behind schedule when I got home from the run to discover Samantha Dale and Haldis Pike standing on my front porch talking to each other.

Keep calm, I told myself as I approached them.

"I'd better let you go on up," I told Samantha, "and I'll talk to my client out here."

I opened the door, ushered Samantha in, and turned back to Haldis.

"Oh, it really wasn't important anyway," Haldis said, and gave me an elegant little touch on the hand. She walked away nonchalantly.

I had handled that situation with all the aplomb of a junior high school student. But as Woody Allen once said: "Your heart knows what it wants."

Samantha was sitting at the top of the landing in the upstairs hall when I went inside. I joined her there.

"Call me an irresponsible mother," Samantha began, "but I didn't feel like bonding with the child of the man who raped me, threw me to the wolves, and tried to kill me."

"I'm afraid I don't know how that works," I replied. "That bonding stuff. What happened? Was the whole thing just an invitation to visit the boy?"

"Yes," Samantha replied. "Mark has a wet nurse now. Yes, 'Mark.' Ogden is really giving him the same name as the monster. He wanted me there to see the boy christened as Mark Anthony Ogden."

"I expected as much," I told her. "But I can see how that could bother you."

"That was the least of it," Samantha continued. "The nurse handed the child to me. It was like holding a big rat to my breast, expecting it to chew into me at any moment. Have you been out on a case?"

"Had to," I replied. "It was for a cop."

"That's okay," she said. "Go ahead and take more of them if you want to. As long as you don't stiff me on the stories."

"Agreed," I told her. It was nice to see that the way I'd handled the rough work in Colorado had given her some confidence in me. We went up to my bedroom and lay down. Fully clothed, we snuggled like puppy dogs for an hour.

I dozed off and awoke to see that Samantha was looking at the sheets I'd bought as a replacement. She seemed to be measuring the polka dots with her fingers. She didn't remark about it, though.

I dressed and drove down to Word to the Wise, just as if I were an actual working man. My tardiness and air of lassitude persuaded Ida that conditions were right, so she hit me up for a raise.

Ida said her piece and I responded. "You're right, Ida," I said, "Word to the Wise Investigations is doing pretty well financially."

"So, what's the problem with a raise?" she asked me.

"A raise is not out of the question," I told her. "Give me some stats on secretaries who are making more, and we'll talk about it." Contrary to her expectations, she'd caught me in a defensive mood. I'd been walking on eggshells all morning to avoid woman trouble, and I was trying to achieve an equilibrium.

"But I'm not a detective, Mr. Turley," Ida replied. "I'm a secretary. The secretaries I know don't want to talk about what they make."

"There you have it, Ida," I answered. "Secretaries at hospitals learn something about medicine. Secretaries at computer stores get all digital and techy. That way, they learn about what makes a business tick, and it makes them more valuable to an employer. Do some detective-work. Bring me those stats and you'll be in a good position to get that raise."

"But I still say . . ." Ida began. "Oh, it's almost time for your first appointment. Mr. Worthington will be here in five minutes to see you." She was a little off-balance, because she'd let an appointment sneak up on her and had to announce it at the last moment. I was almost always in the office before her, and I had thrown off her timing.

I went to my office door and looked back at her. "Send him in as soon as he gets here, Ida," I said. In truth, I hadn't counted on getting a secretary as good as Ida was, and I wanted to give her a raise. All I needed was to see that one little thematic twist that identified her as not just a secretary, but a P.I.'s secretary.

I sat down, wincing at the lumpy souvenir of North Carolina that one Lamont Morgan had kicked into my ribs. I made a quick phone call to Matt Jacobs to see if he'd thought of a way I could get at Milburn Howard without blowing the whole case, but Matt hadn't come up with any inspirations.

As I hung up the phone an elegant-looking man about my age strode into my office with a jaunty air. He had wavy hair and was dressed in a finely-tailored pastel-colored suit with cane to match. He may have been attempting to take on the appearance of a sophisticated English actor between pictures, but to me he looked more like Donald Duck's lucky cousin Gladstone Gander.

"My name is Temple Worthington, Mr. Turley," he told me. "Perhaps you've heard of me."

"The name is familiar," I replied. "You're a writer, I think."

"I am indeed, Mr. Turley," Worthington said. "Writer, artist, and the inventor of the Random Poultry Effect."

"I knew it had something to do with chickens," I told him.

"Indeed," Worthington replied. "R.P.E., as it is popularly abbreviated, is a current media phenomenon. One sprays the keyboard of one's word processor with an edible adhesive substance. It could be sugar-based or (a subsequent refinement of mine) made to be entirely opaque, as with wallpaper paste. One then writes by scattering birdseed on the keyboard and releasing a given number of chickens into the environment. Later, one comes back and pushes the print button."

"I see," I replied. "And does one actually make a living doing this?"

"I do it almost exclusively at art galleries," Worthington explained. "The Happening still lives. I get paid a set fee to show up, and then the viewers pay for copies of the signed printouts. For a pretty good price. But this 'Crankpot' killer has me worried. He has been making headlines, shooting people who've been doing a lot less annoying things than the gig I'm into."

"The guy who's been making the papers with random killings," I said.

"Right," Worthington replied. "So, I have to worry about this nut walking in on one of my performances as much as I have to worry about him potting me as I go inside."

"Have you tried talking to a regular security agent?" I asked.

"It's too inhibiting, Mr. Turley," Worthington answered. "I'm walking a fine line here. It's a delicate balance. Any one of these eccentrics who attend my shows could decide that the presence of security guards queers the whole deal, and then spread the word to the other élite consumers. Pretty soon, no more chicken show. I went straight from playing elevator pop in a piano bar to this, and it could go south on a thin dime. I've got to cash in on it while it's hot. It's like printing money, but how long could it possibly last?"

"I see your quandary, Mr. Worthington," I told him. "I could take a good look at the entrance and exits to your show, and put a man on each. They'd be inconspicuous. Then I could go in with you and keep an eye out. How would that be?"

"That would take a huge load off my mind, Mr. Turley," Worthington replied. "And leave scope for creativity as well."

"All right," I assured him. "You've got it covered."

The event went off as planned. I entered with Worthington, pretending to be some anonymous goof interested in chicken writing. And I didn't feel guilty about it. This "Crankpot" murderer was a real threat to anyone doing something generally annoying: throwing chewing gum on the sidewalk, driving with a bad muffler, or wearing pants that dragged along the ground. He had killed at least one person in each category and stated the reasons for the shootings in matter-of-fact letters to news outlets.

When honest con-men like Temple Worthington begin to have their creativity stifled by psychos, it's time to do something about it, I thought. But I didn't want to ask Samantha for her help. After what had happened in Colorado, I wasn't going to get her involved in future cases in any way. I decided to get some advice from a psychologist who was working on the government dime.

The city had recently switched to a new approach to an old problem: how to get trained staff to all the police precincts that were in need of psychological consultants. When a perp was brought in raving, somebody had to help figure out what was wrong, and how to get the offender processed without automatically conceding a mistrial. The hit-or-miss process of guessing which degreed psychologists were needed at which precinct wasn't working. The new plan was to assign each precinct a graduate student from Columbia or New York Universities, under the supervision of one man in a central office at City Hall.

The project was housed in one big room with dozens of carrels in it, each belonging to a student who was earning credits and helping the city save big money at the same time. Most were empty because the occupants were on the job at one N.Y.P.D. precinct or another.

I had come to see a man who was overseeing the project at the moment, Dr. Lang Andrews.

"What about the copycat element?" Dr. Andrews," I asked.

"I believe the city is suffering the effects of that right now, Turley," Andrews told me. "The Crankpot started the ball rolling by choosing a few of his pet peeves to work on, and now the copycats have shouldered their way into the act. They're whanging away at minor annoyances and old grievances. And they're all trying to blame the killings on the Crankpot."

"I thought as much," I told him. "What seems to be motivating the Crankpot, Dr. Andrews?"

"He seems to consider himself a social engineer, Turley," Andrews answered. "It took time enough for this to come across to us. The killer assumed at first that his motivation would be self-evident, but of course it wasn't. He finally hired a vagrant to distribute circulars that explained what he was doing."

"Can the vagrant identify him?" I asked.

"No," Andrews answered. "The Crankpot shot him. The vagrant was a dead man from the moment he agreed to take the job. He had worked his way around the perimeter of the park before he attracted official interest. Then the Crankpot shot him from long distance."

"Is there a clear pattern that distinguishes the Crankpot from the copycats?" I asked.

"Apparently so," Andrews answered. "We have similar groups of dead gum chewers and smokers. The chewers were either popping or stringing out their gum. The smokers were emptying ashtrays at intersections. The individual killings stand out as copycat murders. For instance, we've already identified the killer of an antique store owner as a patron who knew where the murder weapon was kept. It was a Walther P38 nine-millimeter Parabellum automatic. The killer circled the supposed annoyance, the notation 'Pontius Pilot' on the glass of a framed print of a Passion scene. It was the owner's nephew. We have a confession."

Small world, I thought. The victim was someone I'd met on a previous case. There couldn't have been two such inscriptions. That poor guy who'd thought he bought a Rembrandt for the price of a bottle of wine got rubbed out. Bad luck.

"The copycats are as much a problem as the original, then, right?" I asked.

"Neither one is a picnic," Andrews replied. "It's making people nervous."

"Right," I said. "I had to babysit an artist last night, so he could kid people that chickens were using a typewriter."

"Yeah," Andrews replied. "I've heard about that crap. What a way to make a living."

"I couldn't even enjoy the gag," I said, "because I was watching the crowd. I'd rather be doing something more productive."

"You should talk to the reporter who was just in here," Andrews remarked. "He's been asking the same questions."

"When was that?" I asked.

"Five minutes ago," Andrews answered. "I think he's still around here."

"What did he look like?" I asked.

"Hard to say," Andrews replied. "He was, well, nondescript."

"Can you point him out?" I asked.

"I think so," Andrews answered. "Let me look. That's funny. He's disappeared."

I went back to my office. Fifteen minutes later Ida signaled me on the intercom.

"Mr. Turley," Ida said, "someone wants to speak to you on the phone, but he won't give his name. Do you want to talk to him?"

"Yes, Ida," I told her, "thanks. . . . Word to the Wise Investigations," I said.

"I have some important information regarding the Crankpot," said the voice on the phone.

"What would that be?" I asked.

"It's the kind of thing you actually have to see to appreciate," the voice answered.

"I'll bite," I replied. "Come on by."

"I mean you have to go there to see it," said the voice.

"I don't like the way this is turning," I said.

"It'll be worthwhile," said the voice. "Believe me."

"What's the proposition?" I asked.

"Meet me at the park," the voice answered. "That's close enough, isn't it?"

"If there's anything to it," I replied. "Who am I talking to?"

"The reporter who was at City Hall when you were there earlier today," the caller answered. "Go to the corner of the park nearest to your office, and straight up the walk. The third bench, facing a big oak tree, has a cell phone taped to the bottom. Take it out and punch redial. Then I'll tell you what I've got."

"This better be good," I said.

I did as the voice instructed. "All right, we're connected," I said when I had found the phone. "What's going on?"

"You spoiled my game last night, Mr. Turley," the voice said.

"Who is this?" I asked. "Suddenly your voice is not all that friendly."

"I have been absurdly referred to as the Crankpot," the voice answered.

"Okay," I replied, "what now?"

"Now, Mr. Turley," the voice said, "I have you trapped on a park bench, with my rifle zeroed in on your head."

"If you do," I said, "you're set up at quite a distance."

"I wouldn't recommend trying to leave, Mr. Turley," the voice said. "Take a look at the beer can across from you."

The beer can exploded. I waited for a report in the distance, but there was none.

"You have a rifle with a silencer on it?" I asked in a dubious tone.

"You bet," the voice answered. "I can stay here as long as I want to. Until I'm through with you. If you make a break for it, I'll shoot you first, and then a few other people. Like that artist sitting across from you, painting a picture of the park."

"So, what do you want?" I asked.

"I have a publicity problem," the voice answered, "and I want it straightened out."

"Okay," I said. "What does that have to do with me?"

"I need an agent," the voice replied. "Someone to help me make decisions about who gets eradicated. Sometimes I think my emotions may be influencing my judgement."

"There's something damn fishy about this," I said.

"Er . . . I'll start with the gum-popper," the voice said. "I began with one who was not only popping her gum, but pulling it out in a string and looking at it. I shot her in the middle of the forehead. She won't be doing that again."

"Honk, honk, chirp?" I asked. I leaped to my feet and gave the artist ahead of me a ringing slap across the head. "Hey . . . What . . . do . . . you think you're doing, Worthington?" I growled.

"Ow!" Temple Worthington exclaimed, "You slapped me, Turley. Right . . . on the head! That hurt!"

"I oughta do more than that," I said, "you . . ."

"Don't hit!" he said. "Don't hit! I'll sue you if . . ."

"Gimme that!" I said. I grabbed his camera, popped out the video card, and crushed it.

"My camera!" Worthington protested. "My card! Leave that alone. I'll sue you for everything you . . ."

"A video camera poking through your canvas," I said. "You're lucky I don't do the same thing to your camera that I did to the card. What the hell do you think you're doing?"

"It is performance art, once removed," Worthington explained. "I have every right."

"Not with me you don't," I replied. "I don't remember giving you permission to sit there and use me as an experiment in terror. If you hadn't set your mike up so close that it caught feedback from the traffic and birds, I'd still be sweating."

"Think of the relief you'd feel, after . . ." Worthington began.

"You had those beer cans rigged to explode, didn't you?" I interrupted. "Didn't you think it would look a little suspicious to place full beer cans around the park? What if some kid had picked up one of them?"

"The cans couldn't go off without this remote control," Worthington countered. "See?"

"Let me see that," I demanded. "How do you do it?

Worthington made another can explode.

"I see," I told him. "You need to see a shrink, Worthington. Don't try a gag like this again, all right? Somebody could get hurt, and for no reason."

"Mr. Turley," Worthington protested, "you've got me wrong. What I was after here wasn't as frivolous as you seem to think. I was trying to get you interested in going after this Crankpot fellow. Once I made it look personal, I knew you'd get on board and nail him. The two of us could get the job done, and in the process, I could capture it on video. We'd have the eye of all New York. We'd be set up for life."

"Or at least you would be, right?" I replied. "Don't underestimate this Crankpot guy, Worthington. And don't mess with him. I've looked at his M.O. He's as mad as a cliff diver, but he's also brilliant. That's a deadly combination. Keeping you safe for a night is one thing, but if you pull this guy's chain, he'll kill us both."

"Okay, Mr. Turley," Worthington replied, "okay. If you put it that way, I'm convinced."

Worthington gathered up his gear and I checked my suit for beer spray. I went back to the offices of Word to the Wise.

Inside my inner office I looked at the big window behind my desk, considering for the first time the fact that it made me vulnerable to attack from long-range rifle fire. I decided to order some blinds for it. I had just started to reach for the phone when Ida rang in.

"It's a busy day, "Mr. Turley," Ida said. "Another one wants to speak to you without identifying himself. Shall I pass it on through?"

"Sure, Ida," I answered. "Word to the Wise Investigations" I said.

The person on the other end of the line waited for the click that indicated Ida had hung up, and then spoke. "Do you know who this is, Mr. Turley?" a very relaxed voice asked.

The voice gave me chills. I'd heard a lot of cops on the range use just that tone as they sighted in a rifle. In addition, the voice was being channeled through some subtle but effective synthesizer that made it unrecognizable. "Unfortunately, I believe I do," I replied.

"And yet you remain seated at your desk," the voice said.

"I have more respect for your marksmanship than to believe that a little juking and jiving would help me," I answered.

"You're a man of good judgement, Mr. Turley," the Crankpot said. "And a man of good taste. I have enjoyed

examining the appointments of your office. You wouldn't mind
if I elaborated on that statement, would you?"

"No," I answered.

"First of all, there's an intercom on the desk in front of you
that is set to 'off'," the caller said. "I'm sure you know what
will happen if you change that setting."

"Message understood," I said.

"Good," the voice said. "Let's see . . . that's a mounted
model of the Twenty Mule Team Borax wagon and team on the
wall at your left, isn't it?" the voice inquired.

"Yes," I answered.

"There's a movie with Wallace Beery driving one of those,"
the voice said. "Same title. Have you seen it?"

"No," I answered.

"Perhaps you shall one day," the voice said.

"I'd like to," I replied."

"At your right there's a reproduction," the voice said,
"painted by a fine copyist, I must say, of Jan Bruegel's The Fall
of Icarus."

"That's right," I answered.

"Have you noticed the bird in the tree at the right, in that
painting?" the voice asked.

"I've seen it, yes," I answered.

"Can you identify it?" the voice asked.

"It's a partridge," I answered.

"And what has it to do with the flight of Icarus?" the
Crankpot asked.

"Nothing that I know of," I admitted.

"It's an illustration of the cycle of life, Mr. Turley," the
Crankpot told me. "The carpenter Daedalus, the father of Icarus,
tried to kill his nephew Perdix when that young man showed
him up by inventing the saw. Daedalus tried to drown the boy.
Rather than letting him die, the gods changed Perdix into a
partridge, known now as *Perdix perdix*. So, you see, when at the
end of the story Icarus falls into the sea and drowns, it is part of
the cycle of life and death."

"They had partridges in ancient Greece?" I asked.

"Indeed so," the voice replied. "The partridge is a transplant, brought over by the Pilgrims."

"You learn something every day," I remarked.

"What's behind the painting, Mr. Turley?" the voice asked. "On the other side of the wall?"

"My secretary, Ida," I answered.

"Ah, and in a position of distinct peril, too," the Crankpot noted. "I'm using double-tap technology. Two shots with one trigger pull. The first bullet breaks the glass ahead of the kill shot, both in my window and yours. They are separated by only a millisecond, but to the second bullet it is as if the glass had never existed. The first bullet goes wild, of course. I wouldn't want to be seated behind that wall."

"I'll grant the short putt," I told him. "I'm sure you could put a bullet through the partridge if you wanted to."

"Thanks," he replied, "And that will also save you a pane of glass. At least for now. You have nerve, Mr. Turley. Many people would have jumped away, to one side or the other. Or they would have gone over the desk. The latter alternative would have injected a note of humor into the proceedings, in the present case."

"From your point of view, at least," I admitted.

"It would have made an irresistible target," the voice replied.

"How'd you get locked onto me?" I asked.

"When I tapped the artist's phone," the voice answered. "That gave me access to you as well."

"Temple Worthington?" I asked.

"Also known as Morey Levitz," the caller replied.

"Morey Levitz?" I repeated.

"Yes," the Crankpot confirmed. "The 'Temple' is a rather arch acknowledgement of the man's ancestry. At any rate, Mr. Turley, while I have your attention, I'd like to vent a little. You don't mind, do you?"

"No," I answered. "What's bothering you?"

"Straight to the point, then?" the voice asked. "Very well. I've been unfairly accused, Mr. Turley. I've been called a racist. The accusation is totally unfounded, of course. It isn't my fault that the targets who offered themselves for the demonstration of the moment happened to be black."

"Now that I think of it, Crank . . . may I call you Crankpot?"

"Oh, why not?" the voice replied

"Most of the gum poppers who've been shot recently were black as well. That's your work, right? Is there something to the allegations after all? Think about it."

"I have already, Mr. Turley," the Crankpot replied. "Pacing through my house and watching the slow drip of the rain down the windows. I pondered for hours about my whole program of social improvement. I have to admit that it is not having the effect I intended."

"Then why do it?" I asked.

"Why, indeed?" the voice replied. "Instead of being a force for the betterment of society, my campaign is becoming divisive. Recriminations assail me. I must admit that I have simply been too ambitious. I should have addressed just one issue at a time. The situation would have been different, of course, if I'd had the freedom to just set up on any street corner and put together a demonstration. However, lamenting over conditions that can't be changed will not help."

"So, what's your decision?" I asked.

"It's a very difficult realization to come to," the voice replied, "but the conclusion is unavoidable. I'm strictly a hobbyist. I am working with forces that are too difficult to manage. Social experimentation on any level, even this small project, is fraught with difficulties. I remember pausing at the window that gives upon my . . . well, never mind. It's not in my interest, or yours either, to get too specific."

"I agree there," I said.

"I stared at the image of my face in the window," the voice said, "at the shadows of the raindrops rolling down the glass, at the teardrops running down my cheeks in the reflection, and I wasn't sure which was which. I admit to having a sensitive side, Mr. Turley."

"Most people do," I said.

"The public's mistaken view regarding my campaign is partly my fault," the Crankpot continued, "and partly that of an uncomprehending society. So be it. I admit it. I am simply a tyro. But I'm no racist."

"People make assumptions," I said.

"Just so, yes," the voice replied. "And in doing so they've missed the point entirely. Due to this foul assertion, my best stand has gone unappreciated. A whole family walked from their seats at the back of the bus, through the bus, to get off at the front. To make some ridiculous point to the detriment of the buss company's attempts to keep their coaches on schedule. So you see the object was to select those targets, and those targets alone, bringing into clear focus the idea that those offenders alone were to receive the appropriate reprimand."

"Tough but fair, eh?" I asked.

"Very droll, Mr. Turley," the Crankpot replied. "Yes, the chosen vehicles for my statements are invariably in for rough treatment. That's the nature of the game, I'm afraid."

"I still don't understand." I said.

"I chose to apply my skills to a specific problem," the voice explained. "Exiting the bus by the front door is appallingly wasteful. It's a shocking reversal of logic. Riders who do so impede the process. They are, in a small but appreciable way, reversing the course of civilization. These riders thus suggest themselves as appropriate targets, converting the problem into a largely mechanical process involving such considerations as wind flow, trajectory, priority of selection, etc."

"Sounds complicated," I said. It seemed he was somehow drawing a distinction between thrill-killing and murder as a test of marksmanship. But I didn't have the nerve to ask if that were the case.

"It can be," the voice replied. "Very much so. That's what makes it an art. The combination of elements, that is. All woven into an intricate skein that is complicated greatly by the immutable factor of time."

"And yet you didn't shoot the driver," I said.

"An astute observation," the voice replied. "Yes, the safe course would have been to take the bus driver first, so the others wouldn't bolt back on, making the whole shoot more difficult. But that would have been a mixed message. I tend to be a bit of a purist, and there is nothing in my nature that would allow me to take the safe course. I started with the smallest target, a boy, perhaps three years old, who stumbled as he jumped off the bus, and then bounded back to his feet. A clean kill. The big woman next to him started screaming. Clean kill, dead center. Two quick shots took out the two females at the far right, evidently sisters of the first target. Just as I'd feared, an older woman, quite a bit overweight, lumbered back aboard the bus. I took a chance on hurting the driver, then. But the job had to be done. I wasn't going to break up a family. It just wouldn't be right. The bus driver got sprayed a bit, but he was untouched by the bullet. It exited cleanly through the window to his right. What a shot that was! If I do say so myself. Finally, the driver started out in panic acceleration, right through the light, which hadn't changed yet. Tires screeched and horns blasted, as the final target danced around and around with her hands in the air in front of her. It was a very difficult shot. I had to time not only the motion, which was erratic, but also the rhythm of the dance. So many variables. Slowly, I pulled . . . Yes! I had done it. What a stand! Six head shots. Six clean kills. No incidentals. I had reached a stage in my work that few others had ever attained, I realized, with a flood of strangely mixed pride and humility. And yet my efforts lie in the dust, as dross."

"Because nobody really understood the point of what you were doing," I said. "They just jumped to the conclusion that you were potting black people for the heck of it."

"Quite so," the Crankpot said. "Let me tell you about the aftermath of the bus incident. It is an embarrassing and annoying situation, this not being able to defend oneself in print. They have raised such an uproar that the issue to which I directed the killings seems almost petty. They are calling me a bigot! People who know nothing about me are exhibiting the effrontery to put a label on me, based on a single isolated incident. I have shot hundreds of targets in my career, and a mere ten of them . . . no, twelve . . . or so, have been black people. Racist indeed! I have shot as many Japanese, for Jove's sake! The idea is overwhelmingly offensive. I am so far from being appreciated, that there is obviously no hope. If they are going to put this kind of slant on it, the uproar is going to be totally counter to the purpose toward which my actions have been directed. Such sensitivity! If I have to rule out black people, what next? Hispanics as well? It will inhibit my selectivity. The whole thing is becoming such a burden. Carrying a pistol with a silencer, in case anyone stumbles across me while I'm shooting, is an annoyance. In some strange way I haven't ever been able to put my finger on, it is offensive to me to shoot someone close up. The act is so strangely personal. It requires more intimate contact than I care for, and I don't really relish contact with people. Then there are concerns, so recently developed, about infectious agents that can be transmitted through airborne drops of blood. This project is changing my outlook about the people around me. I feel more critical. I'm beginning to see faults in people I hadn't seen before. The whole project has become burdensome."

"Sounds like you're not having any fun," I remarked.

"Indeed so," the voice conceded. "I've been reviewing, Mr. Turley. The fault is essentially mine. I'll accept that. I'm guilty of hubris. It was ambition that prompted me to skip around in my target selections. Confined to one single target group, it seemed to me, the program would not be as effective. Only one specific group of offenders would be deterred from their anti-social activities once notice was given. I wanted to build up a body of incidents I could point to when I brought my campaign to public notice. And that was my mistake. Smokers, litterbugs, gum chewers, I tried to make an impression on them all. And the campaign was doomed from the start. I was beginning to gain some focus as I turned to the bus riders. The plan (an eminently logical one) was to persuade them to use the bus more efficiently. I would take out a few offenders at various bus stops, create a pattern that couldn't be missed, and then make an announcement that no one was to get off the bus at the front any more. I felt that the suggestion would be attended to very seriously by a large percentage of the ridership. Now, with this new factor having been thrown in, the whole plan seems pointless. I certainly am not going to set myself up for the allegation of racism again. I thought you might want to know that I'm leaving town. I plan to return to my hobby of potting hunters. I have an impressive number to my credit. I won't bore you with details."

"What do you have against hunters?" I asked.

"Nothing, really," the voice answered. "I shoot from ambush. That is my identity. Young in the war (I won't tell you which war, as a safeguard to both of us), I was assigned as a sniper. This assignment was made solely on my merits as a sharpshooter, and without benefit of a preliminary psychological examination. Had certain tests been administered I would have been diverted and sent home for care, or detained in some stockade behind the lines. Mad? The term is meaningless, Mr. Turley. No living person is truly sane. I took the lives of more of my fellow soldiers than of the enemy. Working forward of the lines, I was assigned repeatedly to counter the devastation that I myself was visiting upon my officers, my platoon, and even my own squad members. Any clear target, under the proper circumstances, that came within the cross hairs of my scope died. The excitement I later felt, viewing the remains, was interpreted by witnesses as outrage at the enemy, and I was never suspected. I was promoted, decorated, honored. The end of the war came in time to prevent my detection, for the charade could not have continued much longer. Sooner or later one chance witness would have surfaced, and my little hobby would have been revealed."

"So it's back to the woods, you say?" I asked.

"My business ventures take me to many parts of the country," the voice continued. "And the woods are often conveniently nearby. However, I hope you won't be wasting your time checking statistics on hunting accidents from now on."

"Not unless somebody calls me to take up a case," I replied.

"I like that attitude, Mr. Turley," the Crankpot answered. "It shows courage. A lesser response would have caused me to pull the trigger. But in any event, you wouldn't have a clue. I am very careful. When at my chosen pursuit, I've never parked a car that could be traced to me. When hunting, and when doing the background work in preparation for a hunt, I always use an assumed identity."

"Very thorough," I remarked.

"Quite so, Mr. Turley," the voice replied. "I'm feeling much better for our talk. Before I go, I'll reminisce a moment about the troubling aspect of my transition from carefree woodsman to failed social reformer. Or does that interest you at all?"

"By all means, say on," I invited.

"And so I shall," the voice replied. "I recall clearly the moment of crisis. I'd been hunting at the edge of the woods. I lined up the cross-hairs for the tenth time. An easy shot, but the target wasn't posed just right. I wanted the man to lower his head a little more. I was using a deer slug with an underpowered package, to simulate a hit from greater range. I was using just enough powder to penetrate the skull. The target would then fall backwards out of the tree stand, always an artistic touch. The slug would match up in its ballistics with the shotgun of the hunter another two hundred yards behind me (I dug it out of a dirt bank earlier in the day). This was not a necessity in regards to averting suspicion in this case, but it was another pretty point."

Too much information, I thought. Sooner or later the Crankpot was going to lose track of all the facts he had laid out for me, and then he would kill me to make sure I hadn't heard something I could use to track him down. I tried to put myself back on the firing range, during the relatively few hours we'd practiced with the rifle in the N.Y.P.D. Could I have talked to anyone and kept my eye on the target all that time?

"Then something unusual occurred," the Crankpot continued. "I noted that the target had seen something interesting, but had not raised his rifle. I switched to binoculars and picked up the distraction. A group of people of varied description were approaching the hunter. Environmentalists. I'd heard about these spoil-sports on the radio. Strangely, though, I found myself sympathizing with the people who were harassing the hunter. In my years of hunting, I had never shot a deer, rabbit, squirrel, or . . . come to think of it, I had never shot any game animal but humans. It was a revelation. I had never really thought about it that closely, but suddenly I realized that I had some basic similarities to these people who had just saved the hunter's life. They cared about making this a better world, and so did I. Maybe I hadn't been giving enough thought to social issues. I felt a little ashamed of my insular existence. I didn't even have a television set. I had quit when the newscasters started exchanging insipid pleasantries in the middle of newscasts. Radio allowed me to pursue my hobbies of gun repair, gun modification, gun study, and making preparations to kill people. To pursue this last pastime seriously requires much groundwork. One has to prepare many levels of identification, in case one gets interrupted during a shoot. Even the process of arranging travel is necessarily complicated by concerns for secrecy. How very difficult life must be for people who are forced to do such work for a living. The fun would be taken out of it."

On the other hand, the Crankpot wasn't a normal man. Maybe his psychosis enabled him to concentrate for long periods of time.

"I had devoted my life to the collection, study, care, and use of guns," the voice went on. "The hobby presented an extra challenge, since I didn't want to get involved with gun registration. It seemed a lot of bother in the first place, and then of course it would make killing needlessly complicated. The basic point of a purchases is to obtain guns with which I can kill people, not the acquisition of a few complicated chunks of metal to look at. No malicious intent underlies the shootings. I simply like to kill people by agency of various firearms. I like killing enemies, of course, although I have never really had many, but I also like killing friends. The apparent loss evokes sympathy from others, and then there is the challenge of making new friends. This way, people don't start getting uncomfortably close to me. I realize, however, that this suggests an avoidance, even a fear of forming intimate relationships that isn't very healthy. I'll have to live with it. I decided so years ago. That's just the way I am."

"Sounds kind of lonesome," I said.

"I wouldn't say so, Mr. Turley," the voice replied. "With my hobbies I've been quite content through the years. I've never been one to boast, so it didn't really bother me that no one knew about the really interesting part of my pursuits. Perhaps one day I'll write a book. An anonymous work, of course. A wealth of interesting incidents could be related. My widely based system of operations, for instance. I hadn't planned, at the beginning of my hobby, on establishing bases in a number of hub cities in the country. Such a network has grown by accident. Unexpected acquisitions have given me property in areas that are rather populous. In consequence, there is no necessity to carry guns with me as I hop around. That wouldn't be possible today. Things have changed. Are changing. Like that situation with the hunter and his antagonists."

Or maybe the Crankpot had set the rifle aside. Or maybe it was Worthington doing a really good impersonation of a psycho. Or maybe I was just losing my nerve with these maybes.

"I watched the drama of the animal protection associates and their confrontation with the hunter play itself out," the voice continued. "I was not at all disturbed by having been denied my own kill for the day. On the contrary, the affair had put me in a philosophical mood and prompted a self-analysis that was long overdue. The incident had changed me, I was to reflect later, from a person who killed for the thrill of the activity to a killer with a purpose. The following week I shot a person in the act of emptying the ashtray of his car in a parking lot. That shot was the longest I could remember making. My era of the city kill had begun."

No, the stakes were too high to take a chance. I'd just have to wait him out.

"Rain fell the next morning," the voice continued, "and the forecast was for rain all day. I had planned to kill someone that day, and this was no weather for the job. I went out to the airport and took a shuttle to Nashville. By four o'clock in the afternoon I had gotten everything squared away and had made my first environmental kill. I wasn't quite sure, but I thought it might have topped my shot of the previous day in distance."

Sweat had trickled down my back and into my underwear. It was uncomfortable, but I wasn't about to change position.

"My City Kill plan was an ambitious one," the speaker went on. "A coordinated program to alter people's patterns of behavior. Too many people are on the earth, anyway, so it offered benefits in population reduction as well. This is quite apparent from population statistics. People are eventually going to be fighting for a square foot of land to stand on."

"Things are tough all over," I replied. "No question about it."

"Our chat has been quite therapeutic, Mr. Turley," the voice said. "And now I'll let you off the hook. I'm not going to kill you today. However, if I ever have occasion to come back to New York I shall come looking for you."

"No offense intended," I told him, "but you could skip that part."

"You worry too much," the voice replied. "So as not to keep you in a state of unrest, I'll be sure to let you know in advance."

"Thanks," I said. "But just one more thing. Did you go to the park to kill me or Worthington?"

"Most intuitive," the voice said. "But I think I'll leave you guessing about that, Mr. Turley. Ta-Ta."

"So long," I said. ". . . Whew! That may be the best sounding dial tone I've ever heard in my life."

Sweat was working its way down my legs now and dampening my socks. At least I hoped it was sweat. I got up to bathe my face at my private restroom. Nausea overcame me before I made it there.

Five minutes later I turned on the intercom. "Ida," I said.

"Yes, Mr. Turley?" Ida answered.

"I'm going to take the rest of the day off, Ida," I told her. "And you can do the same."

"Wonderful, Mr. Turley," she replied. "By George, I'll take my kid to the zoo, that's what I'll do! Any special occasion?"

"No, Ida," I answered. "I just have an urge to go home and lie down."

"Sorry to hear you're not feeling well, Mr. Turley," she replied.

"It's not exactly that, Ida," I told her. "It's just that once-in-a-while, things get, shall we say, too insane to deal with."

"Yes, Mr. Turley," Ida said. "Oh, please don't leave yet. There's the phone again, and I think I know who it is."

"I don't see how you could tell that, Ida," I replied. "Look, I don't want to handle any more calls. I'm tired enough to . . ."

"It's the police, Mr. Turley," Ida interrupted. "They've caught the man you were just talking to. You know, the Crankpot."

"Say what?" I replied.

The next hour was a struggle. Being on the phone with that killer for so long had worn me down, and I was in no shape for a prolonged interview with the cops. But I had to go through it anyway.

I can't even remember the first few exchanges of the discussion. My recall of it starts with something Ida said to the police. "Mr. Turley was suspicious from the beginning," she was saying, "and he signaled me to listen in on the line, didn't you, Mr. Turley?"

"I have a headache," I replied.

"So, I just flicked the receiver a couple of times with my letter opener to make him think I had hung up," Ida continued. "And he started chattering away. You couldn't stop him."

"Tell us again, Ida," Lieutenant Tom Dench requested, "how Turley figured out where the guy was." Tom and his partner Sergeant Jack Boozer had figured out early on that Ida had saved my bacon and was giving all the credit to me. I couldn't admit as much because of masculine pride, and Ida was not going to show up the boss. The two cops were having a world of fun at my expense.

"Sure," Ida agreed. "Mr. Turley's Twenty Mule Team Borax wagon is mounted very high on the wall, so he knew the killer had to be no higher than the floor we were on."

"Is that right, Mr. Turley?" Dench asked.

"I need an aspirin, Lieutenant," I repeated. "I think they're in that desk."

"Come on Ida, let's hear the rest of it," Dench prompted. "Jack, you carry aspirin with you, don't you?"

"The killer mentioned that he was planning to shoot through the actual glass of the window where he was," Ida continued, "so Mr. Turley knew that the man wasn't in the old office building over there that has windows that open."

"Here you go, Turley," Boozer said. "Come on, Ida. Give."

"I need to get past you to the water cooler, Sergeant" I told him.

"And, of course," Ida went on, "it was plain from that statement that the killer wasn't set up on one of the buildings a little further on that have roofs to the level of this story."

"How's that again, Ida?" Boozer asked. "How did, ah, Mr. Turley figure that out?"

"Mr. Turley's desk is in the middle of the room," Ida explained, "with the painting and the model wagon equally divided at each side. To see them both, the way the killer described to Mr. Turley, it meant he had to be almost directly across from him."

"How about it, Turley?" Dench asked. "Is that the way you figured it?"

"Ask her," I answered.

"That's what we're doing," Dench replied. "Tell us more, Ida."

"Well," Ida continued, "when Mr. Turley signaled me to call on the other line and I found out that a single occupant was lodged in a room between the only two vacant rooms on that floor, I knew exactly where to send the police."

"It was a good thing the old motor-mouth gave us plenty of time to get here," said Dench.

"Yeah," Boozer agreed, "but a bad thing that we couldn't take him alive."

Too bad you couldn't have let me know that a little sooner, I thought. Then maybe I wouldn't have lost my lunch on the carpet.

"Yeah, we may never know what was motivating him to . . ." Dench began.

Then he stopped as Ida handed him a piece of plastic she had popped out of her console on the desk. A memory-card. Samsung, one hundred twenty-eight gigs.

"Oh, of course you did," Dench said. Ida had recorded the entire ordeal.

"Word to the Wise Investigations is a full-service organization, Lieutenant," Ida told him. "Right down to the training of the secretarial staff."

"Is that right, Turley?" Boozer asked.

I gave up. "I've told you before, Officers," I said. "This is her game. She did the whole thing. Would I be doubling her salary if she hadn't pulled my fat out of the . . ."

But Ida was intent upon having the last word. "Isn't he wonderful?" she interrupted. "The best detective in Manhattan, and modest too!"

CHAPTER FIFTEEN:

BORN YESTERDAY

SAMANTHA AND I RELAXED the next couple of days
following the turmoil around the Crankpot case. The nerve-
wracking session sitting under the gun had been bad enough,
but when the cops had told me afterward that they had identified
the shooter as Norman Granville I felt even worse. Ballistics
had matched his rifle to nearly all the Crankpot murders. I had
underestimated the guy.

For the entire weekend Samantha and I walked arm-in-arm
and pretended we were tourists. We hit the usual sights and
gawked at them to see if we could fool people, just for the fun
of it.

That exercise in relaxation was good preparation for the
week's events. The Crankpot case was a bizarre one,
particularly in light of several supposed confessions of murders
that nobody else seemed to know about. I wasn't surprised
when Lieutenant Dench and Sergeant Boozer showed up again
at Word to the Wise, wanting some of my time.

"Haldis Pike has turned up missing," Dench informed me.
"Certain assets supposedly collected for the Save the Elephants
Foundation have come up missing as well. Bearer bonds, stuff
like that."

I stepped over to the water cooler to shut Dench up for a
moment. I needed a chance to absorb the flood of new
developments.

But Dench didn't stop. "It isn't clear whether Haldis or
Granville was responsible for the loss," he continued. "Harley
Pike had set the organization up in such a way that both the

brother and daughter could get to them. With Granville dead and Haldis nowhere in sight, the case is in turmoil."

Dench had delivered all that info right in front of Ida's desk. He hadn't even bothered to accept my invitation to go into the inner office. I figured that meant he'd just dropped by to update me on the case and move on, so I gave him what I naively thought was helpful advice.

"I wouldn't jump to conclusions," I told him. "It sounds like two cases to me. The killings and possibly a kidnapping of Haldis."

Dench and Boozer looked at each other in a way that made me think I still had 'tourist' stamped on my face. "But we can still count on your cooperation, can't we?" Boozer asked.

"It isn't my case anymore," I told him, "Because I've already done my job and gotten paid for it, but I'm willing to help you in any way I can."

"Good," Dench replied. "To begin with, can you think of any reference, any clue, that might give us a lead on Haldis Pike's whereabouts?"

"No," I replied. "But I can tell you that she struck me as kind of a mouse. Not the type to grab the dough and run."

The two cops looked at each other again. I didn't remember police work being quite as much fun as they seemed to be having.

"I mean, it looks to me as if you're more interested in Haldis than in Granville," I continued. Behind Lieutenant Dench the door to the hall opened. Samantha Dale came in and stood in silence so she wouldn't interrupt the conversation. She had evidently shown up early for our lunch date.

"Yeah?" Boozer replied. "Well Haldis Pike is suspected of the murder of her previous two husbands."

"Husbands?" I gulped. How had she pulled off that sleight-of-hand trick in the bedroom? And why?

You can't be prepared for everything all the time. I was so surprised by Boozer's revelation that Samantha caught me with my mouth hanging open.

Samantha spoke up. "Excuse us for just one moment, gentlemen," she said to Dench and Boozer. "Let's go into your office," she continued, touching my arm.

Samantha and I retired to my inner office. "Oh, so that's the little detail you were trying to hide," she said as soon as the door closed. "Now I understand why those polka dots on the sheets looked different. Well, Haldis Pike put one over on you. And I would never have taken her for *virgo intacta* in the first place, even if she'd left the sheets there."

"All I can say is that the woman was very practiced in deception," I replied. "She could make a living coaching that act. Is that all you brought me in here to talk about?"

"Yes," Samantha answered. "Now I'm going to walk back out with you and smile pleasantly, so you won't get laughed at."

To my relief, Samantha pulled it off nicely, and I continued my discussion with the cops.

"When Granville disappeared," Dench told me, "we found a video studio in one of Harley Pike's office buildings."

"One of them?" I asked. "I knew he was wealthy, but I thought it was inherited money."

"No, the guy was into half a dozen businesses at once," Boozer replied. "Including the one we found the studio in. It's got floor after floor of offices with people in them monitoring security cameras all over the city. A surveillance firm."

"And it's equipped with a private studio Haldis Pike and her father were using to fool around with old security footage," Dench added. "The way I see it is that it was a creative endeavor for him, and practice for murder for her."

"That's an intriguing statement," I replied.

"Good," Dench said, "Because we came over to invite you to look at the place."

Samantha had already left, without explaining where she was going. "Inform Dr. Dale we'll have to miss out on that lunch date," I told Ida in a face-saving tone, and left with the cops.

Jordan Deaver, who'd signed back onto the force, was at the Pike studio when we got there. Maybe Headquarters wanted him to sketch somebody from video footage. "The print guys went through this stack of cards," Deaver told us, "and he says it's all right to view them."

Deaver was talking about memory cards. Behind him were two heavy metal cabinets full of video equipment, including file boxes of memory cards. The cabinets had counters, were bolted together for stability, and were set flush against the back wall

"Are all those cards from security cameras?" I asked Dench.

"Most of them," Dench answered. "And a lot of footage from them has been used to put together a kind of documentary of big city life. Show some of it, Deaver."

For the next five minutes we viewed a montage of interactions between people on the street, in alleys, and within various interior settings. It was done by somebody with a good eye and good editing skills. It was powerful as in was, in silence, and I wondered what the effect would be with a script behind it

"There's no title on the video," Dench told me, "so we don't know who put it together, but here's something Haldis Pike did herself."

Deaver ran a video showing Haldis backing away from the camera she'd just switched on, turning around, walking away from the camera thirty feet, and then returning to turn off the camera. The scene was repeated several times, with Haldis walking with a slightly different gait in each. Deaver turned off the video.

"So, what's she doing?" I asked. "Trying to look like Charlie Chaplin?"

"I think I know," Deaver answered. "And that'd what we're looking for. Show him the scene in the hallway, Deaver."

Deaver inserted the next card. "That's the hall leading to the room in the building across from you where we shot Granville," Dench explained. "The security camera shows Granville walking down the hall. But not alone. He is being steered by a person dressed as a man. We think it is Haldis Pike."

Deaver paused the video. "Granville looks like he's sleepwalking," I commented.

"No surprise there," Boozer replied. "With the chemical stew in Granville's veins he couldn't have told you his own name. He was doped up like a hype in Washington Square Park."

I didn't even consider the idea that Haldis Pike could have been the Crankpot impersonator who had terrorized me in my office. But if Dench was right, it had to have been someone other than Granville. "And it couldn't have been anything but a setup?" I asked.

"No," Dench replied. "The perp had propped Granville up in a chair with his hand super-glued to the stock of a rifle pointed at the door. And the forestock was resting on a chair back. The way the real shooter had it rigged, no cop in New York would have stood there arguing with Granville. You see a rifle pointed at you, you shoot."

I thought about the image of the figure steering Granville down the hall. My mind couldn't make the leap yet. "I don't know," I replied. "These days it's hard to tell a man from a woman out on the street. That could be a woman, I guess, and the perp is tall enough to be Haldis Pike. But there's no way that view would do you any good in court."

"No," Dench agreed. "But we're looking for more. There's plenty of material here to look through."

"About that," Deaver put in, "we've determined that the stuff in here is pretty well-organized. There's straight security footage, and hours of this art film project. I don't think we're going to find anything else."

"Aw, nuts," Dench replied. "Well anyway Turley, take another look at that perp hustling Granville down the hall to make sure. You tagged Haldis Pike, didn't you? That's what I got from looking at your girlfriend's reaction at your office."

It's dangerous to lie to a cop, so I evaded the question by attracting Dench's attention to a suspicious stain on the otherwise clean counter beside us. "What's this?' I asked.

"Don't change the subject," Dench replied. "That's dried mango juice. The can it came from was in the trash."

"Yeah, but look at the groove," I replied. The mango spill had trickled over the edge of the counter, into the space between it and the counter next to it. The spill had an inch-wide rectangular depression in it where something the size of a memory card had slid over the edge and between the two shelving units."

"Crap," Dench said. "And headquarters told us not to unbolt these units.

I picked up a metal yardstick from a nearby desk and stuck it between the counters, next to the stain. It fit snugly. I raked it forward and a memory card fell to the floor beneath the unit.

Boozer examined the card with a magnifying glass and made sure there were no fingerprints. The print man had already left.

There were no prints, so the card was okay to view. It was the evidence Dench had hoped to find. In it Haldis Pike appeared once again, dressed exactly as she was in the security camera video that showed her controlling Granville. As it opened, she backed away from the camera she had just turned on. She practiced her walk, came back toward the camera, and the picture went out. It started again. Three times she did this. One version was undisguisedly feminine, not just swishy. The second was an exaggerated masculine clumping walk, nearly comical in effect. The third looked convincingly like the walk of a man.

I had no doubt I had just seen Haldis practicing up to march Norman Granville to his doom.

"Perfect," Dench said. "Convinced?"

Sometimes you have to rip away the invisible hand clutching at your throat and go on. Everybody gets ice in their guts once in a while. Yes, I was convinced.

"What about the other killings she mentioned in her act?" I managed to ask. "Or did Haldis throw in a few killings based on habits that annoyed Granville?"

"The other shootings were totally fictitious," Dench replied. "She made them up just to pull your chain a little harder, I guess." I deserved that crack, so I let it go.

"We figure she saw us nosing around this setup here," Boozer put in, "and took it on the lam."

"Good thing she was on a tight schedule," Dench added. "The security camera here records that she searched this room shortly before we got here this morning. She must have missed this card by accident."

"You guys through with me?' I asked.

"Yes," Dench replied. "You've done us a favor here Turley, finding that card. You've redeemed yourself in my . . . well, that's going too far. Let's just say you came away with a little less egg on your face."

CHAPTER SIXTEEN

WHAT GOES AROUND

I ARRIVED HOME that evening aware that I'd have no room to argue with Samantha about resuming the story–telling program. And then again it was cheaper than bringing her a dozen bouquets to make up the ground I'd lost. I skipped the nonessentials and picked up my autobiography at a point three days after Monique had put me off at the jetty on the coast of southern France.

A psychiatrist is a different kind of audience than most. As I told the story I was once again sitting at Charles de Gaulle Airport waiting for my plane. My conscience was kicking the walls of my skull like a show horse that wants to go home.

I wasn't proud of what I'd done to get the fare back to New York, but it was too late to undo. I had caused Darlene King, a tourist from Wyoming, to feel ugly and useless. No, make that used. I'd hired out as a gigolo, her look told me, but she hadn't known it until I asked her for the loan.

Once again, I had failed to look at all the possible consequences of my actions. Or maybe it had something to do with meeting Darlene only three days after Monique handed me my head on that jetty.

In addition, some dipper had picked my pocket inside the terminal. The money, not the papers, but they'd taken it all.

"Turley?" a voice beside me asked.

I turned to the man who had just sat down. He held a cell phone with a picture of me on it. People were behind me in the photo, talking to each other. Further back was the Rockport, tied to the single dock of the little sailing village at the east edge of the calanques.

I figured the stranger for a plainclothes cop, Paris style. Well, at least from the evidence of the photo he had used to find me, this wasn't about that affair with Darlene. But then maybe the De Lafontaine brothers were trying to charge me with piracy.

"My name is Ferenc Carette," the man told me. "I'm a private investigator, and I have come to ask a favor for Georgette and Marie."

"They need me as a witness, then?" I asked.

"That is correct," Carette answered. "A simple deposition will do."

"I should have thought of that," I replied.

"It would cause you to miss your flight, of course," Carette continued, "But another will leave tomorrow at this time. I've already ascertained that there is a vacancy."

If Carette's English was this good, how much better was his French? I wondered.

"I don't have money for a hotel," I told him. Or even a flop house for that matter, I thought. And I didn't want to spend another night on the street.

"I can put you up in my apartment," Carette replied. "It will be more convenient than a hotel, and I could get you back to the airport in time tomorrow."

I agreed and we left. "We just need a record of the circumstances under which you met the two women," Carette told me in his car. "Their state of mind at the time is important to their case."

He didn't elaborate. He wasn't trying to influence my testimony; he just wanted to get me primed for the deposition so as to save time.

I could have had a guided tour on the way to his apartment, which was sixteen miles away, but I didn't want to be a pest. It was enough to look out the window and see if I recognized anything.

Carette lived in Belleville, a section of Paris that was relatively tourist-free. It was a crowded working-class neighborhood that reminded me more of New York than any other part of Paris I'd seen.

Before we got to Carette's apartment he pulled to the curb beside a woman walking ahead of us on the sidewalk.

"Delphine," Carette called.

"Carette," she said, "I was just coming to see you."

"I know," he answered. "I have Mr. Turley with me. We'll escort you."

I got out, gave her my seat, and climbed into the back. It was a small car. I speculated that Delphine was to serve either as a witness or notary to my deposition.

A notary, I found when we got inside. Carette lived in a modest fourth floor walk-up apartment overlooking a street that was lined with the same mixture of shops you'd find in Brooklyn. In addition, you could hear the rumble of the Metro train that had brought Delphine to the nearby stop.

We went over details of my seizure of the Rockport carefully, with me answering questions that were subtly calculated to catch an exaggerated claim or outright contradiction.

Delphine, who was not much older than me, was very good-looking. She had olive skin and an aquiline nose that seemed to suggest both strength and intelligence. She seemed fascinated by Carette, and watched him when he wasn't looking. This is for me, I thought. So what if the guy's apartment was cheap and his car an old one? Call it hero worship if you like, but from that moment I wanted to be a private detective even more than I wanted to be a cop. But that would be a tall order in New York.

Delphine notarized the deposition and got up to leave. "Delphine is reading for her law degree at the Sorbonne," Carette informed me as he opened the door for her. "Having her name affixed to this document will be significant for her, due to the aggravating circumstances of the case."

At that Delphine tucked her head against Carette's shoulder, hugged his upper arm, and left. I was surprised at the little-girl bashfulness of the gesture, coming from a woman with those strong classical features.

"Are you sure they won't need my actual testimony?" I asked Carette. Rape plus abandonment at sea was a vicious combination, I thought, but you couldn't blame me for wanting to get away from the calanques. And hitchhiking in France is no easier than it is in the U.S., so I'd been occupied with the process and not thinking much about Georgette and Marie.

"Oh, I'm sure," Carette answered. "This way the defense won't get a crack at you to try and get you to say something that would help the defendants."

Carette treated me to a meal at a nearby restaurant. The food came without the usual magic show, and it was cheap as well as good. Carette knew his stuff.

I hit the couch back at Carette's apartment for a solid eight hours of sleep. "Cereal for breakfast," he said early next morning. "Then we go to the laundromat, if you don't mind. Do you have anything that needs to go there?"

"Yes," I answered. Sure, I'd go with him, I thought. I wouldn't have wanted a stranger hanging around my apartment for two hours, even if he seemed on the level. And I had kept a few items from the Laughing Dove.

The laundromat was just down the street. Carette fished some coins out of his pocket on the way and handed them to me.

"You can feed the machines if you don't mind," he requested. "That way I can look over your deposition one more time and make sure there isn't some question I have forgotten to ask."

"Sure," I agreed. I was young enough then that machines of any kind still fascinated me.

Two men were blocking the door of the laundromat when we got there. One was a policeman and the other had his back to us. It didn't take me long to find out that they were talking about a homicide.

That's because I asked Carette, afterwards, to translate the whole incident for me so that I could write it down. We got it all translated and written in a notebook Fournier, the policeman, gave us while we were getting Carette's laundry done. When you find me asking people questions in the story, I was doing it with Carette acting as interpreter for me as we went along.

The man with his back to us was asking: "Please, Officer, can you wrap this up so that I can get back to business? It's been all morning."

"Can I help it if they're fouled up downtown?" asked the policeman. "Oh hello, Carette. Want to play detective? I'm short-handed and upside down on this one."

"Got troubles, Officer Fournier," Carette asked him.

"Right out of the starting gate," Fournier replied. Inspector Bonnet folded up ten minutes after we got here. It looks like appendicitis. He'd already had a blowup with the Smurf doctor, so he refused to ask for their help."

"Smurfs are S.M.U.R, or Service Mobile d'Urgence et Reanimation," Carette explained to me. "A blowup?" he asked Fournier, "what about?"

"It's this way," Fournier explained. "A woman came in to do her laundry and saw the victim. She ran out screaming and called the Smurfs. So then of course they sent a crap load of doctors who arrived just after Bonnet got here. He wouldn't let them in, because whatever he had was making him short-tempered and he didn't want to deal with complications. No reanimation needed here, he told them; the guy was dead, so get the hell out."

"That kind of a day for you, eh?" Carette asked.

"That's just for starters," Fournier replied. "We're running Mr. Laurent here out of business. People show up with their dirty laundry, and then they have to move on."

"What's holding up your case?" Carette asked Fournier.

"Visiting dignitaries all over the city," Fournier replied, "and no help from anywhere. The street's blocked up at the corner. The Smurfs are hanging around, but they refuse to push the gurney down here this far. Don't know why; can't read their minds. Something about not wanting to start a precedent. Everyone's either a lawyer or they're the next president of their union."

Laurent, who had just sampled a frozen ice drink, made a face to show he didn't like it. He put the lid back on the Styrofoam cup and set it down on a dryer. "I'm going across the street," he said. "Anybody want coffee? Inspector Fournier? Carette? You, young man?"

I didn't even have the price of a cup of coffee. I looked at Carette to make sure I wasn't committing a breach of etiquette and then said "Yes, thanks, Mr. Laurent. Black for me."

"Black for me too Mr. Laurent," said Carette. "I'm buying. Here, ask the assisting officer, too. That's Officer Legrand isn't it, Fournier?"

"Right, Carette," Fournier answered. He continued filling Carette in on the problem: "And then Inspector Bonnet put Legrand and Mercier next to the suspect, who's passed out in a chair in there, and told them to wait till the guy wakes up to arrest him. Then Bonnet got sick and forgot to rescind the order. He went out of here with Mercier in a patrol car, but if you ask me, he should have been in an ambulance."

"How about giving me a rundown on the case?" Carette asked.

"Okay," Fournier answered. "It looks simple. The victim was in a dryer. He got spun, burned, and asphyxiated. A little guy. It looks as if the drunk in the chair, a big guy, stuffed the victim into the dryer and turned it on."

"Couldn't the victim have put himself in there?" Carette asked.

"How about it, Mr. Laurent?" Fournier asked. "Why don't you tell these guys what you told me?"

Laurent turned back away from the door. I wasn't going to get that cup of coffee after all. But at least Fournier had included me in the discussion, because I was with Carette and I was eyeballing the whole scene with obvious interest.

"Sure, Officer Fournier," Laurent answered. "These machines have a safety feature. First you put the money in. Then you turn the crank on the coin slot over, and you can't release it to start the machine until the door is closed."

"What about when you feed it several coins?" Carette asked.

"You can feed it fifty Francs if you want to," Laurent answered, "But each time you have to close the door and then turn the crank. I'll show them one of these down the line, Officer Fournier, okay?"

"Sure, Mr. Laurent," Fournier answered. "This is the only machine we can't touch."

"So you've got the victim on the drying table," Carette repeated thoughtfully, "and you're waiting for the gurney."

"Hell of a way to do things, isn't it?" Fournier asked. "It looks like our suspect is waking up. Read him his rights, Officer Legrand."

Read him his rights? I wondered. The Miranda law was just an American ruling, wasn't it?

"Oh, God," the man in the chair groaned. "What a way to wake up. Where am I, anyway? Looks like the basement of hell."

"You are under arrest," Legrand informed him. "You have the right to notify a relative or an employer."

"Oh, my head!" the man complained.

"You have the right to notify consular authorities if you are a foreign national," Legrand continued.

"Ow," the suspect said again. "Please, Officer, skip the rest. I know my rights. What's the chance of getting a drink here? Hey, let go of my hand."

"What's the matter, Turley?" Carette asked me. "Why were you feeling of his hand?"

"You can tell Officer Fournier to let this guy go, Monsieur Carette," I told him. "As strange as it may seem, this was suicide."

"Suicide?" Fournier repeated. The word is the same in French.

"How do you figure that, Turley?" Carette asked.

"That's impossible, young man," Laurent said to me. "I just told you how my machines work."

"Anything," the suspect pleaded. "A cup of coffee. My head."

"Hey, Officer Fournier," Legrand asked, "Should I cuff the suspect or not?"

Officer Fournier looked at Carette questioningly.

"Let's allow Mr. Turley to explain," Carette suggested.

I hated to be a show-off, but we needed to get Carette's laundry done so I could catch my plane.

"Here's how it happened," I replied. "Mr. Laurent, you offered us coffee from the all-night shop across the street, right? Is that where you got that Slushie you were sipping when we walked in?"

"Uh, yes," Laurent answered.

"But it's a little too sweet for your taste, right?" I continued.

"Yes," Laurent answered. "But what does this have to do with . . ."

"You got the idea from that empty cup on the washing machine, right?" I pursued.

"Yes," Laurent answered, "I thought I'd try one."

"They give good value there," I said. "They put in lots of syrup in proportion to the ice. I can tell that from the smell. You can also see the traces of the sticky flavored syrup on the victim's right hand, and the patch on his right thigh where he wiped it off as he was reaching for the door. But the guy who just woke up has clean hands. Those prints that are visible on the door to the dryer will be the victim's. The smudge around the coin slot is obviously a patch of the same substance, as is the pool of liquid on the floor beneath the coin slot. Watch."

"Watch what?" Laurent asked. "You're just feeding coins into an empty dryer."

"Keep watching," I replied.

"You're turning the switch to the right," Laurent said. "So what?"

"So this," I answered. I picked up the still-cold Slushie that Laurent had sampled.

"'Huh?" asked Fournier. "He's grabbed a handful of that Slushie."

I slapped the clump of Slushie against the coin slot.

"Damn," said Fournier. "It's holding the switch over like a piece of clay."

"I see," said Carette. "And the victim would have had plenty of time to climb into the machine if he wanted to, before . . ."

Carette was interrupted by the whirr of the machine.

"Before the machine starts up," Fournier continued.

"And now the Slushie is starting to melt into a dirty pool," Carette observed, "just like the one in front of the dryer where the victim died."

"Hey pal," Fournier said to the suffering man in the chair. "Sleep it off somewhere else next time, okay?"

"Oh Jeez, anything" the suspect answered. "Just let me get out of here and do something about this head."

Carette looked at the victim on the drying table and then at me. "I have an idea, Fournier," he said. "Let's get Turley to push that gurney up to the ambulance. He'll be breaking the law, but that's all right. I'll be putting him on a plane in about two hours. He's too much competition."

CHAPTER SEVENTEEN:

JUDAS GOAT

SAMANTHA HAD ENJOYED the morning's story so much
that she was whistling to herself as I left the house. But as for
me, my mind went back to the problem that had been bothering
me for days. A week had gone by since Denise Black had
turned up at the morgue, and during every minute of it her death
had been picking at me like a schoolyard bully. Except that
there was no way to strike back. No way that I could think of to
kick Milburn Howard's feet out from under him.

What burned me the most was to be stuffed by a mere
amateur.

A first-time murderer should not be able to lash out in a
killing spree like that and walk away with all the usual slipups
covered.

I checked into Word to the Wise and sat at my desk thinking
about it. A motive wasn't hard to find. The insurance on Denise
Black wasn't much, but Milburn Howard was going to inherit
from her, and it was a lot of money.

So, there it was: clear motive, means, and opportunity for
three murders that were logically connected to one man. And it
was all based on evidence that a defense attorney would laugh
at. The prize witness for the defense of Milburn Howard would
be me.

"Mr. Turley," the defender would ask me, "You say you own
a detective agency?"

"Yes," I'd reply.

"Then as a detective yourself, when you heard about this
supposed phony wedding confrontation . . . Why didn't you
have Milburn Howard followed?"

And for that question I would have no answer. There would be no way to convey to the jury the desperation, the sincerity, and the concern that Burlin Frederick had conveyed in my office when he had come in for help. Of course, I should have had Howard followed, but I'd been as wrapped up in searching for Denise Black as Frederick was. I'd put all the resources I had into looking for her. And as a result, Howard had been at liberty to cover up one murder with two more.

Yes, there might be enough evidence for an indictment, but my incompetence had given Howard a chance to erase his trail. And with a merciless psychotic efficiency no one could have anticipated.

What next? Sure, there were other avenues to try. Maybe he'd left bloodstains in the house. Maybe he'd taken Deborah Lancaster's body to the river in a car that still had evidence in it. Or maybe not.

But the humiliation that comes from being outmaneuvered came in handy for the next move I made. I put away pride and used some of Temple Worthington's typing-chicken, fright wig tactics.

After buying a ten-year-old car in so-so condition, I took it to a sign painter. "Left rear squeaks a little," the painter said as I pulled it in.

"Yep, just bought it," I told him. "The bearing should have been repacked before they put the car on the lot." To prove it I stuck my arm under the car and pulled out a lump of brown stuff from the leaking grease cup.

I told him what I wanted on the car and rubbed the grease thoroughly into my hair as I walked to a nearby thrift store.

While I shopped for the second-best used suit at Goodwill the sign man was painting "Manhattan Insurance" on both sides of the car. I came back in my moth-eaten finery with an old briefcase under my arm. After paying for the sign-work, I kicked a dent in the side of the car and drove to the Denise Black estate.

I parked out front and sat in the car, fumbling with my phony paperwork. A few minutes later I walked to the door, started to push the doorbell, stopped and fumbled through the briefcase, and went back to the car.

I went through this process three times, knowing that I would eventually get a hearing. Maybe Howard would see through the ruse at once, but in that case, I'd be no worse off than I already was.

At last somebody responded. I made sure to beat the footsteps to the punch, ringing the doorbell a second before the door opened. That way I could pretend that I had finally summoned up the nerve to ring the bell, and had failed to notice that somebody was coming.

When Milburn Howard opened the door, he saw a man in a disheveled state of dress clutching a briefcase he had just managed to keep from dropping. "What do you want?" Howard asked, looking at me down his nose.

"Oh, sorry," I said, "I . . . I guess I shouldn't have called. I mean I suppose I should have called you before I came, but I didn't want to bother you."

By this time Milburn Howard had gotten a look at the car I'd come in. Two things had been apparent about the way he had covered up Denise's murder: first, he was quick-witted; he'd found a way to turn certain disaster into a big win; second, he was an exploiter. And the situation I'd just painted for him was too appealing to turn down.

"You're from my insurance company, aren't you?" he asked.

"Yes, Sir," I replied, "and, well . . ."

"I understand," Howard said, with sudden empathy. "You don't want to bother me at a time of loss. Come on in. After all, the world has to go on, doesn't it?"

"Uh, yes Sir," I replied, and shambled in, gaping in awe at the conservative but expensive Empire Style furnishings. Howard had laid claim to the main house now, and was luxuriating in his triumph. He was even wearing a purple velour smoking jacket.

"You have a beautiful place here, Mister Milburn," I told him. "That paneling, or I guess they call it . . ."

"Howard," he interrupted.

"Wainscot . . ." I continued, and then "Oh, I see, I got the name wrong."

"Yes," Milburn replied. "Tell you what, just get the paper out and I'll sign it."

What he wanted, of course, was the statement I would give him to sign that agreed that his wife's death had been a suicide. He'd be happy to do that, I knew, because the statement would further insulate him from suspicion of murder.

I could only carry the deception so far, though. Sure, I had a briefcase full of papers I could fumble through, but no such document. Once he caught on, he would spit the hook and I'd have to go back to the beginning.

"So, by 'statement,' that would be the, uh . . ." I temporized.

Howard stopped me with a look and picked up a bell from the end table beside his chair. He rang it so loudly that it hurt both our ears. Evidently this was his first time using it with company. A woman appeared at the door to an inner hallway.

"Sherry?" Howard asked me.

"Me?" I asked. "Is she . . .? Oh, I see. Yes! I would like a glass of sherry very much. Thank you."

Howard laughed indulgently and signaled to the woman, who returned almost immediately with bottle and glasses on a tray. She was dressed in the outfit of a French maid. Black skirt, white apron and all. It fit exactly with the smoking jacket. Howard was playing the Lord of the Manor already.

"What a beautiful woman," I said, after she had left. My down-at-the–heels insurance salesman had been plainly awed, and Howard liked that. It was time to introduce some complications into the game. Just in case, I kept my meek, beaten-down posture as I did so. If he pegged me for a cop, private or otherwise, he'd just throw me out.

"You did a terrific job of play-acting in the church with that actress you hired," I told him. "And it was a good idea to mess up her face when you put her in the River."

It was a better move than I had expected. Howard jumped to his feet, and his face turned red. He wanted to shout, to order me out of the room. But he also didn't want to attract any attention from the maid in the back of the house. He was a knight pinned by a Bishop, and he had to wait for the next move.

With a gesture almost comical, Howard put his left index finger vertically in front of his pursed lips and flagged me to silence with his right hand, palm outward. The woman reappeared.

"Michelle, you may go to your quarters now," he told her. "You won't be needed tonight."

"Oui, Monsieur," she replied, and curtsied. Maybe she actually was French.

With Michelle gone, I started again. "Breaking into the fur storage locker was good, too," I continued, "so it would prompt a search that uncovered Denise's body before her temperature dropped too far and ruined your alibi. Shooting the guard was a no-extra-penalty killing after those first two murders. Maybe he caught you by surprise, or maybe you planned to do it. No difference either way."

"Whoa," said Howard, sinking back down into his chair. "Stop. For a moment there I thought I was actually talking to an insurance man, and I couldn't figure out the angle. What are you talking about?" He was struggling for a defense, and nothing was occurring to him. His eyes were darting around the room as if he were looking for a secret door in that nice walnut wainscoting.

"I'm talking about the warehouse where you kept your wife's body stable in a meat locker at twenty-eight degrees for a few days," I told him. "Then you transferred her to an ice cream locker at minus ten degrees, making it look as if she had been in there just a few hours and had not yet reached ambient temperature."

Howard had been clutching himself as if cold while I talked about the work he had done in the freezers. Maybe there was something in him that could visualize the suffering of others, after all. Or maybe he just hadn't dressed for the job.

"Anyway, like you said, the world has to go on, doesn't it?" I continued, emerging from my meek persona. Hunching over so long was killing me. "Four degrees an hour, that's the index you were using. Yes, the tragedy for you was that when you blew your cool at home and killed Denise with a knife, it left defensive wounds on her hands. No more smooth murder plot. You had to go to creative means to get rid of the body and still collect on the inheritance."

I'd scored on several points. I knew too much, Howard could tell, and he'd have to deal with me. "What are you," he asked, beginning to regain his composure, "a private investigator?"

"Bingo," I replied. "If I were a cop, you'd have handcuffs on at this point, wouldn't you?"

Howard didn't answer at once. He fumbled for the glass of sherry I had left untouched on the tray and slugged it down. If I had to guess, I'd say he was wondering how much it was going to take to buy me off.

"And Deborah Lancaster was not hard to trace at all," I continued. "Maybe for someone else, but not for me, after I'd figured out the cooler business. I can give you particulars about that if you'd like."

Howard looked at me appraisingly. "That won't be necessary," he told me. "You've convinced me that you know enough. How much do you want? I can give you a deposit that should satisfy you for the moment, and then pay the main fee after the inheritance is settled. Will that work for you?"

It was delicate, the way he'd put that proposition. "Fee," instead of "payoff." But in context, it would clearly show that he'd confirmed the accusation.

I took the recorder out of the breast pocket of my cheap suit and keyed it to replay the conversation we'd just had. I laid it on the couch next to me and watched him as it played, so I could keep my hands free. Sometimes in a situation like that the person you're dealing with will reach for a gun.

Howard didn't say anything, just listened. By the time the recording was finished he had his elbows on his knees, propping his head up on his hands.

"What do you really want?" he asked.

"I'm going to give you a break," I answered. "The police are right on my heels, putting together a chain of evidence even stronger than the one I've just outlined for you. With the rundown on the coolers, the blood evidence . . ."

"Blood evidence?" he interrupted wearily.

"Yes, that much Warfarin in her blood would be a lethal dose in itself," I lied. "Plus, there's the info on Deborah Lancaster, this recording, and the security camera shot of you leaving the warehouse. With all that, you're a sure bet for the gurney. The best lawyer you can get will save you only by getting you to cop to it, so the state can save some trouble. You might as well pick up the phone now, and save yourself the stress."

Howard thought about it that way for a minute, head in hands, not saying anything. Then he gave a little sigh.

"You have a point," he said, and reached for the phone.

At least with one hand. With the other he brought a gun up from seemingly nowhere and shot me.

It was sleight–of–hand; misdirection, and I fell for it. He hit me right in the middle of my faded breast pocket handkerchief. The impact was like getting hit by the biggest heavyweight, smack in the heart.

The gun was a forty-five. The force of it, or maybe my reaction to it, knocked me off the couch.

The vest under my shirt saved me. It was the single concession I'd made to the authenticity of my shabby disguise. I'd only put it on in a last second flash of intuition.

I must have passed out for an instant, because the next thing I knew Howard was bending over me with the gun in his hand, ready to finish me off. He'd rigged up a home-made silencer from a soft drink bottle taped to the muzzle. He had stuck it down beside him with the gun balanced on the bottle. I had reached for my gun when he came up with it, but I wasn't quick enough. There's always a new trick.

The shot had taken off the bottom two inches of the bottle. He'd stepped close to me in order to take a second silenced shot by pressing what was left of the bottle close against my head.

Never stick a gun in the face of a person who knows how to take it away from you. I wrested the forty-five from his hand and motioned him back into his seat.

It was his gun, so I couldn't do to him what I wanted to do. Instead, I good-copped him to death. I had absorbed so much technique from Samantha during her sessions with me that it was easy.

Grabbing that gun had taken all the fight out of him. I stayed and shepherded him through the whole process of surrender. Or maybe I should say that I led him through it like a Judas goat. When the police got there, he waived his rights and confessed to the whole thing right there in his living room. He even gave up the gun he'd used to kill the guard at the warehouse.

Sometimes a bluff will work. I hadn't really been able to find any connection between Deborah Lancaster and him. There was no security camera view. I'd been compelled to save the reference to Deborah's tattoo for later, since he had obviously missed it when he stripped her. It was the gun that nailed him; the one component of his confession that he couldn't take back with words.

Maybe what I did to him was unfair, like the teacher who heaps discipline on one of her more controllable delinquents because she can handle that one, but Milburn Howard had it coming to him. The fact that far more heinous acts were escaping punishment all around him didn't make it any easier on Denise Black, Deborah Lancaster, or the guard at the fur storage unit.

And after all, Howard couldn't really blame me. I couldn't have assigned any particulars to his universe if he hadn't defined it himself.

CHAPTER EIGHTEEN:

THE UNINVITED GUEST

AFTER GETTING Milburn Howard squared away, I went home. The house was still. I had just cleared the first step on my way upstairs as the lights went out. It distracted me just enough that I failed to notice the noose slipping over my head from above. The rope tightened, hauling me to tiptoes.

It was a thin rope, and my skull threatened to pop loose from the top vertebra. I reached up blindly to get a grip on the balusters of the stair railing above and behind me. As I did so, someone snapped handcuffs on my wrists, behind the rope.

A second rope whispered over the railing above to hang beside me. Someone quickly climbed over the railing and descended the rope to my left.

The climber paused momentarily to nuzzle my cheek and plant a gentle kiss. Haldis Pike, I realized, from the faint trace of lavender perfume. That and the athleticism she had shown in my bedroom. Plus, the fact that she was nude helped jog my memory.

Her brief touch had revealed that Haldis was wearing some kind of goggles, most likely infrared night vision glasses to maximize her advantage. I was beginning to understand how she'd been able to control her uncle on his way to the final sacrifice in the room across the street from my office.

Haldis slid down the length of my body, holding the all-important choke rope in one hand. Her six feet of Mitzi Gaynor curves pushed her over the lightweight limit, so she had the heft to back up her move.

She made it to the floor, keeping me balanced on my toes with the rope. Something happened in the darkness behind me, and then she lifted my right foot just enough to get a rope around my ankle.

Where was Samantha? I wondered. I'd expected her to be home. Had Haldis done something to her as well? Samantha was six inches shorter than Haldis, and twenty pounds lighter. Plus, Samantha wasn't a psychotic serial killer.

Haldis made both ropes fast somewhere in the darkness.

"Now the other foot," she said. I hadn't much choice other than to comply.

Haldis walked back upstairs at her leisure, passed a belaying rope around my chest, and lowered me backwards into the downstairs hall. I took advantage of my new position by attempting to get the handcuffs in front of me, but she surprised me by dropping over the railing in the darkness and preventing the move. Night vision gave her all the advantage.

Soon Haldis had the cuffs off and both my arms secured behind me with rope and tackle she had stowed somewhere out of sight before I got there. The click of metal teeth told me she had at least one geared cable-puller of some sort back there helping her.

"Don't tell me you have four horses hidden in here too," I said.

"It's not that bad," Haldis replied. "I'm just here to finish that little liaison we had earlier, remember? You still owe me one."

"I can't recall anyone having to tie me up before, to get that done," I replied.

"Oh, I tied you out of consideration for your notions of fidelity," Haldis told me. "But we're missing part of the setup. I'll be right back."

Haldis disappeared and returned two minutes later, preceded by the sound of creaking wheels and the muffled protestations of someone apparently wearing a gag. She did something to restore the lights. She had brought in Samantha Dale, tied in a wheelchair, with some sort of rubber ball device strapped into her mouth.

"Now we have a quorum," Haldis announced. "Be sure and take notes, Miss Dale."

Haldis got to her knees astride my hips. "What can you tell me about the investigation?" she asked.

"I can answer that better if you tell me what you want to know," I answered.

"I know I'm a suspect," she continued, "and I know they're after me. I need to know exactly, and I mean precisely, what they think they have on me."

So that was it. Haldis had missed the memory card and she wanted to know if they had found it. For Samantha's sake, if not for mine, I couldn't gamble on Haldis' reaction if I told her the truth. If she were truly psycho, she might go kill-crazy at the bad news. I had to keep her guessing.

"Because you turned up missing at about the same time Granville held me hostage with a rifle, some of them think you were in on it with him," I said. "Since you and Granville both had access to the negotiable bonds that are missing."

"But on what evidence?" Haldis asked, gazing meaningfully at the choke rope. "Why were they so interested in my video studio?"

"Because they thought it might give them some clue as to your whereabouts," I replied. It wasn't a lie. They had investigated the studio for that reason initially.

Haldis fingered the rope thoughtfully. "I'm not satisfied with that answer," she said. "I think I'll give you a little motivation to answer in more detail."

Haldis stripped me down far enough to make access easy, and positioned herself astride me. Having made the seating comfortable for herself, she began her work. The room was silent except for some creaking for a while, and then she looked at Samantha. "I went to great lengths to spare your feelings last time," she said to Sam, "so I thought I'd just . . . even . . . things . . . up . . . this . . . time . . . arrr . . . ou . . . nnd!"

Haldis paused for a breather, much to my relief. But it didn't last. In a little while she was monkeying with that rope again. Traffic moved in the street. A couple of cats railed at each other outside. The sounds had something to do with sex and something with violence as well. A fit accompaniment.

I'd be lying if I said I didn't enjoy the first one. But Haldis wasn't in the mood for long intermissions. She tugged at the rope around my neck. I realized she had rigged it to run through a sheaf somewhere behind me for convenience sake. When it produced the effect she wanted, she mounted up again.

"A woman can't rape a man," the old saw goes, but it plainly isn't true. We had a long night of it, what with Haldis' versatility, my growing discomfort, and Samantha's muffled protests. Plus, winter had rolled around, and the floor was cold.

"I'm going to lean forward," Haldis said once, before changing positions. "If you bite me, I'll kill you." After that she didn't talk much, just grunted her satisfaction.

At the end, when the ant had decided there was no more sap in the aphid, she rose with a sigh.

Haldis retrieved her clothes and put them on. She knelt beside me and squeezed my lips into a pucker between her fingers. "The next time we meet you may well be a daddy," she said in the kind of voice you'd use on a cute puppy dog. She turned to Sam. "And your little rich baby will probably have a younger brother walking around somewhere." She paused at the door and turned back. "Or maybe it will be a girl."

The wheelchair vibrated and thumped at this, but Samantha was still helpless.

"It's been loads of fun," Haldis concluded, and left.

Samantha shifted in her chair an inch at a time and eventually passed out of sight, headed for the kitchen. Half an hour later she reappeared on foot. She liberated me and we both drank bottled water for a long time, belching but not bothering to say "excuse me." Then Samantha helped me up the stairs. How had Haldis Pike managed to pull off such an epic string of wanton murders? I wondered as I dragged myself up the steps. Maybe some mysteries are not worth solving. Neither Samantha nor I said as much, but both of us had had our fill of Haldis Pike.

We hadn't spoken a word since the door had closed behind our unwelcome visitor. Samantha finally broke the silence as we crawled into bed. "I thought she'd never leave," she said.

CHAPTER NINETEEN:

THIRD BEST

"I'M GLAD YOU DECIDED to stay home today," Samantha told me the next morning.

"I was afraid the wind might blow me over," I replied. "Is there any more vitamin E in that bottle?'

"You shouldn't have any more," she answered. "Anything over fifteen hundred I.U.s is considered an overdose."

"So, what happens if I take more?" I asked.

"You could experience blurred vision, weakness, nausea and diarrhea," it says on the package," Samantha answered.

"I've got most of those already," I complained.

"Here, have some more vitamin C," she suggested.

"I'd already had three," I said. "Won't I overdose on that?"

"No," Samantha replied. "Vitamin C is a water-soluble antioxidant, and the way you're drinking water you need some more of it. How does the neck feel?"

"Not nearly as bad as it did after we got away from that trap on Fifth Avenue," I answered, "but I guess it's back to the turtleneck again for a while."

"I like you in the turtleneck," Samantha said.

"I did, too, until I saw Temple Worthington wearing one," I told her.

Samantha fluffed up my pillow, pulled up the ratchetting footboard, and sat at the foot of the bed facing me. My bed has a headboard at both ends when you do that, with a good light attached to each. Maybe I should patent the idea. "You must like intellectual girls," Samantha had said the first time she saw it. She thought she was kidding.

"Okay, now back to the story," Samantha said. "But I'd like you to skip the four years you served on the police force, and go to the part where you broke out and became a private detective."

"That actually happened twice," I told her. "Do you want to hear about the first one, where I got stiffed, or the second one?"

"Got stiffed?" Samantha repeated. "Well, I guess you'd better tell me that one, so I can get an explanation of what you mean."

So I told her.

When I got back to New York from the ill-fated trip to the Middle-East I swore I'd never leave the city again. I finished college with difficulty and picked up some momentum in the police academy. I was really good at all the physical stuff involved in getting onto the force, but the Minnesota Mining or whatever they called the test that was supposed to gauge your attitude about things was a problem.

That test was a safety net to keep guys with a chip on their shoulder off the force, and my chip was a big one. I had to keep uppermost in mind what it was they wanted me to reveal. It was clear that the police were interested in culling out candidates that might have some kind of a compulsive disorder. The "counting" questions were a tip-off to that: "Do you find yourself counting street signs, lamp posts, etc.?" and "I wish I could stop counting such and such." Those are questions you have to stay away from. The test makers were really hung up on questions like that. I counted twenty-seven of them.

So I managed to out-guess that test, and make it onto the force. I was carrying those fifty lashes around with me every minute of the three years I played backup and flunky for a dozen other cops, low man on every duty roster. It was looking as if maybe I had painted the wrong profile of myself by cheating on that test.

I got a chance to make a move, though, because one cop had seen right through me. It was a chance that almost changed my career from police Officer to private detective in the space of a few hours. A year later the real thing happened on a bridge in Turkey, but this event got me ready for that one.

When it started, I was standing at a lane in the indoor firing range in the basement of the precinct house, South Manhattan patrol district. Captain Dowell Childress came in. He made a show of looking around, but by the way he came up to me I knew he had really come there for me specifically.

I was expecting "hello Turley." Instead, I got: "A big shot's daughter has been kidnaped by terrorists. They're calling for two million in ransom."

I'm not superstitious ordinarily, but I felt a little twinge at that moment, like when a black cat gets in your way in the street.

"Will he pay?" I asked, wondering why Childress was confiding this to a lowly plainclothesman at the bottom of the list to make detective.

"He can afford it but he can't pay it," Childress answered. "If it came out that he was handing money over to people who were killing citizens of the U.S. he couldn't get elected meter maid." Childress told me the man's name, a famous politician. And a guy who could pay that amount out of petty cash.

Okay, maybe Childress needed some low-profile guy he could trust to keep his mouth shut. I didn't really think so, though. How much did this guy really know about me, anyway?

"So, you want me to deliver the ransom?" I asked.

"No," Childress answered, "I want you to kill the terrorists and save the girl."

I glanced toward the two cops on the end of the firing line. Both consistently shot higher range scores than I did. I was going to play dumb as long as I could.

Childress read the look, but he was way ahead of me.

"I picked you because of what's in your locker," he told me.

That explained it. I couldn't even gripe about the fact that he'd been nosing around in my locker. Childress could only be referring to the Arab headdress and the special holster I kept in there. A fake Koran with a gun inside it.

"Yeah, I know about that little murder kit," Childress told me. "You're the wannabe who studies Hamlet in case an actor breaks his leg."

I had no comeback for that remark. There was no disguising the intention behind a pair of objects like that in a police locker. As long as you knew about those lashes across the back, that is, and the captain obviously did. He had come to the correct conclusion that I was waiting for just the kind of proposition he was talking about.

But now that the opportunity had actually arisen, the burr under my saddle that I had expected to goad me on, make me impervious to fear, was gone. A cold chill had hit my gut, because people were going to die and I'd probably be one of them.

But maybe I had a way to back out of danger without giving away just how scared I was. I'd impose a condition Childress couldn't agree to.

"I keep the money," I said.

"I . . . you what?" Childress returned, astonished.

"I kill the perps, save the girl, and keep the money," I answered.

Childress couldn't speak at first. He wanted to hit me so badly it hurt him not to.

"If you've got the nerve to tell him that," he answered through his teeth, "then tell him." He turned on his heel. "Let's go," he said. "I've wasted all the time I can here."

We started toward my locker so I could gear up. "Either way," Childress seethed as we walked, "you'll be off the force."

The headdress was an authentic keffiyeh, well-worn. Seaman Kalid Ben-Ali, misplaced desert nomad, had given it to me the day after I saved the Morning Dove; one of several gifts of clothing I'd received from grateful crew members.

I was as annoyed at Childress by this time as he was at me. Out of sheer bravado I stuck the .357 magnum revolver I'd been shooting with into the book.

"Six, huh?" Childress asked. "Think you'll get them to line up for you?"

I put on my tactical vest, an extra–large shirt, and stuck a Glock down the back of my pants for insurance. "Line up?" I wondered. How the hell many of them were there?

"What are the odds?" I asked. It was about time I thought of that.

"Four to one," Childress answered.

I looked at him.

"Maybe more," he continued, watching for my reaction.

I switched the revolver out for another Glock. Let him have his little victory. "What's the setup?" I asked.

"They've got her somewhere on a stretch of adjoining rooftops," Childress answered. "Six-story tenement buildings on the lower east side. They have lookouts in every direction, including high buildings a mile away. And the time element is critical. It's impossible to get an effective force in there without being detected. At least not in time. They'd kill her and maybe even get away. Although that part doesn't seem to really matter to them."

"Then the exchange is supposed to take place up there?" I asked.

"Yeah, up there," Childress answered. "They've agreed to let one cop follow behind the go-between to keep the trade-off honest. One cop, and all he gets to use is a riot gun, which probably won't do much good. They can pick their range up there on the roofs."

"I'm the go-between, then?" I asked. "As well as the Trojan Horse."

"Something like that," Childress answered.

"What happened to the original go-between?" I asked.

"They killed him," Childress replied. "But not before he planted a microphone on the leader. We're monitoring them now."

"Why did they kill him?" I asked.

"Probably just for the heck of it," Childress replied. "They're a weird bunch of characters."

How well I knew it. I'd thought about that, night and day, for the past seven years. Long enough.

"Just one more thing," I told Childress. "Let's go out through the office. I need to make some last-minute preparations."

The Client was waiting in his limousine. I hit him with my demand that I keep the ransom at once, so I wouldn't lose my nerve. He accepted that condition, as time had almost run out. It was take a chance with me or lose both daughter and any chance at a future political career.

There were five of us. The client's chauffeur and bodyguard rode in front. The client, Childress and I rode in the back. Matt Jacobs, the cop who was to follow me with a shotgun, would already be on site waiting for us. There was no double-cross in store for me then; Matt Jacobs was the best, and he could be trusted. I wouldn't get it in the back at least

As we pulled out into traffic the client handed me a duplicate earpiece that was receiving the signal from the microphone the go-between had planted. The plan was to listen to the conversation of the terrorists on the way, but we weren't picking up a signal.

We touched down, I exchanged a few words with Matt, and he followed me up the fire escape. It was on.

We were vulnerable to attack at each section of the stairs. I was carrying a twenty-two-pound block of hundred-dollar bills wrapped in clear polyethylene. Matt was carrying an identical one, plus the wheeled carrier they would go into, and his riot gun.

A few feet up the stairs the transmission cleared up. I listened through the earpiece as we climbed.

"I don't like this, Burhan," a voice said. "Why does the meeting place have to be a rooftop surrounded on all sides by the police?"

"Rest easy, Yoosuf," Burhan answered. "They haven't deployed yet. We are guarded by patrols of children with telescopes on roofs in every direction."

"So that's why you were giving those things away like candy?" Yoosuf asked.

"You are beginning to understand," Burhan answered, laughing.

"You could have told me," Yoosuf replied hotly.

"Your report, Yoosuf," Burhan answered. "Did your call get through?"

"Yes," Yoosuf replied. "It's confirmed. The money is real, and moving toward us in a limousine."

"Good," said Burhan, "as he has parted with the money so readily, we will kill the emissary and ask for more. So far, the press has not even broken a rumor that his daughter is missing. He will pay again."

"Especially as he is imagining what is happening to the girl during the night," Yoosuf replied.

"But you haven't heard all of it yet," Burhan said. "After the second payment he'll get his daughter back. And we will speak to him personally about his feelings in regard to the experience."

"Are we to die as martyrs while our job at the paper is working so well?" Yoosuf asked, surprised. "Surely the girl would see us during the process."

"Without eyes?" Burhan asked him.

"Oh, now I understand," Yoosuf answered. "And that is why we must kill the emissary as well."

"Exactly," answered Burhan. "And speak of the devil, here comes the one we are waiting for."

I had just poked my head above the parapet of the roof. I threw my leg over the edge and sat there, re-tying my square of cloth into a keffiyeh, the scarf used throughout the Arab world to protect against the sun. I was getting my bearings and at the same time creating what I hoped was a favorable impression for the men on the roof. At least I had learned something on my world tour with Arnold Gassner.

"It is a sign," Yoosuf said.

"Yes, you don't learn to do that in an hour," Burhan replied.

They'd wait until I brought the money to them. I knew that. They weren't going to get within range of Matt's shotgun.

"He's stopped," Yoosuf said. "He's waiting."

"No," Burhan answered. "He has accepted a book from his backup man. A book with a golden clasp."

"And a piece of silk," Yoosuf added. "How carefully he wraps it in the cloth. In many layers."

It was half of a silk skirt from a high-class hooker in the lockup.

"Yes," Burhan replied. "And he holds it with reverence. He is loath to place it on the parapet or on the roof. He hands it back to the follower while he accepts the case that holds the money."

"A case on wheels," Yoosuf said.

"Of necessity," Burhan replied. "Such a sum takes up space."

"He has taken the book back from the follower," Yoosuf said. "It must be the one true book, for only a believer would know to hold it so."

I wouldn't even have needed my expensive gun carrier. What Matt handed back to me could just as easily have been the other half of that skirt, wrapped loosely around a cigar box with a gun inside. The old switcheroo.

And that test told me something. These guys were the real thing, and their minds were absorbed by the idea of divinity. I had a tiny edge.

"We shall see," Burhan replied. "Holding a Koran under his arm will not save him if he is not what he appears to be."

"Then we spare him?" Yoosuf asked. "What of the plan?"

"We shall see," Burhan answered.

"He's not moving," Yoosuf observed. "He's waiting for the girl to be brought up for the exchange."

"Signal for the men to bring her, Yoosuf," Burhan ordered.

Yoosuf signaled. "It is done," he replied. "Here they are."

Two men had been holding Melissa just inside the stairwell entrance.

"Here he comes," Yoosuf continued.

"If it is indeed the money he pulls behind him," Burhan instructed, "you three take it to safety at once. Hasan, stay with Yoosuf and me. I'm not sure I like the look of this man."

"He carries the book clutched against his heart," said Yoosuf. "As if it is dear to him, but he pulls the baggage cart behind him as if it was of little value."

"Keep an eye on him as he sets it down," Burhan warned.

I let go of the cart. Those forty yards or so had seemed like a mile, and the tiny stones in the asphalt had felt like concrete blocks. I had heard all they were saying to this point, but the feedback was getting louder as I neared them. I adjusted my keffiyeh as a signal, and the transmission was shut down. And I almost lost the gun from under my arm. That yellow streak had come back.

"Praise to the name of Allah," I said, in a voice that was startlingly loud. All the Arabic I had studied had left me. I should have said the Shahada, the believer's oath, immediately, but I had forgotten even that. Suddenly the relative positions of the other men on the roof was all I could think of.

And a further complication had arisen, that I hadn't expected. Instead of thinking of the men in front of me as targets, I found myself thinking about who might be waiting for them at home and their reactions to the news of the killings. It wasn't a good mood to be in when I'd crashed a party I couldn't leave in one piece without blood being spilled. Childress had been closer than he'd thought with that Hamlet crack. Conscience had made me a coward.

At that point I would have turned and walked away, girl or no girl, if I could have. But there was no way to say "Hey guys, I was just kidding."

"Stand very still, and speak when you are spoken to," Yoosuf told me.

"Let me look," said Burhan. He bent and opened the case. "Help me inspect it, Yoosuf. Careful. It is . . . it's the money. And real. There could be no mistaking it. I feel its power."

"I felt it myself," I replied, disregarding Yoosuf. "The power to persuade in many ways."

Yoosuf glared at me, but I had heard enough to know that Burhan was the leader. The lookout at the edge of the roof to my left had heard Yoosuf's warning as well, and was pointing his gun at me. I managed to take this in with my peripheral vision and keep my eyes on Burhan. His was the only opinion that mattered at that moment. He was watching me carefully, waiting for me to say something else.

The book with the gun in it was starting to slip again. The silk was soaking up my icy sweat and clutching the whole mess against my chest had caused the gold latch to spring open. I stalled for time, trying to collect my wits.

"You can't be near this much money without feeling the potential for what it can do," I managed to continue. "I'm glad to be rid of the burden of responsibility."

"Well spoken," returned Burhan. The wheels were turning. He still hadn't decided about me.

"There are six of you," I said. "I was told there would be four."

"The others are clerics," Burhan replied. "It is necessary, to do proper respect to your burden. Take it away, Fareed, and you two as well."

"Then the bargain is concluded?" I asked. "I am required to take a good look at the girl."

Without prompting, the two men escorting Melissa held her in place in response.

"Yes, that's her," I said. "Very well, let's bring the meeting to an end."

"There is something else," Burhan replied. "How did you come to be sent for the exchange?"

"Something else?" I repeated. "But your men have walked away with the money."

"What are you?" Burhan asked. "It is possible that you are in a position to be of service to us. Or have you ignorantly approached us in a manner that profanes the name of Allah? We have to know."

I was experiencing a total mental blank. I stalled some more.

"I anticipated your question, my friend," I told him. "And I have come prepared with the answer."

"Fortune smiles on us both," Burhan said wryly. "Speak."

So that was it, then. Burhan had tumbled to me. But if I was going to die it was still possible that I could get the girl out of harm's way. I tried one more dodge. It was all I had left.

"What I have to say is not for the ears of this young one," I told Burhan. "May I send her to the end of the roof now?

Burhan looked at the gun in his hand and heaved a weary sigh. He was a man burdened with decisions, and he was only ninety-five percent sure he was going to kill me. He didn't believe I was the real thing, but was still entertaining the idea that I might have something important to tell him.

"Yes, go on," Burhan answered. "Walk slowly, girl, but not too far. Stop just out of earshot. We are not quite finished with you yet."

"Go on, Melissa," I told her. Burhan was only playing with me, but at least Melissa was a few feet closer to Matt.

"But I, ah," Melissa said, "think there's something you should know . . ."

Bad luck. She was trying to warn me about them, and that would be sheer disaster.

"No more talk, Melissa," I interrupted. "Walk on by."

Melissa obeyed. She had passed by me only a few yards before Burhan quit playing.

"That's far enough, girl," Burhan ordered. "Stop there."

"Please, easy with that gun," I told him. "I have worked hard to gain the trust of these people. It will reflect poorly on me if they see you pointing it at her."

"They can't see it," Burhan replied. "They're too far away. All right, now you can talk without fear of compromise. Who did it?"

"Did what?" I asked.

"Sent you here like this," Burhan returned. "You're not a believer. Why are you pretending to be?"

Suddenly I remembered something from that trip with Arnold. I pretended to be insulted. "Am I not?" I answered haughtily. "I have touched the Hajar-al-Aswad. Have you?"

That threw him off guard. "How do you even know . . . ?" he began. "You have touched the Black Stone?"

"By Allah's grace," I answered.

"What do you see on the other corner of the Kaaba, before you reach the Black Stone?" Burhan asked suspiciously.

"The stone wall of the building is exposed in a spot the size of the area around the Black Stone," I answered. "This is the Yemen Corner."

"And the other two corners?" Burhan pursued.

"They are shielded by the rounded enclosure at the back of the Kaaba," I answered. "The building was once rectangular, and when it was cut down this area was saved and enclosed for prayers."

"One final question," Burhan continued. "Is there anything else behind the Kaaba?"

"The Footprint of Abraham in a glass and gilded metal enclosure," I answered.

The mental block was gone. Other names were coming back.

And that was good, because Burhan hadn't finished. "The three devils?" he asked quickly. "Name them."

"Al-Aqaba, al-Wusta, and al-Ula," I answered as quickly. I couldn't forget those names. I had watched several hundred people lose their lives in an attempt to throw stones at them from the Jamarat Bridge. The Stoning of the Devil.

And it came back to me. The Shahada in good Arabic. I stood tall and looked toward the sky. "Ash-hadu . . ." I began. It takes a long time to get the phrase out when you're being dramatic about it, and I was.

It was the looking up that did the trick. Misdirection. It works doubly well with people who think there is something to see up there. I slipped the gun out of its carrier and shot Burhan under the chin and Yoosuf in the forehead.

That cleared my line of sight for the other two near me. Two snap shots and square hits.

I shot the fifth one before he had dropped the money case, but the sixth, the man beside the parapet, was faster than I expected. He shot me in the chest at the same time I fired at him. I didn't see where I hit him, because he went off the roof from the impact.

I flew back across the tarred roof, hit by a high caliber pistol shot.

I must have blacked out for a second or so. "Mr. Turley. Mr. Turley!" came a voice.

I grunted in pain, trying to get my breath. "Melissa," I said. "What are you doing here?"

"You're shot," she answered. "I came back to help you."

"I'm all right," I told her. "I'm wearing a vest, but it still hurts." That wasn't half of it. The Glock I'd stuck down the back of my pants for insurance had gone off and burned a groove down my left buttock. I got to my feet and snatched up the money case. To heck with the wheels.

"Let's get out of here," I said. "Or we may have some others up here."

"You killed them all," Melissa replied. She hadn't moved yet. "They . . . look so different, lying there. What were you telling them?"

"Lies," I said, pushing her along. "I cheated."

"They had it coming, believe me," she said. "They . . . did things to me. Both the ones you were talking to."

"So that's how it was?" I asked, coming to a halt. "Can you handle some advice, Melissa?"

"I'm listening," she answered.

Your father is sitting in a car about half a block down the street," I told her. "He's had a tough time. Save the details about what happened for a therapist. Spare him the grief."

"You're right," Melissa replied. "Thanks for the warning. I'm kind of off balance. I'll do that."

I got her moving again. "That's what I wanted to hear, Melissa," I told her. "Let's get you home."

Then it turned out there was so much heat I didn't get my payoff at all. Or rather, my payoff was that I didn't get prosecuted for the shootings. It wasn't fair, and I didn't have an easy time adjusting to the fact, either. "Things aren't that simple, Boy," Captain Childress told me. "A lot of money goes through a lot of hands to straighten out a situation like this, and there's not going to be any left for you." He watched me carefully to see how I was taking it. If I was going to blow up, now was the time I'd do it.

"Eighty to life, that's what you'd be looking at instead of a promotion," Childress went on. "A good job and an opportunity to do your twenty with a lot of good will surrounding you is the alternative. A smart cop would jump at that."

I kept my cool. The hitch was that two of the men I shot were local recruits, young guys. They had family in that very building. To protect the Big-wig there had to be payoff, on the spot. Yes, the cops stiffed me for the reward for saving the girl, but I stayed on the force anyway. And from that point on I set out to prepare for the time when I'd run my own agency. Sometimes incentive will take you farther than money. I hung around communications and asked questions about the computers. The brass gave me a lot of leeway, because they had put away a lot of cash when they ripped me off. I'm no geek, but within a year I was able to look through police files on my computer at home. That was going to come in handy.

Matt Jacobs got some of the money, though. He was content with his small payoff. Why was he due a reward at all? Because it hadn't been my bullet that hit that final terrorist. It had been a deer slug from Matt's shotgun that took the perp out of action. I hadn't been the best marksman on that roof after all. I was the third best.

"Some story," Samantha said. She was now lying next to me. "Like the others. But due to the nature of some of the acts you're admitting to I'm beginning to feel a little like Scheherazade in One Thousand and One Nights. Except that I'm the one who has to keep you telling the stories so I won't get bumped off."

Was that a cry for comfort? I wondered. I rolled over and wrapped her gently in my arms. "Then maybe I should point out that a wife can't testify against her husband," I told her.

But we still knew that we hadn't worked out the one final question that could serve as an obstacle between us: who was boss?

CHAPTER TWENTY:

NIGHTMARE RALLY

I HAD PUT IN A PRODUCTIVE week, or perhaps I should say that Ida had. She had accepted a number of routine security accounts and checked on their progress without any input from me except for an occasional okay. No new strange cases had popped up, and no threats had appeared.

Samantha had been busy, too. She'd opened her practice again, accepting a new doctor who was nominally her partner but in essence an employee. She probably wouldn't practice again, though, she told me. And she had subleased her apartment.

Then, Saturday morning, I woke up screaming. It wasn't a new thing. I'd done it often. Beside me, Samantha woke up, too. She turned on the light and looked around, trying to orient herself. Maybe she'd been dreaming too, I thought.

I had woken Samantha this way once too often. "Turley, we have to deal with this," she told me. "What was the nightmare about? You know, I think I could help you with them. The cause is probably an unconscious conflict."

I knew what she meant. Stories are one thing, but what she was talking about meant giving her deeper access. Well, I wanted the bad dreams to stop, so maybe it was worth the risk of getting my tether shortened another notch.

"And what do you shrinks do about that?" I asked.

Samantha rubbed her eyes. "We'd use free association for a first meeting," she answered, "But knowing that latent content is being revealed in your dreams will help here."

Samantha had decided for both of us. She got up and took a seat in a chair to the left of the bed, out of my line of sight. I heard paper rattling and the cap came off a pen.

"Describe your dream in detail," Samantha instructed. "It may take us to the source of the problem."

"How does that work?" I asked.

Samantha stifled a yawn. "We all constantly censor what we say," she answered, "And this goes double for people who have to deal in confidential matters as private investigators do."

"Makes sense," I said.

"This process allows us to hide some of our thoughts from ourselves," Samantha continued.

"I've heard that it isn't good practice to psychoanalyze somebody you're shacking up with," I said. "That makes sense to me, too. What if it turns out that I'm somehow psychologically allergic to you?"

"That's a chance we'll have to take," Samantha answered. "You want the truth, don't you?"

I felt the finely woven cotton sheet with my fingers. This bed was a good place, a comforting place, for more than one reason. But Samantha had the deciding vote, for the same reason I'd paid four hundred bucks for that set of sheets.

"Okay, I'll tell you about it," I agreed reluctantly. "Yes, the same nightmare has happened before. I dream that I am some kind of animal. I have been shot, and I am running around in circles in an enclosure that is made up of people holding pieces of plywood in front of them, forming a wall.

"What kind of animal?" Samantha asked.

"I don't know," I answered, becoming more relaxed. "No, it's a . . . I'm a pig in the dream."

"A personal pun, I'd say, for your profession," Samantha remarked. "Your subconscious doesn't differentiate between a policeman and a private eye."

"I guess that's right," I allowed, relaxing even further.

"What do the people in your dream look like?" Samantha asked.

"They're smiling," I answered. "And their heads are way above me."

"Is it an evil, or a benevolent-looking smile?" she asked.

"It . . . seems kind of neutral," I answered.

"Their heads are above you, and they seem to be looking down on you," Samantha repeated. "That's it: they think they're superior."

I agreed, with a faint murmur. I was running in a circle below the faces now, slowly.

"Try to see the enclosure more clearly," Samantha instructed. "You say it is plywood?"

"It's dirty," I answered. "It's coated with the dust I've kicked up as I ran around."

"What's behind the dust?" she asked. "Can you see?"

"I see designs," I answered. "Curls and squiggles. All geometrically balanced. Oh, my God. It's . . . they're prayer rugs."

I jumped off the bed. Tears were streaming from my eyes. I felt as ashamed of that as I had the first and only time I had backed down from a bully in grade school

"I know what's wrong," I said. "I've been hiding the fear that gripped me on that rooftop in the Lower East Side."

Samantha had crumpled the papers. She set them aside. "You've only been hiding one part of it," she replied. "Isn't that it? The part where the pig dies. The part where five guns swung toward you at the same instant."

She was right. I hadn't described that part to her.

"Do you think this . . . uh, breakthrough will stop the nightmare?" I asked.

"That has been the pattern in my practice," Samantha answered, "But there are no guarantees. Now would you like to go for two?"

I wasn't sure what she meant, but I kept myself from looking at the bed. Instead, I steered by context.

"You know about the second dream?" I asked.

"Yes," Samantha answered. "In the nightmare you had just now you were guarding your chest with your hand. The other one seems worse. You just make tormented faces and change position, but it goes on and on. Are those two your only recurring dreams?"

I had to think. "I believe so," I answered.

"Want to describe the other one for me?" she asked.

I settled back and relaxed. I could hardly refuse, after the demonstration she had just given me.

"I've had this one for a dozen years," I told her. "In the dream I'm walking down the sidewalk, mid-town, and a massive safe just misses me, falling from about fifty stories above. A huge egg falls at the same time. It splatters on the sidewalk to the other side of me, covering me with muck."

"How big an egg?" Samantha asked.

"The size of a man," I answered. "Then a huge white wolf smashes through the door of the safe and buries his head in the remains of the egg."

"The remains?" Samantha repeated.

"Yes," I answered. "Then the egg turns into the body of a man. He has no head, but a turban, a Hindu turban I think, unrolls itself onto the sidewalk from where the head should be."

"And them?" Samantha asked.

"The wolf turns into a creature that is half wolf and half man," I continued. "It is wrapped in cloth with a kind of flower design on it. Suddenly it is back in the safe and is gathering the broken fragments of steel around it. It looks at me and says 'Better safe than sorry.' And then I wake up."

"Such puns are not unusual in dreams," Samantha answered. "Dreams are essentially all puns, in fact."

"What pun?" I asked.

"The turban implies an Indian man," she answered. "The flowered cloth is a sari."

That hurt. "I'd hate to admit to a groaner like that one even in my sleep," I told her. "I'd have to vote against you on that idea."

"We'll see," Samantha replied. "Have you had any significant dealings with an Indian National?"

I paused to think. "There were several of them on the ship I served on," I told her.

Samantha paused, too. "You wouldn't have gone calmly to that answer if that were the latent content we're looking for," she said. "Let's go back further. Why don't you begin by telling me what motivated you to become a detective? Not your childhood play, but whatever event led you to the profession."

"You mean tell you how far back the beginning of Word to the Wise Investigations goes?" I asked her.

"Yes," Samantha replied, "take me to the root, the origin."

"That's about fifteen years of story," I told her. "It probably starts with the time I had to step in at the University's free speech area to help a scrawny little guy who was being threatened by a football player for something he said."

"Was this a violent intervention?" Samantha asked.

"Yes," I replied. "I ended up knocking a few of his teeth out."

"Oh, an actual fight?" she asked.

"Yes," I continued. "We left the speech area because he challenged me to go behind the building. The funny part was how he explained the damage to his teammates and coach."

"And how did he explain the injury?" Samantha asked.

"He said he was practicing wind sprints in the botanical gardens," I answered, "and he hit a piece of wood that was suspended by a guy wire that ran through it."

"Suspended?" Samantha asked.

"A tree branch had grown around the guy wire," I explained. "When the groundskeepers removed the tree, they had cut off the ends of the branch. A chunk of wood was hanging there. Actually, it was a pretty plausible story."

"I see," Samantha told me.

"But the funny part was that I did him a favor," I went on. "He didn't do well in the pros, but he replaced those teeth with some beauties. And he's a sports commentator on TV right now. Cable."

"And that incident, you say, influenced later developments?" Samantha pursued.

"Yes, in a way," I answered. "Because the guy I protected ended up hiring me to be a kind of bodyguard, caddy and orderly for him."

"You mean Arnold Gassner," she noted. "Resulting somehow in your eventually becoming a detective?"

"That's right," I answered.

"Let's go over those experiences in linear order," she directed.

I retold the events of the Haj in Arabia, the voyage up the Red Sea on the Laughing Dove, and my trip through France to Paris. Nothing seemed significant enough to her to cause that dream about the wolf.

Then I got to a part I hadn't mentioned before. The part where I was coming out of the Laundromat in Paris with Ferenc Carette. Actually, the day after, because I hadn't made it to the airport. Carette had miscalculated about the striking medics and the gurney. They had calmly watched me push it down to the laundromat and then they'd had me arrested by a cop from around the corner.

To make up for his mistake Carette got me released on his recognizance at the station and kept me from going to jail. I wasn't twenty-one yet, and he lied and said I was a relative from the States. I wasn't familiar with the customs of France, he said, and he'd keep an eye on me at his apartment until I was ready to be shipped home.

Scratch one more airline ticket. Carette would replace that one for me too, he said. And until the S.M.U.R. complaint was cleared up I could help him with a case by doing some research for him.

Delphine was helping on the case as well. My job was to assist her by making follow-up inquiries to various archives, libraries, and private collectors she had contacted. We were searching for the source of a certain letter, an old one. Carette had a copy of it. One page, with no salutation, no signature, and no real clue in its context. All Carette knew was that it held the key to whether or not a client of his went to prison for life.

What the letter did say, however, was pretty attention-getting. It claimed that a second version of a certain painting by Raphael existed. A painting that would be worth tens of millions.

The case was one I had some background to help with, because my aunt had been a docent at the Metropolitan Museum of Art. She was often steering tour groups through noisy crowds, and she liked to lecture to me while I was working out on my karate practice post. It was a home-made Wing Chun, constructed from salvaged wood and padded with discarded hawser rope. It popped and rumbled as I struck it. That challenged her concentration, she said, and in the process, I had absorbed some of the material from her lectures.

"A client of mine has been convicted of murder," Carette had explained. "He was accused of killing an art dealer for a painting that was a second version of Raphael's Portrait of a Cardinal that's in the Prado Museum in Spain. Supposedly, the second painting was also an original Raphael."

"How does the letter we're trying to track down enter into it," I asked.

"Either my client, Michael Parness, is guilty," Carette answered, "Or the man who got him convicted, Mario Carducci, is. But I'll start with a third person, the victim. He was an art dealer named Paul Bazelli. And he was Carducci's partner in a gallery they owned."

"Got it," I said.

"Now Bazelli claimed he had a page of a letter, a single page of it about five hundred years old. A letter that established the existence of a copy of the Raphael."

"Raphael's Portrait of a Cardinal?" I asked, just to be sure.

"Right," Carette answered. "So then Bazelli came up with a painting he thought was the missing one. He got in touch with Parness, art expert, to help authenticate it. Showed him the letter. This is according to Parness."

"Okay," I said. "I'm following."

"But Carducci says he came into the back room of the studio the next day and found Bazelli dead and Parness unconscious. Locked door mystery stuff, witnesses and all."

"And you think it's a setup, right," I asked Carette.

"One of them is lying," Carette answered. "Parness woke up confused. Circumstantial evidence, fingerprints and such, was against him. Stuff that can be faked, if you're clever enough. Carducci, I think, set it all up so he'd not only get the gallery, but maybe an authentication of the Raphael as well."

"A pretty risky play," I said.

"A very nervy one," Carette replied. "Carducci threw in a slick psych job on Parness that clinched it. 'Must be some other explanation,' Carducci said, there at the scene. He pretended he didn't know about the letter; a letter that would establish a strong motive. And there in the middle of the room was a dinner plate with the ashes of a sheet of paper. Very old paper with one tiny corner left. Parness, confused, took the bait and clammed up about the letter."

"I think I see what's coming," I said.

"You guessed it," Carette continued. "In the courtroom, just at the psychologically best moment for the jury to see it, the prosecution produced that single page. The authorities had dug it up from a hiding place in the room, still under police cordon. Clear chain of evidence. Case closed."

"I suppose they had run a drug test on Parness," I said, "To see if they could account for the state he was in?"

"Sure," Carette answered, "but it was inconclusive."

"Right," I said.

"I got in on the case late," Carette continued. "I think I could have helped if Parness had called me in before he did, but maybe I'm just bragging."

"How much was the gallery worth?" I asked.

"Doesn't matter," Carette answered. "People have been known to kill for pocket change."

"True," I answered. "So now you're down to finding the source of that letter, to see if you can connect it to Carducci?"

"That would be great," Carette replied. "But we've got something else, too. Delphine has found another portrait, possibly by Raphael, of the same person."

"Same unknown Cardinal, right?" I asked.

"That's what Delphine thinks," Carette answered, "And so do I. But the owner identifies the subject as Matthew Lang, Bishop of Gurk. Early sixteenth century politico."

"Doesn't sound Italian," I said.

"German," Carette replied, placing a couple of photos of known portraits of Lang on the table. One was a painting, and one was a drawing by Albrecht Dürer. In both Lang had floppy jaws and small squinty eyes. He looked nothing like Raphael's Cardinal from the Prado Museum.

"Which brings us to another aspect of the letter," Carette said. "It's written in Italian, as you'd expect from a Cardinal, but part of it is in German as well. Mixed in are a few Latin phrases and a few French terms."

Carette placed a sheet of paper onto the table. "This is an English translation of the letter," he told me.

The letter read: *". . . you for the gift of the excellent wine by courier. We all enjoyed it at table that very night, and some were so impudent as to compare it with that of my own vineyard. At length I began to suspect their contest was a ruse by which to repeat the testing of one vintage against the other. I indulged my assemblage until the moment at which I felt they had reached the pinnacle of receptivity but had not yet for the most part descended into drunkenness. Then I sprung the trap, for I wanted them to speak their true opinions of my new acquisition with tongues unguarded by complete sobriety. It was then that I unveiled the second depiction of me by Raphael di Sanzi, who has by talent and grace risen above that unbathed beggar who designed your costume. At first the viewers seemed unimpressed, but then I realized that they had simply been struck dumb by the unexpected appearance of a second Cardinal in their midst. I had placed the painting in such a position that the illusion of roundness and solidity of the picture had achieved its maximum effect. There followed a succession of individual testaments to the indisputable likeness Raphael had achieved on this second attempt, and expressions of wonderment that I had been able to elicit a second work from a master whose efforts are in such demand that it is impossible for anyone short of the Pontiff himself to beg time of him. I dispelled the mystery by explaining that the magic had resided in the course of the first sitting. Some have told me that my gaze has a certain power to stimulate in the imagination of others the vision of possible discomforts which might befall them should they. . ."*

And the letter broke off as it had started, in the middle of a sentence. "Wow," I said. "He got that much on one page? What about paragraphs?"

I looked up to see that Delphine had arrived while I was reading the letter. I had been so absorbed by it I hadn't heard her knock on the door.

"I think paragraphs are a modern invention," Carette answered. He took a photograph out of a folder. Eight by ten.

"Here's the painting," Carette continued. "Delphine and I think Carducci's painting is a forgery, and that this is the one referred to in the letter."

"Could the letter be a forgery?" I asked, just to make sure.

"Every expert says it's authentic, so far," Carette replied. "Paris has access to the best."

Delphine had brought bad news with her. "Trouble," she informed Carette. "I'm sorry to tell you, but I just got a phone call from the owner, one Peter Margrave. He sold the painting to an anonymous buyer. He refuses to disclose the identity of the purchaser."

"One step forward and one step back," Carette said. "What if I called Margrave?"

"He seemed adamant," Delphine replied. "The buyer wanted its destination to remain a secret. Margrave would only say that it has gone to 'the one place in the world that it truly belongs.'"

"Cryptic," Carette said. "And there's no chance of getting a court order to look at it on the evidence we have."

The three of us sat at the table and examined the photo of Margrave's supposed portrait of Matthew Lang next to the one of Raphael's Madrid Cardinal. It seemed to depict the same subject, but in profile, light against dark. The prominent nose showed evidence of a break that hadn't been apparent in the three-quarter view, but I'd have bet it was the same man.

"A strict profile view," Carette mused. "Why would the master of masters use that simpler and much easier pose?"

"The one in profile looks a little older," Delphine commented, "But that's because of the harsh, chiseled effect that comes from that pose, I think."

"I agree," said Carette. "The lines at the side of his face are accentuated, and that strong nose as well."

I couldn't add anything, but something about the image seemed familiar.

"There's no way anyone who admired Lang enough to buy a picture of him would want that one," I said. "It doesn't look like him in the least." I pointed to the images of Lang on the table. "There's an official painting of him and also a drawing by Albrecht Dürer, so the buyer couldn't be confused about it."

Then I remembered what was familiar about this second painting by Raphael. "Wait a minute," I exclaimed. "I just recalled a conversation at my friend Arnold Gassner's house, about a Dürer engraving. The one called 'Knight, Death and Devil.'"

"And so?" Carette asked.

"Arnold's guardian Hoagland had studied that print for years," I explained. "He thought that the real identity of the knight was a man named Matthew Schiner. Hoagland had a whole list of evidence he thought he could see in the print."

Carette looked puzzled, perhaps suspecting that I was wasting valuable time.

"Wait a minute," Delphine said, "I know where this is going. Sure, Matthew Lang was appointed Cardinal for a brief period of time, for political reasons. But Matthew Schiner was a Cardinal too. And the favorite of Pope Julius II. Are you about to tell us that this Hoagland thought Schiner was Raphael Sanzio's Cardinal as well as Albrecht Dürer's knight?"

"Yes," I answered. "Hoagland was convinced of that."

Delphine pulled an image of Dürer's "Knight, Death and Devil" up on Carette's computer.

"It's hard to form an opinion," Carette said, looking at the print on the screen.

"Arnold's print was an early impression," I said. "Clear and detailed. This computer view is not as sharp."

"I don't know," Delphine said, "Thousands of scholars have examined that engraving and . . . say, the knight does look kind of like Margrave's profile version of Raphael's Cardinal."

"One of Hoagland's main points," I told them, "was that the horse the knight is riding looks a lot like Leonardo da Vinci's Sforza horse."

"Da Vinci's Sforza horse," Delphine repeated. "It was the symbol of Milan."

"So what?" Carette asked.

"Well, in 1513," Delphine answered, "when Dürer engraved the print, Schiner was in charge of Milan, right there in the city."

"Interesting," Carette replied. "Raphael's Cardinal was painted in 1510, so that tallies. Did Schiner have vineyards?"

Delphine tapped at her keyboard. "Yes," she answered, "as Bishop of Sion he did. It's still the city's major industry, and there's a tiny vineyard there now that's named for him."

"Is that Sion, Switzerland?" Carette asked.

"Yes, Schiner was the first Cardinal from Switzerland," Delphine answered.

"The city on the hill in Dürer's print is a reference to Sion," I told them, "according to Hoagland's theory.'"

"Delphine," Carette asked, "What languages did Schiner speak?"

"German, Italian, French, English, and Latin," Delphine answered. "He was fluent in all of them."

Carette turned to me. "Is any of Hoagland's evidence in print?" he asked.

"No," I replied. "Hoagland worked on it for years, but hadn't published it."

"That's too bad," Carette replied, "because. . ."

"But Hoagland mentioned an article that made the direct claim that Raphael's Cardinal is Schiner," I interrupted. "I remember because the author had almost the same last name as the artist. It was Robert Durrer."

"I've found something," Delphine said. "Your Mister Hoagland is going to be disappointed, because somebody just published an article on Dürer's knight engraving, claiming the same thing."

"Let me look," I said. "Yes, you're right. It's in the title: 'Kardinal Mathäus Schiner as the Knight in Albrecht Dürer's

Knight, Death and Devil.' Yes, Hoagland would have killed himself if he'd seen that."

Delphine switched to the other computer while Carette and I read the new article. She read the Robert Durrer article and finished first, even though ours was in English and Delphine's was in German.

"This Robert Durrer makes a very appealing case," Delphine reported, "in view of the fact that there are no known portraits of Schiner still in existence."

"Good," Carette replied. "This other article is written poorly, though. Too bad."

"Yes," I agreed, "but still, the author has brought up a number of points Hoagland used in his study."

Carette looked over Delphine's notes and came to a decision. "I need to find the painting Margrave sold, Delphine," he said. "With the evidence of these articles and the painting there's a chance I can get Parness a new trial."

"Sion's a good bet," I offered. "That's usually how Schiner is referred to in history: 'the Bishop of Sion.'"

"So, Margrave's reference to 'the one place in the world where the painting truly belongs' could mean Sion," Carette agreed. "If Margrave knows the identity of the subject, and it sounds as if he does."

"Sion is a tourist destination," Carette said. "Medieval buildings, vineyards on steep slopes, and high prices. If they could connect Cardinal Schiner with a famous Dürer engraving, they would have one more tourist attraction."

"Then the Raphael could very well be in Sion," Delphine agreed. "And I think I know why Margrave has just recently found a buyer, when he's had the painting for years."

"I'll bite," Carette said. "Why?"

"Because Margrave showed the buyer that new article," Delphine answered, "which claims Schiner is the knight. It referred readers to the article by Robert Durrer, which claims that contemporaries got portraits of Lang mixed up with those of Schiner."

"Why would anybody back then make that mistake?" Carette asked.

"Because of a museum started close to that time," Delphine answered. "The Giovio Museum in Como, established some forty years later. Paolo Giovio mislabeled a drawing of Schiner as Lang."

"Let me see that again," Carette said, bringing up Robert Durrer's reproduction of the drawing from the Giovio museum. It looked as if it had been sketched from Margrave's painting. "And nobody else corrected Giovio?" Carette asked.

"Anybody who knew the difference would have been afraid to admit it," Delphine explained. "It's like the political correctness of today. Schiner's enemies had already destroyed every known image of him. They claimed he was a warlock. The museum would have been burned if Paolo Giovio had labelled the drawing correctly."

"They hated Schiner that much?" Carette asked.

"Absolutely," Delphine answered. "Schiner had urged Pope Julius II to enforce the so-called Donation of Constantine. Schiner recruited so many Swiss soldiers for the papal army that as a result, tens-of-thousands of French, Swiss, Germans, Austrians, English and Italians died in battle. It was the first real bloodbath in Europe. Strictly between Europeans, that is."

"So, at the end of it, Schiner wasn't so popular, eh?" Carette asked.

"Right," Delphine confirmed. "The Swiss learned a lesson about neutrality, tucked their heads in, and have prospered ever since."

"So . . . when the author of that recent article pointed out the parallels between 'Knight, Death and Devil' and Cardinal Matthew Schiner, it suggested to Margrave that Sion would want the portrait."

"Right," Delphine answered. "Sion was his home venue, and the one place he's viewed as a hero. But Margrave doesn't suspect it's a Raphael, or he'd have been bubbling with joy when I called him."

"Let's hope these conclusions are accurate, Carette said. "It will save an innocent man from a life sentence." He made a phone call to the seat of the diocese in Sion, Glarier Cathedral. He spoke with the Bishop's secretary, explained the need to find a certain painting, and that he had reason to believe it was in Sion. Carette explained that he had information that could add millions in value to the painting. Then after . . ."

And that's when Samantha stopped me.

"ONE MOMENT," SAMANTHA SAID, bringing me back to the present. "Just to clarify a point, are you telling me that this Carette dismissed the idea of obtaining the Raphael for himself without even considering the proposition for a moment?"

"That's right," I answered. "That's the kind of a man he was. I mean, is."

"Even though he was well aware that he would realize tens of millions in the process?"

"That's right," I answered. "Carette had given his word, and that was the end of it."

"I see," Samantha replied, and made an entry in her notes. "Please continue."

I put myself back at the scene, in Carette's apartment once more, waiting for the call to Glarier Cathedral to be returned. After leaving Carette on hold for a while the Bishop's secretary admitted that the Bishopric had purchased a painting like the one Carette described. The Bishop, the secretary told Carette, had been saving it as a surprise for city officials at an upcoming wine festival. And yes, the purchase had been motivated by the appearance of a recent article connecting Cardinal Schiner to the Albrecht Dürer engraving "Knight, Death and Devil."

Carette agreed to keep the Bishop's secret, as well as possible and still do justice for Parness. They arranged a meeting for the next day in the Valère castle, which would be closed to the public for the day.

"What's the Valère castle?" I asked as Carette hung up the phone.

"It's a fortified basilica," Delphine answered for him. "Built on top of a steep hill in the Rhône Valley."

She pointed to her computer screen. Two fort complexes were perched atop twin fang-like hills. It looked like something cooked up for a medieval warfare movie.

"Which one is the Valère?" I asked.

"The one on the right," Delphine answered. "The other one is Tourbillon Castle, the Bishop's residence.

"Need any help?" I asked Carette. I was hoping to see the place.

"I can't go," Delphine informed Carette. "Classes."

"You're elected, Turley," Carette replied. "We'll go by train, and that takes close to six hours. You can do some research on the way."

We left early the next day. The seat of the Bishopric of Sion had been moved to a newer building, the Glarier Cathedral, far lower down in the city than the thirteenth century Valère castle. It had been shifted downslope for the very good reason that it didn't have to be run from a fortress any more. But for our meeting with the Bishop's committee, we'd be climbing the hill to the old castle. It was a tourist attraction now, but for this special occasion it would be closed to the public. As for the Bishop himself, he couldn't come to the meeting even if it were held down in the Glarier. He was in the hospital with a bad case of gout.

A guide met us at the train station at Sion, and introduced us to the sexton, who was waiting at the foot of the hill. Out of courtesy the Bishop's secretary was going to let us go up first and wait for the committee. They were accustomed to climbing that steep hill, and would let us go up and recover for the meeting.

I knew better when we began the climb. The church officials were giving us time to absorb the grandeur of the place, and be sufficiently impressed once the meeting began.

The sexton loaded us up with facts about the place as we walked. It was hard not to gape in every direction. We were surrounded by the highest peaks of the Swiss Alps.

We entered the Valère through a wide portal with a small door set within a larger one, both made of planks over two feet wide. The sexton seated us in wooden pews that were dramatically modern-looking, but had been there for centuries; just good design.

A few minutes later a committee of eight, headed by the Bishop's secretary, followed the sexton into the Valère to join us.

"Shall we begin?" asked the secretary. The sexton disappeared into the sacristy and emerged with the painting they had purchased from Margrave. It was oil on wood panel, the same size as Raphael's Cardinal in the Prado. The portrait was much more impressive than it had looked in the photo. We were convinced.

Carette responded by showing the committee his photo copy of the single page of the letter. They were astonished. It was in the hand of Cardinal Schiner, they agreed, and the content was clear. Schiner had been talking about his own vineyards, and the 'unwashed beggar' mentioned turned out to be Michelangelo. Cardinal Schiner had recruited and organized the original Swiss Guard for the papacy, and Michelangelo had designed the uniforms.

And there was no doubt that Schiner had been talking about Raphael in the letter. Schiner, who later had missed being elected pope by one vote, had served as the main recruiter of Swiss troops for Pope Julius II. Hence the desire of the pope to keep Schiner happy with the gift of works by Raphael.

The letter would go far toward authenticating the Raphael, and in return for its recovery the committee would make the painting accessible to French authorities. Seen next to the forged painting Mario Carducci had paid somebody to make, Sion's new Raphael would expose Carducci's fraud. It would convict him of murder and free Parness.

At least that's what we thought would happen. The committee left with the painting, to show it to the Bishop.

"Enjoy a visit in the Valère alone," the secretary invited. "It is a rare privilege. When you are done, ring for the sexton."

Carette and I were both pleased, but for different reasons. He wanted to rest from a stressful trip, and I wanted to tour the place. I made a circuit, viewing paintings and sculptures.

I stopped before a huge structure that looked like the bow of a ship sticking through the wall. It was a five-sided mass of polished wood, sticking out of the wall twelve feet above the floor. It held up the base of the Valère's organ, the sexton had told us. An organ so big that the wall had been built around the pipes for support.

The top part of the structure was a massive wooden barrier designed to conceal the organist. According to the plaque on the wall beneath it, it was the oldest playable organ in the world, dating from 1380. Too bad Carette and I wouldn't be able to hear it played. Its protective panels, medieval works of art themselves, were closed over the pipes.

At long last, I thought, something had gone right in this Odyssey of mine. Carette and I had come to the end of a difficult quest that accomplished several goals at once.

Then, like the big ugly insect unfolding itself in Alien, a creaking came from the wooden enclosure surrounding the hidden instrument. Had someone gone to sleep while polishing the pipes of the organ, I wondered. And so did Carette, who had just arrived to see if I was ready to go. It was then that two men in tailored silk suits finished their descent down a hidden stair within the wall and into the nave.

"It's Carducci," Carette told me, as the two men approached us.

The man on the left glared at Carette while the man on the right looked me over. "Do you have any idea how much damage you've done to me?" the one I took for Carducci asked Carette.

"You have some options left, Carducci" Carette answered calmly. "A deposition from you will free my client. After that, whatever you do will . . ."But Carette didn't get to finish the statement. Carducci was in the process of drawing a gun from his jacket.

I HAD FINISHED THE STORY, nearly. "That's when I panicked," I told Samantha, "despite all the training sessions at home and the free lessons from martial arts experts in the park. And I killed my first man."

The story had absorbed me in the telling, and I found that I was looking at the wall instead of at Samantha. "It wasn't necessary," I continued, turning to face her. "I could easily have taken the guns away from them, and the problem would have been resolved."

"Guns?" Samantha asked.

"Yes," I answered, "But the other man hadn't drawn his yet. He never got a chance to."

Samantha watched, waiting for me to complete the story.

"I could tell by their stances that neither man knew the first thing about martial arts," I continued. "They had no defense as I swept the backup man's leg and broke Carducci's larynx. I had lost control completely, and I added to the carnage by accelerating the first man's fall toward the stone floor. His skull split and . . . the floor got very messy."

Samantha stirred in her chair. "And the other?" she asked.

"Mario Carducci survived," I answered. "But he had no fight in him after that. He confessed to the murder of Paul Bazelli, and Michael Parness was released. The Raphael is still being evaluated for authenticity."

"I see," Samantha replied.

"Carette didn't say much on the train ride back," I told her. "I had the idea that he would have preferred to deal with them in a different way. Knowing him, I think he would have talked them out of it."

"And how did you feel about that?" Samantha asked.

"I wanted to tell Carette the truth: that I had panicked," I replied, "that it hadn't been a considered course of action I'd taken. Instead, I kept up the pose that I had gone into action with a cool head and deliberately inflicted the damage. I thought about it a few times after I got back to New York, and almost picked up the phone to talk to him. But for some reason I never have."

"Call now," Samantha said.

"Call?" I repeated. "But it's the middle of the night where he is. It's only. . ." I stopped because I had looked at the clock on the wall. It was noon.

"We've been talking for four hours," Samantha informed me. "The incident you've just described, combined with your nightmare, clearly indicates latent content."

She paused. She'd been right before, but I didn't feel cured this time.

But Samantha wasn't finished. "Carette is a father figure for you," she continued. "You have substituted him for the father you barely knew. Your anger at yourself for disappointing him is illustrated by the egg that has broken on the sidewalk in your dream. It represents the smashed skull of the man you fought. The wolf stands for the savagery you attribute to your actions."

I didn't argue. I called Carette. He was home and he was glad to hear from me. We talked for fifteen minutes.

Samantha watched me in the mirror as this went on.

"Your face turned pale at the end of the conversation," she said, as I hung up the phone. "Tell me about that."

"First," I said, "Carette told me that he hadn't talked much on the train back to Paris because he was absorbed with a problem: How had Carducci managed to monitor his calls to Sion and get into the Valère Castle ahead of us? Carette told me he hadn't even given a thought about how I handled Carducci and his helper, and he regrets that I ever troubled myself by coming to such a conclusion."

"And I believe he said something after that, didn't he?" Samantha pursued.

"Yes," I admitted. "He rang off by saying . . . 'when a gun comes into view, it's better to be safe than sorry.'"

CHAPTER TWENTY-ONE:

DESIGNATED HITTER

AN EARLY PHONE CALL at Word to the Wise informed me that Milburn Howard had killed himself in his cell downtown. He'd been facing a life sentence, and he'd balked at the prospect. The message had come from his attorney. She was a young, very idealistic woman who thought I might like a guilt snack an hour or two after breakfast.

I didn't bite. I was pretty sure Howard hadn't hanged himself out of conscience. He'd just gotten mad at himself for shooting off his mouth in front of the police.

I was mulling that over as the door to my inner office swung open and a woman walked in unannounced.

The visitor was a striking figure, tall and blonde. A long heavy braid, tied with a bow, hung down each side of her head. Super pigtails, I'd call them. They dangled just above a low-cut bodice that was emphasized by a push-up bra and bulked up by the tight laces of her three-piece dirndl dress. Silk, hand-pinned. Two rich shades of blue, fringed at the hem to caress a set of legs that would have made Betty Grable puke with envy. Set against the fluffy fur wrap she'd brushed casually back from her shoulders and onto the chair behind her, the impression was of the most spectacular Tyrolian beer girl you'd ever set eyes on in a lifetime of Oktoberfest. It was a sight more suited to a Wagner opera than a detective's office. The face was vaguely familiar too, and I suspected I'd be talking to an actress about some problem with a masher on a movie set.

Not until she spoke did the gears mesh. It was like taking a snow shovel across the face. The flat side at least. "Haldis Pike!" I croaked.

"The very same," she replied in an even tone.

"How did you get in here?" I asked, "Without Ida . . ."

"Ida is all right," Haldis interrupted. "I'm good with security cameras as well as locks. I waited for Ida to go pee."

Haldis as a blonde, with completely different makeup, was nearly unrecognizable. She'd been good-looking before, but no beauty contest winner. Miss Congeniality maybe. Now her face was a vision of arresting beauty, perfect in symmetry, youthful and glowing. I would have passed her on the street without the slightest suspicion that she was as dangerous as a cobra.

"Did you bring your lasso this time?" I asked her.

"Sorry about the extreme measures I had to resort to when we met last time," she replied. "I was in a pretty confused state of mind when I invaded your home that night, and I'm sorry I was so hard on you and Samantha."

I must have made a face at the mention of Samantha. She'd gotten a bad deal all the way around. You can't even get credit for a threesome if you're tied in a wheelchair at the time.

"And about Samantha," Haldis continued, "well, we'd had a little tiff before, you know. And I didn't really hurt her."

Maybe not physically, I reflected, but that was no credit to Haldis. Samantha had been raped herself, repeatedly, shortly before the two of us had gotten together. Although seeing Haldis work out on me for several hours had put Samantha and me on an equal basis in a way, I was tired of getting jerked around by this doll.

Regardless of sex, sitting across from a person who has hoodwinked you, outfought you, and ridden you like a rented mule far into the night is uncomfortable. Potentially pregnant blonde bombshell or not, I reached for the phone.

"Before you complete that call," Haldis cautioned, "you should look at these." She opened the thin ostrich-hide clutch she had been holding and removed a sheaf of photographs. I picked them up as she slid them across my desk, but I had already seen what they were when she took them out. They were photos of me standing in an alley over the dead body of Neron the Pimp. One showed me wiping prints from a gun. Damning evidence, and from the angle I could tell that they were stills from a security camera. There would be a video somewhere, ten minutes of it showing the whole event.

I repositioned the phone and placed it in perfect alignment with the desk. It was a nice phone, a gleaming black acrylic digital version of the old-fashioned rotary executive model. There wouldn't be any phones like that available to me in San Quentin. I decided to listen to Haldis. "Well, you weren't exaggerating about the security cameras," I admitted. "Is this sequence shown in any of those memory cards the cops confiscated from your studio?"

"No," Haldis answered, "but I do have to move things along here so that I can pick up a copy of it before it goes out in the mail."

It was a threat I couldn't ignore. "What's your proposition?" I asked.

"First of all," Haldis replied, "I need to explain something so you'll stop thinking I'm an ogre. You're looking at an innocent woman. Except for, well, setting my uncle up for the kill, that is."

"That in itself is kind of illegal," I pointed out. "Plus, Granville got it in the neck, what with that zombie walk and the whole suicide-by–cop setup. You'd be in just as bad a spot as I was if you turned me in."

"Not so," Haldis replied. "If they really believed I committed the Crankpot murders, my way out would be to plead insanity. Then after a short vacation in which I demonstrated that I had shaped up I'd be out in time to visit you in Attica."

I suddenly realized she was right. And why.

"You know the court system we have," Haldis elaborated. "As long as you're not a cop you can use baby chickens for tennis balls and get away with it. Plus, I'd have plenty of lawyers and asylum guards to have fun with all along the way."

"This doesn't fit with the picture of a woman who wants a baby to raise," I told her.

"Oh," she replied, remembering something. "You can tell Samantha I was just kidding about that baby thing. It just seemed like a good exit line. Now open your mind a moment and consider this. What if the impression of evil I gave you while you were under the gun was my version of what Granville must have been thinking as he committed his string of murders? Because he did, you know. He timed them to coincide with moments during which I had no alibi."

I recalled that the first time Haldis had come to my office she'd been followed by Granville. That tallied with her charge that he'd been keeping tabs on her.

"Granville thought he was superior to everybody," Haldis continued. "He'd studied Shakespeare so thoroughly that he began to think the writer's ideas were his own. Including the ideas of Shakespeare's characters. It was permissible to him, under his moral code, to kill my father for personal gain."

"And the Crankpot victims, too, on a whim?" I added, almost convinced.

"Yes," Haldis answered. "That's why it seemed fitting to me that a daughter should kill her father's murderer in the only way she could to make sure he didn't escape justice."

One thing still bothered me. "You say Granville shot those people with the intention of framing you," I asked. "Why would he think . . .?"

"I'd had incidents," Haldis explained, interrupting me. "Promiscuous behavior. Lots of it. And practical jokes that got out of hand. 'A prankster without remorse' the shrink called me. While Granville was the perfect gentleman scholar in the world's eyes."

She was right about that. Although indicted for Harley Pike's murder, Granville had probably stood a good chance of escaping conviction. He had enjoyed great prestige within literary and academic circles. He wouldn't want for top-flight legal representation, with all the attorneys who would be eager t to link their names with his high-class reputation.

"Makes sense," I mumbled, trying to cope with the mental images she was throwing at me.

"By the time I caught on," Haldis continued, "I realized he'd timed all the killings to coincide with times I was alone. In turn, I set him up, so he'd be sure to pay in full for my father's murder. I got caught at it myself, went on the run, and got accused of the Crankpot murders. I didn't have a way to prove I didn't commit them. Then it occurred to me that one of the murders my uncle committed, the last one, occurred while you and I were screwing our brains out at your house."

"Just a minute," I said. I checked my records and found that she was telling the truth. So Haldis was not a psycho. At least not a major one.

Haldis had caught me unconsciously rubbing my neck. "I know what you were thinking," she told me. "Only the strength of the insane could enable a woman to take you prisoner in your own house. Don't let your ego confuse you. I was a rock climber at twelve, and I spent summers at a dude ranch in Montana. That's why I was able to hog-tie the two of you. That and a streak of sneakiness that just comes naturally."

"So . . . you want me to testify to your alibi and get you off the hook?" I asked.

"Exactly," Haldis replied. "Or else I'll be convicted of the Crankpot murders *in absentia* and have Interpol coming after me."

"Glad to," I said. It would give me an excuse for bragging under oath.

Haldis looked at her watch. "We're wasting time," she said. "There's one more thing. I want you to track down and deal with the man who made me this way. Deal with him in a manner that will get my attention from whatever safe refuge I happen to be in at the time. That's when I'll destroy the video and all copies of it."

"Made you what way?" I asked. I was pretty sure she meant 'made me a schizophrenic nymphomaniac,' but I wanted to be tactful about it.

"The child molester who got to me long ago," Haldis explained. "I was nine, but he dropped me a year later for a seven-year-old. He's still around. He developed his technique early and stayed with it. They all do. He's still cultivating little girls, practically under people's noses and harvesting them with all the nerve of a TV evangelist."

"Still around?" I asked.

"Somewhere in the New York area," Haldis replied. "It's his hunting ground."

She was a prankster without remorse indeed. Her psychiatrist must have gotten pretty frustrated to call her that within earshot, but I could sympathize with the feeling. I'd been the victim of three of those pranks already, and here came the fourth. A deadly one this time.

"And if he's reformed?" I started to ask. But then I remembered that they never do. "I'm not a hit man, coercion or no co . . ." I began, and she looked at her watch again.

"Okay, watch for the news," I told her. There are times in life when you just have to be adaptable.

CHAPTER TWENTY-TWO:

THE SMELL OF CINNAMON

"WHAT I DIDN'T LIKE about working in a smaller city," Sergeant Roger Newby told me, "was walking a beat where there were so many trees and hedges. Spider webs were strung across them everywhere. They'd cling and stretch, and you'd walk around wiping your face like some grunge who was attracting flies. It's irritating to get one across your face. But I'd never get just one. I'd get them across by eyes or my lips, and sometimes a whole wad on top of my head from an overhanging branch. I collected so many strands of spider silk on my face I could have made a silk purse out of them. Hell, I could have made a whole sow with them by now."

I set down my cup. I wasn't here for small talk. "Yes, they're annoying," I agreed. "And you say you remember arresting this guy, Ford Pressman, a few years ago?"

"Yeah, six years ago," Newby answered. "It was just a chance thing that Poppins, the dad, passed me on the street on his way to Pressman's house. Poppins had a gun with him, tucked down in his coat, and he was on his way to kill the guy. Lucky for him he caught onto himself just in time. Having met a policeman, he changed his mind and decided to have Pressman arrested instead of shooting him. I confiscated the gun, then went along with Poppins to Pressman's house. Knocked on the door and took him into custody. Told Poppins to go home the way he came."

"And then what happened?" I asked, taking a sip.

"Poppins had a phone on him, and he called the school," Newby replied. "Poppins' wife was at the school and she'd been talking to the schoolmaster there. Don't you know that smooth-

talking devil had convinced the wife, in that little amount of
time, not to press charges? Said he'd experienced enough of
those cases to tell her what the little girl was in for if they did.
The wife begged the husband to stand down, the husband got
hold of me through the dispatcher, and I ended up letting
Pressman out of the cruiser a block before I could get him to the
station."

I set the cup down again, very carefully, so I wouldn't end
up sending it into the mirror across the counter from us.

"The world is full of perverts, isn't it?" Newby continued.
"Seems like we're just overwhelmed by a lot of stuff that never
came up in conversation before: sex change operations, gender
reveal parties, corn-hole tournaments. . ."

"Roger, I've got to hit the road," I interrupted, picking the
check up from the saucer in front of us. "Got to keep the lights
on."

"Oh, yeah," Newby said from behind me. He sounded
disappointed. He was just getting warmed up.

I had Pressman's address, but I didn't want to confront him
just yet. I would nose around first and maybe pick up something
current on him. That would have to wait, though. It was getting
late.

I got an early start on the project the next day. Pressman
lived over a little bakery shop in Queens, my lead had informed
me.

Snow had fallen during the night. I'd skipped my morning
run to share some time with Samantha, so I parked a block short
of my destination so I could walk in it. Plus, you don't find a lot
of parking spaces in Queens, so I took one I was sure of.

The bell tinkled and I stepped out of the crisp air and into a
place that smelled like fresh bread. I wiped my feet on a thick
jute mat at the side of the door, under the gaze of a realistic-
looking doll sitting on the floor with its back against a display
case.

"Hello," the woman behind the counter said, seeming
surprised. "You're earlier than the usual customer, but come on
in. I didn't realize the door was open." She was the perfect
image of the baker's wife, hair pinned up on her head with one

stray wisp coming out and a little spot of flour on her cheek she didn't know was there. She was thirty or thereabouts, with the kind of blonde hair you usually only see in the movies. It was gold, then silver, then colorless, like a Technicolor print going bad.

"Sorry," I told her. "I'll come back later." I probably didn't sound very convincing, because I was hungry.

"No," she replied. "Please stay and I'll try to get you what you want."

Okay," I said. "I can be flexible if you haven't taken everything out of the oven."

"You must not be my first customer," she said. "I thought I heard the bell jingle earlier, but then I dismissed the idea because I was so sure that the door was locked."

"There were no tracks outside," I told her. In fact, the street was deserted out there.

"That's funny," the woman said. She looked concerned. I hoped she wasn't worrying about losing one sale. It was hard enough getting along in an all-day job like that without having to do it on thin profits.

"Not really," I replied. "The snow is coming down at a steady rate."

"Oh, I see," she replied. "Yes, it has just started. How pretty. There's nothing like New York in the snow. What will you have?"

"Is your Danish ready?" I asked. The cinnamon rolls smelled good, but the little knob of crust she left at the center of those evoked unpleasant memories. My father had been a drunk, but also an anti-smoker. He'd kept a little plaster rattlesnake ashtray he'd evidently had a long time, and he would take it out to symbolize how deadly smoking was. He'd shove the thing at my face, and not in a playful manner, either. It left me with the fear of smoking, which was good, but also the fear of objects resembling little coiled snakes. Like this pretty lady's cinnamon rolls.

"Yes, pecan Danish," she answered. "You smelled it, didn't you? It's just coming out."

"I think I'll have some of your coffee, too," I said.

"Large?" she asked.

"Medium," I answered. "Just for the Danish. I had some earlier, but yours smells a lot better." It didn't, though. Samantha had some sort of secret formula for preparing coffee, and I didn't want to spoil that experience with too much donut shop java.

"My name's Claire," she said, "and we're the Doyles. Are you one of our neighbors?" She turned her head to look into the kitchen. "Oh, heck," she said, "the coffee's not ready. We'll have to get some more help. The shop's too much for Dan and me. Especially taking care of Tiffany too."

"No, I'm just passing through," I answered. "But I expect to be coming back in here again. My name is Turley." I picked the doll up from in front of the bakery case where it had been out of Claire's line of sight. "Looks like Tiffany left something out here," I remarked, and handed it to her over the counter.

"What?" Claire exclaimed. "Where did you get that?"

"It was right here on the floor," I answered. "Leaning against the display case."

"It shouldn't be there," Claire replied. "I put her to bed with that doll last night. Dan? Dan?" she called into the back. "Tiffany's not up, is she?"

"No, Claire," Dan answered from the kitchen. "This early? Certainly not."

"Go check, Dan," Claire requested. "Her doll's down here."

"Well, she couldn't have come down," Dan replied. "I'd have seen her."

"Not if you were occupied with the oven," Claire told him.

"Oh, all right, Claire," Dan answered. "I'll go check." He turned away, but looked back at the window. "Geez," he said. "One day late."

"What do you mean, a day late?" Claire asked.

"This snow," Dan answered. "April Fool's was yesterday."

"Oh, go on, Dan," Claire returned, "go check," She muttered something that contained "Weather report," under her breath as Dan disappeared.

I stood there awkwardly while this exchange took place, wishing I had mentioned the doll the first moment I saw Claire come in from the kitchen. She clutched the doll so tightly her knuckles turned white. I said something to try and ease the tension. It wasn't time to bring up Pressman's name yet, no matter what wild suspicions had formed in my head.

"That doll looks like a real child, Mrs. Doyle," I said. "Is that one of those special make-up dolls?"

"Yes," Claire answered. "We had it made in the Village."

"That's a beautiful job," I said. "It's about as pretty as she probably is. How old would that make her, four?"

"No, she just turned five," Claire answered. "Excuse me for a moment, Mr. Turley," she continued, turning to Dan.

Dan came in from the kitchen. "Tiffany's not in her bed, Claire," he told her. "She's nowhere in the apartment. I've looked everywhere."

"Oh my God," Claire exclaimed. "Tiffany? Tiffany? Outside! I heard the bell once before Mr. Turley here came in. That sound of the bell I heard must have been her going out."

"But why?" Dan asked.

"Dan!" Claire said. "She was down here. Someone must have come in and taken her."

"Maybe not," Dan answered. "It's snowing. Maybe that's the reason. She wanted to see the snow. Mr. Turley, did you see any tracks?"

"He's already said he didn't, Dan," Claire told him.

Dan made a move toward the door.

"Don't step out, Dan," I cautioned, blocking his path.

"Mr. Turley," Dan said. "Get out of my way. What are you doing?"

"The tracks, Dan," I explained. "We need every indication."

"What are you talking about?" Dan asked. "There are no tracks."

"There's not a track to be seen, Mr. Turley," Claire confirmed. "Even your tracks have been covered over."

"Don't either of you go outside," I told them. "Keep your heads, both of you."

"Dammit," Dan shot back. "It's not your child that's been taken."

I put my hand on Dan's chest to make sure he didn't step out. "Mrs. Doyle," I said. "Bring me a broom."

"A broom?" she asked.

"A broom," I repeated. "Please get one. I know what I'm doing."

"What kind of broom?" she asked.

"A regular one," I answered. "Not a push broom."

Claire left and returned with a straw one. "Here it is," she said, handing it to me like a rifle for inspection.

"Thanks," I said, and put one foot carefully out into the snow.

"You told us not to step out, Turley," Dan protested, "But you're doing it yourself."

"You have to know just how to do this, Dan," I told him.

Dan leaned forward with his hands on his knees and watched as I worked. "You're uncovering tracks," he said. "But how . . ."

"As I stepped out of my car up the street," I explained, "I noticed that the sidewalk was covered by heavy rime. It made a crunching noise. Heavy ice crystals. This fluffy snow is covering up the tracks in the rime, but it is having no effect on them otherwise."

"And it leaves a clear mark," Claire marveled. "Oh my God, Dan. Those are Tiffany's tracks. And they're next to an adult's. A man's tracks."

"Now you two can step out," I told them. "But stay next to the wall."

"Dan, the footprints," Claire exclaimed, "They're . . . they're headed toward the curb."

"Toward the tread marks where a car has headed out into the traffic," Dan said.

Claire put her hands over her eyes. "I can't look, Dan," she said. "It's too horrible."

"Oh no!" Dan said in a hollow voice. "The tire tracks get lost about fifty feet down the road. It's all over."

"It's not over until . . ." I began, and then: "Grab her Dan, she's about to faint."

Dan caught her. "Claire, stay with us," he said. "Are you okay?"

"Yes," Claire answered. "I'll make it, Dan. Why . . . the tracks are turning. They're not going toward the curb after all."

"That's right, Mrs. Doyle," I said. "Now they're going straight down the sidewalk."

"Oh, please be careful Mr. Turley," Claire said. "Please don't lose them."

"Look, Claire," Dan said. "They're changing direction again."

"They're heading around to the side of the building," Claire said.

"To the alley," Dan said.

"The tracks lead to the fire escape," Claire said. "To the fire escape. Tiffany! Tiffa--Mmmph!" She stopped calling then, because I had grabbed her and put my hand over her mouth.

"What the hell are you . . ." Dan began, and then "Ouch," as I put a restraining hold on his fingers.

I hustled them toward the sidewalk out front. "Sorry Dan. Sorry Claire," I told them. "I had to get you to shut up and get back around to the front of the building."

"You've broken my damn fingers, Turley," Dan protested.

"No, Dan," I told him. "It was just a simple finger hold. Rub it. It'll be all right."

"But why did you do that?" Claire asked.

"I had to keep you from shouting up there, Claire," I told her. "And I had to keep you from interfering as I did it, Dan," I told him.

"I don't like having a hand placed over my mouth, Mr. Turley," Claire told me.

"You'll thank me in a minute, Claire," I replied. "The last thing you want to do is attract Tiffany's attention and get her to respond. This guy could be very impulsive. Who lives up there?"

The angry look disappeared from Claire's face as she caught on. "Mr. Pressman has the whole third floor," she answered.

I did my best to keep the emotion out of my face. We couldn't afford hysteria at this critical moment. "Where's his main entrance?' I asked. "It's not the fire escape."

"Part of the third floor is a roof garden," Claire answered. "There's an exit out that way, across another roof."

"We had to get a special permit for that," Dan added.

"But Mr. Pressman's not up there," Claire said. "He's gone away for the weekend."

"I don't think so, Claire," I replied. "Your fire escape doesn't extend to the roof. Whoever took that route went up to a very specific location, Pressman's apartment."

"Mr. Turley's right, Claire," Dan said. "The only other door it goes to is our apartment on the second floor. And he certainly didn't go in there."

"Are there any other entrances to that third-floor apartment?" I asked them.

"No, just the two," Claire answered. "No, wait a minute. There are three. There's a narrow stairwell at this end of the building that leads from our apartment."

"Can we go up that way?" I asked.

"Yes," Claire answered, "if . . . Do you have the key with you, Dan?"

"It's right here, Claire," Dan answered.

"I'm going to go in from the inside," I said.

"You?" Dan replied. "But why you instead. . ."

"I'm a detective," I told him, "private."

"Shouldn't we call the police?" Claire asked.

"Not right now," I answered. "Let's focus on the problem. They'd never get here in time."

Experience counts. Dan saw the sense of it, and he wanted every chance. "Through here," he said. "Follow me, Mr. Turley."

"I'm right behind you, Dan," I told him, "but I need to go through the door first."

"Let me move these boxes," Dan replied. "This door is never opened."

"Is that so?" I asked. I pointed at an object. "Grab that bottle right there, Claire," I told her. The unused stair had served as a storage space for cooking supplies.

"The olive oil?" she asked.

"Yes," I replied. "Slather it on those hinges, Claire. I don't want to get it on my hands."

Claire did the job quickly and efficiently. "It works," she said. "The hinges didn't make a sound."

"You two can follow me up the stairs," I told them, "but don't go past the landing."

"You got it, Turley," Dan agreed.

"And Dan," I cautioned, "be careful with that knife you're holding."

"Right," Dan answered.

I started up. "Give me five seconds before you follow," I told them.

"Do you have a gun, Mr. Turley?" Dan asked.

"Yes, Dan," I answered. "And I'll use it if necessary, but not if there's a chance of hurting Tiffany."

We made our way up silently, Dan and Claire picking up on the technique of placing their feet on the far end of each step as they moved.

I reached the landing and crept down the hall.

"I can't look," Claire said from her post behind her husband's shoulder. "What's he doing, Dan?"

"He's going to kick in the . . ." Dan began.

I kicked. The door flew open, and . . .

Nobody was there except for a little girl sitting cross-legged on the bed. Footsteps pounded down the hall behind me; a man running. I spun back into the dark hallway just in time to see Pressman's retreating back halfway through the door at the end of the hall opposite the Doyles. I ran after him, and made it to the door just in time to catch an empty flower vase across my head. Pressman had good timing.

A smarter man would have been warned by the trail of artificial flowers Pressman had left on the floor behind him. He had been crouching behind a table just past the door I kicked in.

I had to shake off the effects of the blow, and by the time I got up off my knees Pressman had escaped across the roof. The last I saw of him he was disappearing into the shadows as the board he'd used as a bridge clattered into the alley below. Pressman had planned that exit.

"Hi, Mommy!" Tiffany was saying behind me. "Mr. Pressman and me were playing Cowboys and Indians. See what he drew on my nubbies? Eyes."

"Oh, Tiffany!" Claire exclaimed with a mixture of horror and relief.

"Why are you crying, Mommy?" Tiffany asked. "You got that allergy again?"

"Yes, Tiffany," Claire answered. "But it will be all right, now. Tiffany, haven't I told you about going somewhere with someone you don't know?"

"But I know Mr. Pressman, Mommy," Tiffany answered. "He lives with us."

"He just rents the place upstairs, Tiff," Claire told her.

"And he was in the park," Tiffany replied.

"Oh?" Claire said. "I . . . I guess I didn't see him there, Tiff."

"But he was right there close to us in the park," Tiffany said.

"I'll have to watch more carefully from now on," Claire replied.

"And here's a big funny nose he drew around my belly button," Tiffany told her.

"I see it, Honey," Claire answered.

"Mr. Pressman said my Indian name was Princess Pimple Nose," Tiffany continued. "Then he said that next I was going to get a big surprise."

"Well, I'm glad you didn't get that surprise, Tiffany," Claire said.

"But I did," Tiffany replied. "That guy over there came in to play cowboys with Mr. Pressman and me, but it was too loud. I had to cover my ears."

"That guy is Mr. Turley, Tiff," Claire told her.

"Well, he plays too loud," Tiffany complained. "I wanted to run out of the room. I don't like it that loud."

"Hi, Tiffany," I said.

"Hi, Mr. Turley," Tiffany replied. "That's a funny name. It sounds like 'Turkey' and 'Turtle' at the same time."

"Mr. Turley," Claire asked, "are you all right? You're bloody."

"I'm okay, Claire," I told her. "Just a little nick on the scalp.

"And Mr. Pressman?" she asked.

"He galloped off into the sunset, I'm afraid," I answered.

"Cowboys!" Tiffany said. "You had to come in and play cowboys. It makes way too much noise!"

"Now, is that a polite thing to say to Mr. Turley, Tiff?" Claire asked.

"I'm sorry," Tiffany answered, "but next time just come in the regular way, or maybe knock first, okay?"

"Let's go, Tiffany," Claire told her. "Daddy and I have left the shop unlocked."

"But I was having so much fun!" Tiffany protested. "If you and Mr. Pressman are finished chasing each other, Mr. Turley, can I . . . Mommy, can I stay here and play with Mr. Pressman?"

"Mr. Pressman won't be coming back for a while, Tiffany," I told her. "He decided to go running for his health."

"Oh, well," Tiffany replied. "I guess that's okay. But it's cold out there, and we hadn't finished our game."

CHAPTER TWENTY-THREE:

SNAKE IN THE GRASS

I WORKED ON the Pressman problem over the next few weeks, hoping to collect enough damaging material to expose him in such a way that Haldis would be satisfied without actual bloodshed. After all, the media have a way these days of making people wish they were dead.

It was no go, though. On the morning of May the first, a spectacular day otherwise, I got a call from Haldis. I took it at the top of the stairs on my way to Word to the Wise, with my hand on the door to the corridor.

"I can't help noticing," Haldis said, "that it has been over a month since I asked you to do a certain favor for me."

"I've been doing prep work," I answered as I continued into the hallway.

"Don't take too long," she warned. A tapping sound came from the phone speaker. "Know what this is? A thumb-drive. 'Scuse me for chewing. Guavas. Good for breakfast."

She terminated the call.

Motivated, I organized the day for results. I had a conversation with the master of the girl's school where Pressman had most recently taught. I got him to tell me that Pressman didn't work there anymore, and that he wouldn't be working at any school from now on. But I couldn't get him to tell me why.

I wasn't about to give up easily, because the time limit Haldis Pike had given me was soon to expire.

The man eventually opened up. "Dammit," he said. "What can I tell you? There's no room left in the prisons for anybody but the eye-gougers. People like Pressman don't even make it half-way through arraignment before they're given a scented bouquet, a helpful brochure, and a kiss on the mouth for promising to modify their behavior. It's left up to people in my position to address the problem by moving them along to the next school along the line. With a coded message that means 'watch this guy.' After enough moves like that the picture finally becomes clear. And the offender ends up in another profession where the pickings are not so easy."

"I guess I see the problem," I told him.

"For a while it was in vogue to get the kids to tell their stories through dolls and hypnotism," he continued. "That was really cute, but it was getting the nuts cut off the innocent along with the guilty. Kids have even better imaginations than adults, so it was like flinging acid into a dark room."

"Yeah, that was the impression I got from the news," I told him. "Sorry I bothered you."

I'd gotten away from Dan and Claire's place as soon as I could and let the family settle down. It was a good thing for me that Pressman had escaped. What I would have done to him in the heat of the moment would have gotten me into deep trouble.

I hadn't been able to tell Claire Doyle during the ordeal, that the name Pressman had put me on the alert. It wouldn't have helped matters, and later I didn't have the heart to urge them to go prosecute the guy. And when they realized what their daughter would have to go through in court, they'd probably have dropped their case anyway. Why go through it when the end result would be a slap on the wrist and a visit to a halfway house for Pressman? These days, people are hitting the streets after six years for murder. Just check the papers.

I'd picked at the edges of some earlier incidents involving Pressman, in which parents had dropped their cases. Pressman's was a strange history, a mixture of the practical and the perverse. He had started out in the trade of AC repair long ago, entered a community college, and had earned a Teaching degree in English. And most recently, after having been dismissed from the school I had just visited for suspicious reasons a warning had at last been passed around about him. He wouldn't be able to find another post, and he had gone back into AC repair.

I hadn't seen Pressman when he slugged me out there in the dark, and I was pretty sure he hadn't gotten a look at me either. But a peek back into his room on my way to talk to Claire had revealed an AC unit disassembled on a table, so that made him the right guy.

It wasn't hard to find out where Pressman was working. The place was conveniently nearby, so early the next day I decided to tail him and see what he was up to.

Pressman went out on an early call from the AC firm, and I followed. The van he was driving ended up at the Zoo. Pressman was able to go on in with the van to take care of whatever job he'd been called for, but I had to stop and pay the usual parking fee.

It was an even more beautiful day than Tuesday had been, and besides that, Wednesday was free admission day at the zoo. I dropped a twenty into the "suggested donation" box as the person in front of me had done and went past without giving the attendant a good look at me.

The place was swarming. I took off in the direction I thought Pressman had gone, panic-stopping in front of several streams of excited children before I was able to catch up to him.

I had dressed differently from the day at the bakery, and Pressman wasn't likely to recognize me. All I had to do was walk until I saw the van.

Ahead of me a long stretch of tarp obscured a high chain link fence that curved around an unseen animal exhibit house. The AC van was tucked in beside it, parked well away from the curving pedestrian walkway. Pressman stood near the vehicle, arms crossed and glaring left and right. He was obviously waiting for someone.

I walked along the thick grass that grew beside the tarp-covered fence. The grass had been torn up about fifty feet to the left of the spot where Pressman stood, and a hedge had been uprooted.

I knew what Pressman was waiting for then. According to the paper, a rhino had gotten loose the day before and wreaked havoc. Badly near-sighted, it had rampaged past several exhibit houses and ended up smacking into a wall behind a screen of shrubbery it took for a wooded refuge. It had caused a panic and seriously injured a zoo employee. The HVAC system had probably been damaged, and the Zoo officials had called in to have it repaired.

The tarps along the fence had apparently been placed there to keep out gawkers. It was working. The crowd surging past the walkway were headed toward active exhibits, and showed no interest in the closed–off area.

Pressman stood near a flap in the canvas, evidently waiting for someone to open the padlock that secured the temporary gate the zoo staff had made in the fence at that point.

"Are you here with the key?" he asked when he saw me. "Why are you people making me wait? I know more about AC repair than any two maintenance men at this zoo. I would have had the problem diagnosed already if I could just have gotten in there."

"Hey, I've got to get into there, too," I told him, fishing a picklock set out of my pocket. "I won't say anything about it if you don't."

"What's your interest?" Pressman asked.

"Legal work," I told him. "Client got hurt by the rhino and I need to take some notes in there."

I had a little trouble with the lock. Padlocks aren't fixed in place like door locks, so they're harder to open with a bump key.

"Too bad the idiot who got in front of that rhino was some sort of indispensable big-wig here," Pressman complained. "I've never encountered a more undisciplined chain of command. And right on the brink of a heat wave. It's supposed to hit ninety today."

"But exactly one month after we had a five-inch snowfall," I countered, beginning to wish I had caught up to Pressman that day at the bakery. An opportunity squandered.

"No question you're a lawyer," Pressman replied. "You've come equipped with a pocketful of excuses for the Zoo board."

"They have their own steam plant," I told him. "It does most of the work. See that concrete box out there on the lawn? It's one of the maintenance stations." It was a fact that should have been obvious to an HVAC man. A two-foot-wide strip of vivid green stood out from the rest of the lawn, revealing the passage of a heated pipe under the ground. It ran past us, under the AC van, and into the enclosure we were attempting to enter.

"Oh, how fortunate for me," Pressmen replied, with gentle but abrasive sarcasm, "I've encountered an expert. Too bad you weren't in charge here yesterday. Then maybe the whole place wouldn't have been thrown into a state of confusion. They wouldn't have shut a whole exhibit down and had everybody running around like crazy because a rhino knocked itself out on the side of a building."

It wasn't a compliment, the way Pressman said it. From the tone he was using you'd think he had mistaken me for the rhino.

The lock popped. A few seconds later we stepped through the opening and into the enclosure behind the fence. It was darker than I expected back there. The fence was high and evergreens hung over it in some areas. The grass was thicker there next to the building. The zoo had priorities, and keeping lesser-used stretches of grass neat for the use of pending visits by service people wasn't one of them.

Pressman found the defective AC unit and knelt down in front of it. We were all alone. Now could I do it, as Hamlet once said to himself. But I paused, put off by the guy's vulnerability. He was smaller than me, and flabby at that. I walked on down the lane to the left, thinking it over.

The area of the wall hit by the escaping rhino wasn't hard to find. The damaged concrete block wall had been cleared away and replaced by an emergency patch of two pieces of inch-thick twelve-by-four plywood. The sudden change of temperature had warped one of the boards, leaving a considerable aperture. Not certain about what was going to happen between Pressman and myself in the next few minutes, I looked inside to make sure nobody was in the area who'd be looking out at us.

Inside was a six-foot wide corridor, apparently for access to the backs of the cages for the exhibits. The opposite wall of the corridor had been breached as well. That explained the confusion the zoo staff were going through at the moment. The injured zoo employee had evidently been standing in the wrong place when the rhino had hit the outside wall, and had gotten himself punched through the wall behind him and into one of the cages. And even the cage hadn't been repaired completely, as was evident in the dim light.

But there was nobody around in there, and the warped section of plywood I was looking through was well below eye level. Bad news for a certain snippy HVAC man.

Pressman had the cover off the AC unit and was checking out the problem. His stubby little flashlight was working at about half power, and he was having trouble seeing into the box. Plus, there was no place to set down the flashlight, so it was a delicate operation.

Pressman had evidently only brought one replacement part for the AC. He had dropped it and was probing around in the knee-high grass. He found it, dug it out of the sand, cleaned it off and continued with the repair on the unit.

Pressman looked up at me. He wasn't a big man, anyway, and from that position he stood about the height of an eight-year-old. How could anyone look down at a little child like that, I wondered, and think about molesting her?

Yeah, I was making a good try at it, there in the dim light. I was attempting to psych myself up for the act. Trying to convince myself I'd be justified in snuffing out this miserable snake's life. But even with a good motive behind the attempt, it turned out I wasn't a good enough liar to sell myself on that one.

"An attorney?" Pressman asked. "Maybe I'll need a lawyer some time. May I have your card?"

"Well, I'm not fully an attorney," I admitted. "Just a legal aide."

"I figured as much," Pressman replied, and went back to his work.

Despite his dismissive attitude I had decided against giving him the treatment. I'd punched out a few characters in my time, and had been knocked down a few times as well. But I had never yet administered a beating to a man who wouldn't have had a chance to defend himself, as was the case here. And certainly, never a fatal one. I'd have to give up on the idea and just wait for karma to catch up with the guy.

Behind me Pressman had bent over to look for the part that he had dropped again, and something made me look back at that broken section of the wall I'd noticed before. The middle of it was right in line with the greening of the grass that indicated the heat pipe passed through there. I went back over and looked more closely. The grass had been disturbed, as if something inside the building had pushed under the lower sheet of plywood and made a pathway.

Aardvarks and anteaters of various species were housed back there if I remembered correctly. Then I saw something hiding in the shadows that I took for a silky ant eater. I'd seen one a few weeks ago at the zoo, an impossibly cute little fuzzy thing that looked like a puppy dog with a tiny pointed muzzle.

But a closer look told me it wasn't fur I was seeing. Some instinct I can't account for prompted me to reach down and tuck the cuffs of my pant legs inside my socks.

"What are you doing back there?" Pressman asked me.

"The Rhino punched a hole in the wall here," I answered. "Careful. You don't want to step on an anteater or something."

Or was the enclosure for the aardvarks, anteaters and such like one lane over? That would make this the lane behind the snake house.

Make that the latter. I had tucked those cuffs in none too soon, because something hit the cuff of my trousers before I straightened up.

The thing had grazed my knuckles on the way by, but it had been unable to penetrate the fabric of my bullet-resistant pant-legs. I saw it at the edge of the grass, a snake with a big mouth. A black racer if I knew my snakes, I thought. A friend of mine had raised one in a terrarium when I was a kid. This one was holding its head to one side as if wondering why it hadn't been able to grasp the thing it was after with its teeth. That mouth and button-like eyes made it look like an elongated Muppet, but my subconscious wasn't fooled a bit. For some unaccountable reason I smelled cinnamon. I kicked the snake away.

I didn't aim for Pressman, but that's where the snake landed, hooping in the air and disappearing into the grass next to him.

Pressman had been looking at the air conditioner and hadn't seen me kick the snake. "What was that?" he asked, turning around.

"An animal from the other side of this enclosure," I told him. "I kicked it by reflex. Now I'll probably have to pay its vet bill. Don't tell anybody, okay?"

Having been a prep school teacher at one time, and an A-hole since then, Pressman wasn't passing up a chance to moralize. "I'm afraid not," he replied, bending down to search the grass for the injured animal. "We all have to face the consequences of our actions."

"What the . . .?" he continued, and then "Ow, ow, ow, ow, ow," as the snake hit him. It struck twelve times, faster than you could snap your fingers. That kick I'd given it had made it very angry. Plus, I'd made a basic but significant error in animal identification. A black racer couldn't rear itself up like a cobra to strike. As I was to learn afterwards, the snake was a black mamba.

And it hadn't been alone. A tiny nudge alerted me that another snake had settled its head on the toe of my left shoe. It was making its way cautiously toward the series of vibrations Pressman's feet had made as he hopped around to avoid the strikes.

My new visitor didn't have to hurry. Within seconds Pressman had collapsed into the grass, which was now waving on either side of him, rustling audibly. I froze, and the rustling stopped.

I'm no snake expert, but it was clear by this time I'd made a mistake. The animal that had bitten Pressman was not only venomous, but powerfully so. I kept still, because that snake on my foot was moving across both shoe tops now and an attempt to kick it away would present bad odds.

From the corner of my eye came the gleam of two tiny sparks within the shadows. Standing still seemed advisable, so I didn't turn to look. A snake of the same size as the one that had bitten Pressman, rearing to strike? Or just my imagination?

The snake on my shoes had paused. You had to empathize, because how many times had it gotten a chance to rub its belly against polished cowhide?

The grass seemed to be rustling in two places now, behind me. Running footsteps sounded in the distance and . . . no that was my heart beating. But unlike the guy in the Poe story, I was aware it wasn't somebody I'd stashed under the floor.

Oops, and now another set of sparks appeared in front of me. Same height as the other set. And I knew it wasn't shoe buttons, like in the story by Ambrose Bierce. Heart beating louder.

It might have been a minute before the snake on my feet moved away and the sparks settled to the ground and turned themselves off. It couldn't have been as long as it seemed, because night hadn't fallen yet. I moved closer to Pressman, where there was better light.

The stirred-up snake had evidently done its work and left. I bent down with the intention of helping Pressman, but the look on his face stopped me. His skin had smoothed out. The tilt of his lip that had given the appearance of a permanent smirk had relaxed. His features had assumed the innocence of a child. Like for instance a child named Tiffany, or Melissa Bobbins . . . or casting back a few years earlier, a child named Haldis.

I got back up and sidled out through the gateway, making sure I hadn't left any prints. Failure to render assistance? After Pressman had been struck that many times a roomful of doctors probably couldn't have saved him.

I got out of there. I wasn't about to try and convince a jury I hadn't set Pressman up for that treatment. I had stalked him at the bakery the day before, and somewhere in the ether were records of inquiries I'd made about him. I couldn't afford to place myself at the scene of the fatality on top of that.

I walked slowly to my car and headed south. Maybe I should have felt guilty about what had happened to Pressman, but I didn't. Little girls weren't made for sex. They weren't made for the games he played and the poisonous wounds they carried around in their heads thereafter. Nature had evened out a situation the law had failed to address.

As the towers of the city climbed into view, I thought about what Pressman had said a second before the snake hit him: "We all have to face the consequences of our actions." It isn't often that a person's last words can be so thoroughly hypocritical and completely prophetic at the same time.

I thought about it for the rest of the trip. I didn't expect to be talking much about what happened in that zoo enclosure, but it helps to be ready. Haldis Pike was bound to be satisfied. One of God's little creatures had finally bitten back.

But an accounting to Haldis wasn't the only one I'd likely be put to. There remained the next phase of Dr. Dale's Samanthazade. I'd have to prepare for that and drill myself accordingly. It was one step beyond that usual "what are you thinking about now?' question a woman throws at you, and you end up kicking yourself because you hadn't made up an answer ahead of time.

"You'd be proud of me," I would tell Samantha. "I had the strong urge to shoot someone, and didn't." After receiving approval for that statement, I'd go on to the next. "And I also fought back my urge to beat the guy to death, even though there were no witnesses around."

"Good," she would say. "That shows promise. Now how did you finally resolve the issue?"

That's when I would proudly come up with the kicker. "I sat down with him in silence," I'd tell her. "Allowing him to contemplate the issue that had brought us into conflict. Until at length I had come to the realization that he was finally at one with the universe."

Boyen D. Brook Publishing